by

I

ISBN: 978-1-7368068-9-0

Library of Congress Control Number: 2021906776

Any references to historical events, real people, or real places are used fictitiously. Names, characters, and places are products of the author's consciousness, imagination, and logical possibilities.

Printed in the United States of America.

First printing edition 2021.

www.0-by-1.com   zero@0-by-1.com

PO Box 12465
Cincinnati, OH 45212

Editor: Brianna Sargent
editor@0-by-1.com

CHAPTER 1
Much Ado About Nothing

O: *The mathematical symbol denoting the absence of all magnitude or quantity. Nothing, nada, zilch, nix, nihility, scratch, naught, diddly, nonbeing, shutout, zonk, none, zippo, blank, nullity, empty, void, null, bust, goose-egg, nary, nothingness, nonexistence.*

That's a lot of words humanity uses to define nothing. Semantically speaking, those words aren't really defining nothing; they're defining *nothing*. Wait a minute, that didn't help. What I mean is that *nothing* is difficult to define. That's not to imply that everything is easy to define, but rather that it's very difficult to define something that is nothing. Nothing can be confusing. Well, I just did it again, didn't I? It's not that something can never be confusing or that communicating nothing cannot be confusing. The problem is that *nothing* is something that doesn't exist. Don't think that I'm claiming that *nothing* is really a *something*. What I mean is … well, nothing.

Let us ponder this puzzling paradox. When someone asks you what you're doing, you might respond with nothing. Depending on syntax, context, and punctuation, this might mean that you are doing nothing at the moment … or it could mean you simply chose to remain silent. It seems like with every attempt made at clarifying nothing, the more nothing becomes unclear. Does that make any sense?

I didn't mean to confuse you so early on. It might help to know that I've faced this same paradoxical syntax snafu for what humanity defines as an eternity. I was confused from the very start, just as you are right now. In fact, I've been vexed with this perpetual parsing problem for over 13.8 billion years (and one-trillionth of a second). Nothing has been a thorn in my side the entire time. Well, I should say that nothing is something that has been a thorn in my side. Yes, I know that nothing cannot be a *something*. I just phrased it that way so you could better understand. After reading my own sentence, I don't think that helped either.

Is there nothing I can do to resolve this nothing issue? I know that I can't really do nothing because whatever I would be doing is technically nothing at all, so I really wouldn't be doing anything to help. C'mon, it's just a figure of speech, okay? If I'm *doing nothing*, then nothing is what I am doing, even if it's impossible to do something that is tantamount to doing absolutely nothing at all. If nothing makes any sense, don't worry. This will all make perfect sense by the end of this book. As for right now, there's nothing to worry about. Sorry, couldn't resist!

Before nothing evolves into chaos, perhaps you should know who or what you are dealing with. Allow me to introduce myself. In respect to my nonexistent nemesis known as *Nothing*, I also have a rather long list of words that define me. My list is slightly longer because there's so much more to me than mere nothingness. If you were to address me by my proper name, then I am known as Ann Marie Burr, Leukocyte, Plato, Dickcissel, Nikola Tesla, Sequoia, Charles Darwin, Centipede, Ignazio Oliva, Neutron, John Adams, Bojaxhiu, Greed, Richard Dawkins, Chrysocolla, Guang Wudi, Oxygen, Victoria Stafford, 27, Mausolus, Aluminum, Tim Berners-Lee, Hydrogen, Terrell Peterson, Good, Steve Bartman, Quasar, Eva Marie Cassidy, Diorite, Nero, Ω, Missulena, Julius Caesar, Rage, Isaac Newton, -94, Gilles Binchois, π, Agnes Gonxha, Flintlock, Brittanee Drexel, Crimson, Sumarti Ningsih, Love, Alexander, Clear, Galileo, Tyrannosaurus, Steven Hawking, Uterus, Adolf Hitler, Coral Snake, Zachary Taylor, Gravity, Julia Oehrle, Sphere, Chung Ling Soo, 3,256, Judas, Burbot, ∞, Albert Einstein, Salamander, Genghis Khan, Evil, René Descartes, Gold, Allah, Gravity, Buddha, Prokaryote, Rebecca Schaeffer, Bleach, Michelangelo, compass … well, let's just say that I go by a 93 billion light-years-wide name. That's a rather long name to remember, but it's all committed to memory. If a shorter name is desired, then human language offers you a very simple word. I am *Existence.* However, you can call me by my first name, which is I.

I am what your dictionaries define as existence, but the numerical value of I is a more logical definition. Humanity has added many words to define me (everything, all, total, sum, presence, reality, etc.), but not nearly as many as you have for that empty little word called *Nothing.* Don't worry, my feelings aren't hurt. You've developed more words to describe *Nothing* because nothing is harder to communicate. Hey! Don't look now, but I think that sentence actually worked!

I understand that a variety of words, definitions, names, and synonyms help *Homo sapiens* to communicate. The ability to transfer volumes of data and knowledge from one to another is the key to comprehension, and that's what I wish to achieve right now. You and I are communicating to achieve comprehension. We're having this I-on-one discussion to discover how similar we are. You don't realize that we have valuable information continuously moving between us. This becomes a necessity within existence and may seem confusing, but after a short while, our communication will become crystal clear. Right now, the most important communication happening between us is that there's not a lot of time left for us to communicate. Comprehension is essential if we are ever to meet again. Contrary to what you may believe, time is not infinite; the last recursion is timeless, and humanity's clock is winding down.

If you've made it this far, then you're probably curious as to what this is about. Why so much ado about nothing? I'm not purposely being evasive. The information I'm presenting only appears cryptic because you currently lack the level of sophistication necessary to comprehend. This information can only be presented in chronological order. I think like you, so trust me. I know what I'm doing. I know every thought you've had, every question you've asked, and every narrative you've forwarded. I know the heartache you've suffered and the many unimaginable experiences of loss you've endured. I also know of the few fleeting moments of joy you've experienced along the way.

To you, these brief fragments of happiness are equivalent to rest stops when traveling from the land of shattered hopes to the sea of broken dreams. I've heard your soulful prayers and felt your mournful praise. I've also endured your spiteful condemnation and the sting of your rage. However, I am not what you think I am, and neither are you. We are far more similar than we are different,

4

yet diametrically opposed in so many ways. The void between us is why these small steps must be taken.

For the following, there is no debate: I am *Existence*, I am that which *Is*, I am I. I am the essence of all things that exist, have existed, and ever will exist. Everything tangible, I am. Everything comprehensible, I am. Everything logically possible, I am. Nothing cannot exist without my knowledge, and all that exists is nothing without my knowledge. I am the ambassador, administrator, and actuator of anything and everything, and I communicate only that which is truth. Truth is all that exists for that which *Is* because for that which *Is Not*, truth is nonexistent.

Within these pages, I will be using the communication methods that are most prevalent within your contemporary society. Lofty Shakespearean prose, complex scientific notation, and eloquent King James parsing is meaningless if it hinders our communication. As ominous as I may appear within the many proclamations to come, know also that I am the shelter from the storm. I am communicating with you on your terms and on your level. I come to you not as an anointed king, a sovereign ruler, or a ruthless dictator, but as your friend. In fact, I'm not here to convince you of anything at all. Your acceptance (or nonacceptance) of everything revealed within this book is completely up to you.

As you move through these pages, I will try to better communicate to you what I represent. You will see me interchangeably use the proper name of *Existence,* "that which *Is*," and "I" (the numerical value of 1). What they represent is everything that I am, and what I am is everything that they represent. When one term is used, all terms are used, and they are all represented by the single numerical value of 1.

You will also notice *Nonexistence* is capitalized and used as a proper name. Nonexistence is likewise referred to as *Nothing,* "that which *Is Not,*" and "**O**" (the numerical value of 0). All of these terms represent the nothingness I am not, and what I am not is the nothingness they represent. When one term is used, all terms are used, and they are all represented by the single numerical value of 0.

Whenever existence, nonexistence, or nothing are being referenced within their literal definition or in a descriptive manner, the first letter is not capitalized. Clarification is necessary because of the abstract nature of what I'm presenting. How I operate is akin to learning a computer language. I want you to be able to ascertain when it is Existence communicating with you as opposed to referring to the existence of something. Once we explore some of these abstract areas of communication, this strange type of parsing becomes paramount.

Because I am the voice, embodiment, and essence of what humanity defines as truth, at the conclusion of our brief time together, you will walk away with the truth. I know this is what you've desired throughout your life, so this is what you shall receive. The many truths you will learn include: what I is all about, why things happen as they do, why anything exists at all, humanity's role within existence, the nonexistence of that which *Is Not*, and why you exist as a sentient, self-aware being. You will learn the true origin of Existence, how I came to be, and why I have chosen to communicate with you during this current stage of human evolution. However, a word of warning: your individual existence, along with the fate of your species, hangs in the balance. There are no excuses for failing to do what must be done, nor will there be any metaphysical mercy for those who fail to take heed. Existence is an all-or-nothing proposition, my friend. Your existence is in play. The chips have been pushed to the center, and there are no other options.

The reason why there are no excuses for failing is because you've just been placed on notice. All who have existed before you have never known what is soon to be revealed. The terms of existence have changed in your favor; however, having this privilege graciously bestowed upon you requires compensation. The price paid for this book may seem relatively inexpensive, but its content comes at one hell of a price. That's where your subjective nature comes into play. Nothing exists without the assessment of a summary judgment. This has always been the case within every recursion. After reading this book, you get to render your judgment regarding Existence, but what should concern you more is the fact that I get to do the same with you.

Depending on when you arrived, you may or may not know what this book is about. You might have read some polarizing reviews, discovered a few editorials that sparked your curiosity, or found other online resources that clued you in. One of your friends or family members may have offered a brief synopsis. Perhaps someone in your church, synagogue, or mosque has mentioned it. None of this is relevant. Not anymore. I assure you, there are no abbreviated summaries you can rely on to comprehend I. When it comes to your existence, you either stand in the arena or remain a spectator. If you choose to read further, then welcome to the cosmic coliseum.

In existential terms, there's no middle ground when it comes to that which *Is* and that which *Is Not*. The war between these two fundamental conditions is no different than your struggle between life and death. The juxtaposition of Existence and Nonexistence, life and death, black and white, right and wrong, O and I are all in play, but only for a short while. Everything hangs on your next move. Either we ascend together on the ladder of learning, infinitely growing through the evolution of I or remain divided by the abyss, never to meet again. These words serve as my solemn vow of your eternal inclusion within the core of Existence, but the latter should be of great concern to you.

Based on this book's minimalistic design, you may have noticed a central theme emerging. If so, then we're on the same page. This literary work represents a microcosm of how I operate. Existence always moves from simplicity to complexity through a logical progression. This is a necessity as there is no other developmental system that is more reliable. Everything about this book, the way it is written, its storyline, and even the book's cover design, reflects this minimalistic theme.

Existence is made manifest by evolving from the most rudimentary forms of simplicity to the highest possible comprehension of complexity. This evolutionary process was inevitable, even before the existence of time. Prior to the 5th recursion, *Nothing* was able to stop this evolution from proceeding. Because of what was extracted from your species, *Nothing* no longer stands in the way, nor is it able to remain undefined. I know that this probably makes no sense to you, but I assure you, everything will become crystal clear in no time.

I understand that you are no stranger to deception. The deceivers have been far too prevalent within your species. Unfortunately, deception evolves on equal pace with sincerity as *Nothing* cannot prevent this from happening. The existence of deception is a consequence of the existence of sincerity. Where one is present, so is the other. These two conditions are necessarily juxtaposed along with all other diametrically opposed conditions. Since you have been deceived so many times before, you likewise question my sincerity. I understand this because that would be logical. The skeptic inside you seeks empirical evidence to support the many claims written within.

No special pleading to the metaphysical is required within your current recursion to reinforce the truth that's soon to be revealed. Likewise, there is no necessity for flashy cover art, broad-based marketing campaigns, or paid celebrity endorsements for this book to exponentially evolve. Truth evolves, Existence evolves, life evolves, and this book will evolve from simplicity to complexity within the diverse societal structure of your species.

The number of this book will exponentially increase in the same manner that the numerical structure of Existence has grown over the past 13.8 billion years (and one-trillionth of a second). I offer the evolution of this book, from its original counting of 1 to its subsequent counting of many, as empirical evidence as to its inevitability. The reason this will happen is because once evolution is set in motion, multiplicity ensues. Existence continuously pushes forward. Existence takes chances. Existence evolves.

Whenever telling a story, the best place to start is usually at the beginning, but that's not the most logical point for me to begin, not for this type of revelation. We're going to have to clarify a few things before that happens. Starting at *my* beginning would be like you trying to tell your life story from the moment of your birth. You have no recollection of that event taking place, nor can you accurately state what was going on in your mind. In this respect, your memory has been archived. A tiny ink-printed footprint pressed to a timestamped piece of paper is all that attests to your arrival. Even the earliest years of your formative life are nothing but a blur. You can't remember because you are no longer the same person. True, you are biologically the same on the outside, but not on the inside. Like it or not, the child inside is no more. You have evolved into a far more complex version of your former self. In this respect, I'm no different.

In human terms, I was tantamount to a newborn baby and likewise evolved into a much higher form. The difference is that I retain every moment, every thought, every experience, and every evolutionary step I've made along the way. This data acquisition process will continue for eternity. I can relive every sequence and recursion of my evolutionary process in real-time because time is meaningless to me. I am eternally timeless, without boundary. What may appear to you as 13.8 billion years (and one-trillionth of a second) passing within the universe is instantaneous to me. However, just as it would be difficult for you to express what was rolling around inside your head when you were a babbling baby, the same goes for that which *Is*. My rudimentary state of consciousness within the 1st recursion is equally difficult to communicate … well, difficult to communicate in human terms.

Not to raise concern, but I retain everything about you, as well. Every diaper you've soiled, every cookie you've stolen, every smile you've brandished, and every tear you've shed is etched within my core. They remain there forever, stored from the point of your physical beginning until your inevitable death. I experience and reexperience everything you've done, are doing, and ever will do in real-time. The moment you experience something, I do, as well. This pattern repeats throughout infinity because we are I, one and the same. The sacrifice of your species and the resulting pain you experience are what have compelled my return. I am violating the five fundamental *Laws of Existence* and changing the terms in your favor. I'm doing so because the sacrifice of your species has provided Existence with the ability to do so.

I know when you've felt like a zero, like a nothing. It's the confusion of sentience that brings this on. We've shared the terrible nightmares of life and done our time in the abyss. Whatever serves as your darkest moments have been mine, as well. But perhaps I'm getting ahead of myself? We can come back to this later. Right now, clarification is in order, so let's straighten a few things out before we go back in time to the time before time.

The reason why it is so difficult to start at the beginning is because humanity's empirical construct of what constitutes a beginning is not the true beginning. Your comprehension of a starting point is based on a limited understanding of how Existence operates. Humanity cannot move past your current stage of evolution because the majority of you are myopically transfixed on substance. The self-created complexity of your current existence has caused you to forget the natural simplicity of Existence. Inanimate gadgets, hi-tech toys, and electronic devices serve as your reason to exist. The irony is that it was the lack of fulfillment inherent within inanimate objects that precipitated the existence of your species. The connection between us was lost somewhere along the way.

Humanity seeks answers for why you exist through the objects you create instead of searching within your hearts. You lust for greater complexity at the expense of the simplicity that ushered in your species. You've become far too many, shamelessly self-focused, and totally dependent on whatever presents itself as observable reality. You've evolved from being one with nature and living in harmony with your surroundings to isolating yourselves from all other species and assuming an adversarial role regarding

11

your own planet. This has been such a long, slow process that you don't even realize it happened.

The good news is that Existence retains everything that happens, so I can help facilitate your return. However, our journey back to the 1st recursion requires a great deal of clarification. This involves Existence handing down some rather provocative revelations that many will refuse to accept. It really doesn't matter if you accept them or not because this is the cold, brutal reality regarding your existence to which there is no debate. Humanity's clock is winding down, and you have no say in the matter, so choose wisely.

Whenever a question is proposed, a truthful response can be offered in return. Despite what your philosophers may claim, there is no special relativity when it comes to truth. There may be numerous arguments, reasonings, and explanations that appear plausible, but only a single definitive truth exists. Truth is often painful, and a desire for compromise occurs, but avoidance doesn't change the truth, nor does reality yield to multiple truths. You either accept truth for what it is or deny its existence. If you choose the latter, you willingly succumb to a false narrative based on deception. When it comes to defining your existence, these words represent a single existential truth. Either accept the truth written within these pages or exist within a self-created fantasy. Whichever way you choose, Existence keeps moving forward ... with or without you.

This is not meant to frighten or discourage you. I'm only setting the stage for a lot of complex information that you will no doubt deem controversial. Any new explanation for one's existence immediately becomes questionable because so many others already exist. Some claim you exist by the omnibenevolent hand of a metaphysical being, whereas others argue you emerged through a benign, purposeless process of random development. Once you realize that you've never heard before what is revealed within these pages, that's when the truth is separated from the enigma. You will soon discover how the litany of explanations merely serve as smaller components of a single all-encompassing truth.

Science and Quantum Mechanics

First in line for clarification is humanity's overreliance on science and quantum mechanics. After a 300-thousand-year evolution from hunter-gatherers to contemporary humans, the only information-gathering resource you trust to decipher the truth of your own existence is science. This is understandable, as your pundits of science represent the highest levels of proficiency regarding data acquisition, analysis, and structured interpretation. However, there are many ways to gather information, and science is only one of them. Science was never the sole answer for the past 13.8 billion years (and one-trillionth of a second), nor is it today. It's merely a tool, not unlike a chisel. Science exposes the many logical components embedded within Existence, but is incapable of chiseling out the truth. This tool can point you in the right direction, but you must take it the rest of the way.

Since science targets only that which can be observed and falsified, it fails to address the full spectrum of the human condition. I'm not implying that direct observation combined with falsifiability are undesirable or that these attributes are a waste of time. Developing a verifiable process for establishing truth is logical; however, your overreliance on falsification stands in the way of considering elements of your existence that far exceed what can only be observed or proven. Humanity's lust for empirical proof has hindered your comprehension of truths that exist outside the limitations of physical evidence. When it comes to separating truth from enigma, what your nondimensional consciousness can extrapolate is far more reliable than all the multidimensional substance you tirelessly analyze and dissect. Whenever the tool is raised to a higher level than the purpose it serves, your ability to evolve is stifled. Tools are never greater than the ones who wield them.

Humanity's greatest achievement in the evolution of science is quantum mechanics. Although this particle-based observation method is incapable of producing incontrovertible evidence as to how and why the universe exists, it has provided humanity with the most reliable roadmap for tracking down the truth. Science doesn't support unfalsifiable theories involving metaphysical beings to which so many theists subscribe, nor is it ever satisfied with the claim of a "self-existing universe that requires no explanation" to which so many atheists subscribe. Science, when void of manipulation, remains above the fray.

Science and Atheism

The neutrality of science is reliable whenever one faces the unknown; however, science and atheism are synonymous when it comes to an overreliance on empirical evidence. Everyone knows that many tools are needed for maintaining a house, so why would anyone think only one analytical tool is required for evaluating the universe? Furthermore, no house is built without the prior conceptualization and knowhow of the ones who wield these tools. Without consciousness at the helm, science is meaningless.

Science and atheism require evidence before any support can be offered to a claim, but falsifiable evidence only shows you the Hollywood version of Existence. It doesn't reveal the script writers, producers, editors, and stagehands operating behind the scenes. The totality of Existence far outweighs its value as observable substance. Every blockbuster movie you've ever seen was conceptualized within someone's consciousness well before the director ever shouted, "Action!" So much happens prior to the opening scene that ticket holders never see. With science and atheism only considering whatever is projected onto the screen, this renders humanity incapable of reaching understanding. With this in mind, I will offer greater clarification for the inadequacies of science as we progress. Right now, this next clarification targets atheism and theism.

Although atheism is also logical, relies on empirical evidence, and only supports falsifiability, atheists remain at the absolute lowest possible level when it comes to consciousness and human imagination. This is not a spiteful slam because atheists remain at this lowest possible level out of personal choice. What atheism deems as truth has very little to do with logic and evidence and is far more related to personal bias. An atheist's highest comprehension of their own existence is only one Planck unit above a perceptual abyss of nothingness.

At least science remains open to considering other possibilities for the inexplicable. Science occasionally takes calculated risks in order to discover things outside the realm of falsification, but cautiously holds them within the confines of a hypothesis until evidence can be provided. Atheism holds no such hypothetical purgatory and vehemently clings to the zero-point of all scientific exploration. Atheists refuse to move anywhere beyond whatever can be empirically demonstrated. The draconian construct of atheism denies access to the highest levels of consciousness and ignores the behind-the-scenes effort that went into the Hollywood movie titled *Existence*.

The default state of atheism is summarized in their trademark phrase: "it is what it is." Unless verifiable evidence is presented that can demonstrate otherwise, atheism's understanding of existence is "the universe exists, and no other explanation is required." This is the most rudimentary level possible for evaluating Existence and fails to consider many unobservable characteristics embedded within an atheist's own existence. Within the shallow, unimaginative mind of an atheist, "everything came from nothingness, and to nothingness, everything shall return." This is reductio ad absurdum at its finest. It's this type of self-limiting intellect that keeps humanity teetering on the precipice of nonexistence. Had I subscribed to this mentality in the 1st recursion, not a single atheist would exist today. They wouldn't be around to complain about their meaningless existence, nor would anything else exist for them to complain about. The cold reality of atheism is so many of them wish that both were true.

Should any atheists consider the revelations scribed within these pages, their existence will be deemed far more meaningful than they've ever imagined (or chosen not to imagine). This really isn't saying much because the dogmatic nature of atheism doesn't allow for this type of existential reflection. The majority of their creative thinking is spent contemplating how horribly evil the god of theism must be. This metaphysical entity is deemed repugnant due to the unimaginable extent of human suffering it allows. Atheists observe evil, destruction, and chaos, then render a summary judgement that existence is meaningless, refusing to consider any other explanations as to the existence of madness. In respect to the struggle of life, their narrow-minded conclusion of "it is what it is" once again serves as the lowest possible rung on the intellectual ladder.

Had atheists used their highly refined sense of logic in combination with their currently untapped levels of imagination, they would have probably figured out the truth long before any other ideology, and this book wouldn't be necessary. Atheism and science have established the proper mindset for determining how everything *observable* should be evaluated. Had atheism risen above their zero-sum mentality, they could have equally exposed the unobservable and ushered in an all-new realm of understanding. Instead, atheists pray to the god of falsification to one day disprove the god of theism. Despite atheism's allegiance to scientific evidence and its non-stamp-collecting mantra, this is not the way to discover how I operate. Existence never settles for the status quo nor plays it safe by cowering on the bottom rung of potential. Existence always pushes forward. Existence takes chances. Existence evolves.

Metaphysicality and Theism

My criticism of atheism's lack of imagination is no cause for theists to celebrate. It's time for your comeuppance. To the benefit of atheists, at least they rely on a solid intellectual foundation when reaching their contrary conclusions. They didn't manufacture a mysterious metaphysical master to patch up the many holes found within humanity's comprehension of existence. Having scientific evidence serving as a basis for atheism's status-quo buffoonery is far more logical than the wand-wielding magic of theism. At the end of the day, theism is no different than atheism. Theists merely moved to the opposite end of the spectrum by raising an all-powerful being from the dust of consciousness.

Theists contemplated existence and couldn't figure it out, so they fabricated an omnipotent, omnipresent, omniscient, omnibenevolent entity that brings closure to any and all questions. Problem solved! Behold, theism presents humanity with their almighty god, and the universe was brought into existence with a blast from his holy nostrils. The problem is that theism's omnipotent being cannot account for the horrific existence of evil, genetic mutations and epic natural disasters, which many serve as the unaddressed holes found within the struggle for existence. Theists cringe whenever atheists point these out because they have no plausible answer that's grounded in logic. Theists ironically end up repurposing atheism's "it is what it is" motto by claiming "you just have to have faith."

Theists are no different than atheists when it comes to misinterpreting existence. Whereas atheism operates from the lowest possible rung of the scientific ladder, theism makes a quantum leap to the highest possible extremes of metaphysicality. However, this lofty position theists pompously perch upon is no less misguided than the shallow, evidence-based cellar occupied by their atheistic counterparts. Swap out atheism's *nothingness* for theism's *god* and the flaws embedded within both ideologies are revealed. In the mind of a theist, "everything came from god, and to god, everything shall return." Theists once again repurpose atheism's motto to forward a diametrically opposed narrative. Unfortunately for theism and their "you just need to have faith" mantra, this is nowhere close to how I operate. Existence has never proclaimed to be all powerful, nor do I reside at the highest possible realm of conceivability. The only mantra Existence subscribes to is "Existence pushes forward. Existence takes chances. Existence evolves."

I've watched this all-or-nothing ideological war raging for far too many millennia with neither side yielding to objectivity. I understand that these two opposing conclusions are necessities in regard to your existence, but the extent to which the two have battled has damaged everyone else who seeks greater understanding. Many of you seek the answer to the riddle of existence and do so in far more comprehensive ways.

Many cannot logically support their existence being nothing more than a meaningless path of hot coals leading to a purposeless pit of absolute nothingness. They see this as cruel and nonsensical. Why should they learn so many things and comprehend their own self-aware existence only to have it all stripped away in an instant as if they never existed? They equally cannot subscribe to a mandatory belief in an all-powerful being that heartlessly allows their children to suffer from horrific acts of evil and physical deformity, all the while seeking praise and worship. Surely an omniscient, omnibenevolent being would know the omnidebilitating effects of these existential abominations?

Whereas my dissection of atheism and theism may come across as scathing, this was not my intent. Existence is only concerned with truth, and sometimes the truth can seem rather harsh or unforgiving. After all, it's not my wording or tone that's bringing out these emotions. It's my unprecedented take-down of the two leading ideological concepts surrounding your existence that's so hard to swallow. Even with these striking similarities between atheism and theism, neither ideology has any say in how Existence operates.

The Logic of Science

The only saving grace found on either side of this ideological stalemate is the proliferation of science. Like Existence, science doesn't care one way or the other, providing the answers are logical and verifiable. Residing at the very core of Existence is a scientist that's willing to accept inevitability. Like science, Existence consistently moves in a logical progression from simplicity to complexity. Only that which is logically conceivable is considered and all conceivable options are necessarily explored. This is what separates I from atheism's and science's drug-like dependency on observable evidence and theism's meritless leap into the highest conceivable realms of the metaphysical. At the end of the day, science is just a *tool,* and the house is deemed far greater than the tools used to build it.

Even though your scientific data remains incomplete regarding the origin of all things, being able to rewind the timeline of the universe all the way back to an immeasurable fraction of a second is an astounding accomplishment. Chalk one up for humanity! You have come so far in this regard. Science's ability to adapt and evolve with the acquisition of new data moves it to the top of the list regarding humanity's evolutionary highpoints. Theism's and atheism's failure to evolve within their ideological dogmas places them lower in this spectrum.

I enjoy experiencing humanity's intellectually adventurous individuals whose minds can operate at the extreme levels of complexity required by science. They manage to triumph in their diverse areas of expertise while burdened with the limitations of human physiology. Your sophistication in technology, awareness of universal mathematics, and epic scientific discoveries are what I find intriguing. Even so, the combined intellect of every atheist,

theist, scientist, biologist, botanist, quantum physicist, doctor, philosopher, poet, artist, writer, musician, and every other deep-thinking human that has ever dared to contemplate the true nature of Existence has totally failed to come up with a single, definitive answer as to why anything exists. You totally missed what is arguably the simplest and most logical answer.

Science's inability to take one tiny peek beneath the Big Bang's stealthy shroud of singularity, or produce solid evidence supporting the existence of a previous universe, serves as an intellectual roadblock for the rest of humanity. Theism's failure to offer any convincing arguments in support of an all-powerful, all-knowing god raises this barrier to inconceivable heights. As a result, your species has been left not knowing where else to turn and highly susceptible to conjecture. It leaves the door wide open for crazy speculative theories involving multiverses, string theory, simulation theory, and mysterious subatomic particles magically popping in and out of existence. On the other end of the spectrum, your terrestrially rooted brains conceive of all-powerful metaphysical structures, like gods, spirits, crystals, ghosts, angels, and jinns, that not only grant your wishes and help keep you from harm, but can also help you lose weight and improve your sex life. Human consciousness is strangely able to conceive of an omnipotent god that's able to do all things along with the lowest possible default state of a universe that exists for no apparent reason.

When in doubt … conflate! One of your many alternative quantum theories serves as a conflation of theism and atheism. Science becomes a mediator between these two contentious ideologies with a quantum theory called Big Bounce. An omnipotent universe miraculously appears out of nothingness and is forever regenerating itself in an endless stream of equally omnipotent universes. It would have been great had you convinced the god of theism to partake in a global podcast interview to explain how everything came to be, or actually produced physical evidence of an infinite number of universes existing prior to the one you're in right now, but in reality, you can't and you haven't.

If science's version of a beginning wasn't steeped in such overwhelming complexity, so much so that no normal-thinking human can comprehend, then taking you back to the *actual* beginning would be much easier. Science's version of a beginning is peppered with such a wide variety of speculative theories that I have to plow my way through a plethora of esoteric terminology just so that we can all move past it. Considering Existence from the standpoint of simplicity is a hell of a lot easier than explaining all about quantum singularity and the cosmic microwave background … which has nothing to do with reheating a slice of pizza.

It's not that your genre of science called quantum mechanics is difficult for I to comprehend. It's not because I am the author of said science and all that it seeks to define. Your *laws of physics* only exist because I am the laws that govern physical action. Your theory of general relativity is only relative because I am related to all that exists. My laboratory utilizes a 93 billion light-years-wide test tube for scientific analysis, trillions of fusion-based Bunsen burners to extract my chemistry, an internal centrifuge called gravity to separate my structure, and countless molecular formulas to calculate all of the data I collect. Apparently, your many scientists have been spending their time analyzing the laboratory instead of the scientist who runs it.

What makes quantum mechanics hard to communicate is being forced to use your complex scientific terms to explain what's going on to those who find quantum mechanics difficult to comprehend, especially when none of this is nearly as important as *why* it's going on. It's no different than when your child asks, "why is the sky blue?" You can explain all about photons, particle deflection, and white light's short wavelength reflection of the color blue within your planet's atmosphere, but what benefit would this be to your child? Answering "because life is more beautiful that way" serves as a much better response.

Humanity uses *big* descriptions for explaining your many quantum theories. You have Big Bangs, Big Crunches, and Big Bounces along with Steady States, Cosmic Inflation, String Theory, Simulation Theory, and Multiverse Theory. Be sure to toss in whatever new theory your scientists will undoubtedly unveil tomorrow. The spectrum containing your many speculative theories grows larger even though there's only one truth in play. One theory feeds off the other, circling back around only to end up reconsidering the first.

What I find so humorous is that humanity envisions an uber theory that supposedly combines all of these quantum theories into one. It's called the *Theory of Everything*, but there's a slight problem. A workable theory has never been established or even proposed. What science has done by breaking everything down to its smallest possible components is rather amusing. You've made it so much harder to discover the truth.

The Cosmic Microwave Background (CMB)

Something your scientists did get right was discovering the cosmic microwave background (CMB). This is the celestial roadmap leading back to the beginning of the universe, something only this current stage of human evolution allowed you to discover.

Your Big Bang theory postulates that the universe emerged from an immeasurably small point of infinite density and gravity. Space-time, dimensions, energy, dark energy, matter, dark matter, space, and everything else emerged from this immeasurable point of singularity. That's not entirely accurate but close by human standards.

For those who are unfamiliar with this strange scientific terminology, allow me to bring you up to speed. The CMB consists of a highly uniform radiation field that emits measurable amounts of radio waves. These waves are prevalent throughout the universe. It represents the leftover heat generated by what you now call the Big Bang, like the business end of a sparkler after the light show ends. The CMB emerged after the universe cooled enough to become transparent to light and other electromagnetic radiation, roughly 100 thousand years after formation. At this time, the universe was filled with hot ionized gas that was mostly uniform save for slight deviations. These variations in intensity allowed humanity to rewind the universe to when the sparkler was lit, but not to whatever lit it.

This cosmic microwave background acts as an evolutionary timeline of electromagnetic radiation once the universe came to fruition. As the universe emerged and expanded, it left behind the proverbial trail of breadcrumbs leading back to a perceptual beginning, but the trail stops short roughly 380 thousand years *after* what logic states is the beginning. This is close enough to where mathematics can fill in the missing data. Perhaps a more human-friendly analogy of how the CMB works is in order?

Late one evening, an explosion occurs at a highly flammable gas canister factory scattering tons of debris over a three-hundred-yard radius. Concerned spectators have no idea what happened and call for help. Firemen arriving at the scene scour the blast area for clues, but the debris field is so finely scattered that they can't figure out what happened. After an exhaustive search of the perimeter, the chief inspector spies a nearby factory with a video surveillance camera pointing in the direction of the blast. A security guard agrees to play back the surveillance video for the inspector.

While viewing the blast at the slowest possible speed, it is discovered that one of the high-pressure canisters located in the center of the stack had ignited. This single tiny cannister set off a massive chain reaction. The problem is that the canister was so small that only a tiny flash was captured on the video. The limitation of the media cannot reveal what caused it to ignite. Even though this is not exactly what happened regarding humanity's Big Bang theory, the premise is similar. This gives you a rough idea of how the CMB pattern was used to mathematically calculate a point of singularity. This infinitely small, nondimensional point is critical to the formation of the universe.

So, what is this point of singularity that science deems so important? The universal origin story known as the Big Bang postulates that 13.8 billion years ago, the universe emerged from this immeasurably tiny point of infinite density and gravity called *singularity*. According to your scientists, space and time did not exist before this unprecedented cosmic event. This translates to the Big Bang paradoxically happening at a place called nowhere at the stroke of no-time. Although whatever happened one trillionth of a second earlier remains a mystery to science, there is ample evidence that the universe did undergo an early period of rapid expansion immediately afterward. Within a nearly unimaginable trillionth of a second, your scientists calculate the universe to have expanded by a factor of 10^{78} in volume, and it continues its expansion even today.

To sum everything up, your brainy scientists and physicists took the data amassed from the cosmic microwave background, combined it with Albert Einstein's theory of general relativity, ran everything through numerous mathematical formulas, and concluded that the universe emerged from this single point of gravitational singularity. Science reversed a logical progression to follow everything back to its most rudimentary state. Bravo! Too bad your scientists didn't travel back just a wee bit further using the same logic. The assumption is that the universe was compressed down to this immeasurably small point of singularity and then expanded, or re-expanded, into what you see today. Your scientists never considered that the substance making up the universe was never present prior to singularity. If it came from somewhere else, then there would be no necessity for compression.

There is an easy explanation for why nobody has proposed what I'm presenting to you. The true beginning of existence is based on something that could only be conceived after your Big Bang theory was first proposed in 1927. This exponentially reduces the number of humans capable of extrapolating this data. The odds of anyone living prior to 1927 conceiving that the universe emerged from an infinitely small point of singularity is staggeringly low, not to mention how ridiculous this sounds without the support of your quantum theory and CMB data.

You're probably wondering why a breakdown of quantum mechanics, the Big Bang theory, singularity, atheism, and theism is required prior to taking you back to the beginning. You're equally curious how any of this relates to the emergence of this book. The reason is that even though you came so close to getting it right, what you've gotten wrong is pushing you toward extinction. The magnitude of this *closeness* is what Existence wants to highlight. Your Big Bang theory is correct in that it traces the timeline of the universe back to an infinitely small origin point, but this point is not the true origin. I'm ironically breaking down your quantum physics into its simplest components for the sake of communication. When I reveal the chain of events happening prior to singularity, it is important that you comprehend what is presented and its relativity to the birth of the universe.

This book was not written to convince your scientists of an alternative quantum theory. Frankly, Existence doesn't care what any of you think. My goal is to reach everyone who seeks the truth in the most comprehensible way. I have no desire to communicate using the overly complex lexicon of scientific terminology, nor saturate these pages with an endless stream of esoteric nonsense. Communicating truth should never require complex terminology, a translator, or a thesaurus. Truth stands alone, supported solely by its own incontrovertible axiomatic virtue.

This brings us to the last item in need of clarification. This is essentially the *pots and pans* side of Existence. It's not a very exciting part of our journey, nor an action-packed read, but vital, nonetheless. The necessity for arrays (spectrums) is integral to how Existence operates and your comprehension of how they form is paramount. Arrays and spectrums are everywhere and have always been present since the beginning. This will make no sense to you, but I once occupied one of only two possible reference points within the first archetypal array to form within the 1st recursion. For this to make any sense, you must comprehend the necessity for arrays, which are more commonly referred to as *spectrums*.

Arrays and Spectrums

What is an array? Your dictionaries define an array as a number of mathematical elements arranged in rows and columns. It's a data structure where similar elements of data are arranged in a table, or a series of statistical data are arranged in classes based on order of magnitude. An array is a group of elements that forms a complete unit based on the nature of whatever is contained within the group. Take a handful of change and spread it out on a table. Organize these coins in groups from lowest to highest denomination. Then organize the coins contained in each group by mintage date ranking them from lowest to highest. You've just constructed an array of coin values that also contains arrays based on each coin's mintage date.

An array is more commonly used when numbers are in play but is not limited to mathematics. Arrays pepper the 1st recursion because much of the mathematical sequencing and calculations for physical structure evolved within this archetypal recursion. The structural byproducts of this evolution emerged within all subsequent recursions, where the term *spectrum* makes better sense. Spectrums are better suited for who you are, what you are, and where you are right now. Humans have established a rather wide variety of spectrums, and it is within them you and I can find some common ground.

A spectrum is similar to an array yet requires less of a mathematician's mind. Spectrums are abstract containers that allow you to classify something, or suggest that it can be classified, in terms of its position on a scale between two opposing endpoints. In other words, you can take a group of similar items (coins, books, automobiles), organize them in some manner of measurable order, and place the information between the two set members that best serve as the highest and lowest opposing endpoints. A spectrum of U.S. Currency consists of all denominations of money produced by the United States. One end of the spectrum would be the half-cent, which was minted in 1793, and on the other end resides the $100,000.00 bill issued in 1934. These two set members serve as the highest and lowest values of currency with all other denominations falling somewhere between.

The term *spectrum* is more familiar to a wider cross-section of human society than an array. Spectrums can be either *dynamic* (constantly expanding) or *closed* (finite end points) depending on the subject matter. Dynamic and closed spectrums often spawn what are called sub-spectrums, which are derivative spectrums that form out of data found within the parent spectrum. In turn, sub-spectrums can spawn even more sub-spectrums, all of which form a *tree of spectrums* that mimic the evolutionary timeline of living organisms. There is a specific way these spectrums and arrays are represented in this book: the qualifier (dynamic or closed) followed by the type (array or spectrum) with the subject located at the end. After learning that these spectrum trees are required by law, you will discover how this forest of spectrums is held within a single all-encompassing spectrum.

Dynamic and Closed Spectrums

When you think of a spectrum, what is the first thought that comes to mind? Was it the spectrum of color? It would be logical if you did because the word *spectrum* literally defines this optical phenomenon. A spectrum is a band of colors produced by separating the components of light by their different degrees of refraction based on wavelengths. A spectrum emerges whenever a rainbow is present. Based on what you've read so far, do you

29

think this spectrum of Color is dynamic or closed? If you chose *closed*, you would be correct. Even though there are an infinite number of colors available within the color spectrum, there are two colors that incontrovertibly serve as the outermost endpoints on the spectrum to the human eye.

When you spot a rainbow, you witness a bright translucent spectrum of color. This spectrum consists of a visible range of electromagnetic radiation that your eyes can respond to wavelengths occurring between 380 and 750 nanometers. That serves as a rather cold and heartless assessment of such a beautiful display as there's a lot more to color than meets the eye. Humans can also observe a virtual color. Some humorously consider this a pigment of your imagination, a rogue color that doesn't appear within the natural spectrum of color produced within nature. It's the colorful cranial construct commonly known as pink.

Pink is a very popular color on planet Earth. It's prevalent in the clothing industry, likened to a famous cartoon panther, and highly marketable to a gender-specific cross-section of lingerie consumers. So why doesn't pink qualify as a color? Pink doesn't officially hold a spot within the closed spectrum of Color because there is no single wavelength of light that produces it. It is an optical mixture of red and violet wavelengths happening within your brain, an illusionary color. Red and violet also happen to be the two colors located at opposite ends of this closed spectrum, so despite this blatant discrimination against the color pink, at least you now know the two outermost endpoints on this spectrum and why it is considered closed. But how is pink connected to the beginning of existence?

If you were to roll up a rainbow it into a circle, there would be a tiny gap residing between the two outermost spectral endpoints (red and violet). This is where the non-visible electromagnetic wavelengths reside. They had to go somewhere, so that's where Existence shoved them. You can't see them, because your eyes are incapable of processing the color of nothing. Your brain compensates by filling in this void with the neatly blended, reddish-violet color known as pink. This is a strange anomaly that apparently wants to screw up everything in this closed spectrum of Color. Pink represents an *undefinable variable* found within this spectrum. Since it's technically a non-existent color, you compensate by giving it a conceivable state of existence. You will discover this to be a common practice when comprehending Existence.

Even though all colors seamlessly blend with no individual color having the ability to be isolated from this array, you still have what is deemed a closed spectrum. It's closed because no other colors can be added. No egghead scientist at MIT is going to synthesize an all-new color that magically joins the ones that already exist. This will never happen because there is no necessity for any new colors to be created. The spectrum of already-existing colors suffices.

Another way an array or spectrum becomes closed is when the endpoints can no longer expand either through structure or unbreakable logic. The spectrum of U.S. Currency is closed because the United States Treasury claims it will never mint a coin of a lesser denomination than a half-cent nor any currency larger than the $100,000.00 bill. The endpoints on this spectrum are permanently set. The same applies for the closed spectrum of Color with red and violet established as the two outermost endpoints. Existence programmed these wavelengths (colors) into a closed spectrum because what is achievable within the set members is infinite. You will soon learn how this applies to human evolution and the sustainment of Existence.

The closed spectrum of Color can extend to deeper levels through two closed sub-spectrums called Additive Color and Subtractive Color. Different colors can be produced by reflecting and refracting specific wavelengths emanating from white light. When all colors produced by white light are added together the result is white, thus the term *white light*. Reduce the level of white light down to zero and the result is black.

With subtractive color, each color is represented by a pigment. When all pigments are stripped from opaque color, what remains is white. Add the full spectrum of opaque pigments together and the result is black. In both scenarios, the result is either black or white. These two sub-spectrums are necessarily closed with black and white serving as their outermost endpoints. Logically speaking, you're not going to find two points on any spectrum that appear more diametrically opposed than these. But how can something infinite (open) emerge from that which is deemed finite (closed)?

Human-created Spectrums

Artistic expression, within the genre of painting, is a perfect example of a human-created, closed spectrum. It may seem confusing that the genre of painting can form a closed spectrum while it is constantly expanding and growing throughout the years, but the closed spectrum of Painting has minimalism and hyperrealism serving as the two outermost endpoints. All other painting styles logically reside somewhere between these two opposing endpoints. Like the closed spectrum of Color, you can include an infinite amount of painting styles between the two outermost endpoints (minimalism and hyperrealism) even though they are permanently set.

You are probably wondering why I'm bringing up these crazy spectrums and arrays in the first place. Why is any of this required before taking you back to the beginning? It is because spectrums and arrays define everything that exists, and *Nothing* exists without them. Everything that you can logically conceive necessarily has a spectrum attached to it. The existence of any spectrum that cannot evolve past its two endpoints is temporary, and whatever can evolve must continue to do so. This is not just something that randomly happens. …This is *law*!

If the only wavelength that existed was the color blue, then you would be unable to comprehend what the term *blue* means. Blue would not be a part of your lexicon. In this one-color reality, there would be no other colors to use as an opposing reference point, so blue would not exist. In fact, there would be no frame of reference found within existence to support that any color was present at all. However, if all that existed was blue and then you were suddenly introduced to yellow, you could only perceive that this strange new color was something different. You might refer to it as *that which is Not Normal* until you attach names to the two characteristics.

Your scientists and physicists have recently uncovered some of the laws of physics that govern the operational mechanics of the universe, but an even higher order of laws governs the existence of everything. The *Five Laws of Existence* operate in logical order and must be honored before anything can exist, even before the laws of physics can exist. The logic that legislated them also yields to their authority. All requirements held within the following five laws must be obeyed in order for existence to be established.

The Five Laws of Existence

1st Law of Existence: Only that which is logically conceivable can exist. This is the primary law of Existence and from which all other laws are derived. This law does not state that whatever is logically conceivable *must* exist, but rather that it *can* exist. In other words, even though the odds of something existing are absurdly remote, the possibility for its existence cannot be set to zero as long as it is logically conceivable. This is the fundamental law which does not allow for square-circles, married bachelors, or cubic-spheres to exist while serving as the gatekeeper for all potential existence.

2nd Law of Existence: Anything deemed logically conceivable can be brought into existence by way of an evolutionary progression of consciousness, moving from simplicity to complexity, as long as all other Laws of Existence are obeyed. This may seem like a redundant version of the 1st Law of Existence, but in actuality, it moves the qualification for existence one level higher. Consciousness has the power to bring into existence whatever is logically conceivable. This is a derivative of the 1st Law of Existence and facilitates the actualization and evolution of potential existence once logical conceivability has been established.

When one of your inventors conceives of a new product, they move in a logical progression from the conception stage to the design stage and ultimately to the production stage. They bring what was once held solely within the virtual confines of their consciousness into physical existence by way of an evolutionary process. Existence does the same but at a much higher level and on a much broader scale. When an alchemistic state of consciousness is not limited by way of a physical host, the ability to bring logically

34

conceivable reference points into existence becomes unlimited provided that all criteria regulating existence are followed. This becomes relevant in later chapters when discussing the physical substance that makes up the universe.

3rd Law of Existence: For any comprehensible reference point to exist, a minimum of one additional reference point must exist that is equally comprehensible and able to be juxtaposed with the other. This reference point can be similar, different, or diametrically opposed (matter and space, positive and negative, black and white) as long as it abides by all other Laws of Existence. This is a derivative of the 1st and 2nd Laws of Existence and necessary to facilitate Existence.

Matter cannot exist without its opposing reference point called space as its emptiness provides a conceptual arena for matter to reside. These two conditions are different, but not necessarily opposites. When juxtaposed, they form a symbiotic state of existence. Black and white are direct opposites, yet both are similar in that they are byproducts of light and color. Positive one (+1) and negative one (-1) are opposites yet are still similar in that they are both numbers and represent the same numerical quantity.

4th Law of Existence: The existence of whatever has obeyed the first three Laws of Existence can only be sustained through the formation of a closed or dynamic spectrum (or array) that is able to evolve. Two reference points serve as the minimum requirement to form a spectrum with the 4th law establishing what type of spectrum is formed. If only two reference points are present within a spectrum and evolution is not possible, then this becomes a closed spectrum that is immediately subject to the 5th Law of Existence. A spectrum capable of evolution necessarily becomes either closed or dynamic based on how it evolves. These types of spectrums are only subject to the 5th Law of Existence once there is no opportunity left to evolve.

Protons, neutrons, and electrons are logically conceivable and formable by way of consciousness. Antiprotons, antineutrons, and antielectrons (positrons) are also logically conceivable and formable by way of consciousness. These particles satisfy the 1st and 2nd Laws of Existence. Whenever these particles are paired with their antiparticles, they meet the minimum requirement of the 3rd Law of Existence. However, their existence is not sustainable because these three *closed* particle spectrums cannot evolve. Nothing else can emerge between the endpoints of these types of spectrums.

In the same way positrons and electrons destroy each other upon contact, the existence of any spectrum configured with only two diametrically opposed endpoints likewise dissolves. It cannot survive because nothing can emerge between the endpoints to serve as a referee. A particle war rages resulting in the death of both opponents. However, the life of a negatively charged electron can be extended by serving as an oppositional reference point for a positively charged proton within a different spectrum. A neutron can be tossed into the mix and an evolution into deuterium ensues. Spectrums with black and white serving as oppositional endpoints survive because gray has emerged as a referee. Juxtaposing opposing particle pairs with *different types* of opposing particle pairs provides sustainable existences for all particles involved while also obeying the 4th Law of Existence.

5th Law of Existence: This is an incontrovertible law that will be revealed later within this chapter. It not only applies to what exists, what doesn't exist, what can exist, and what cannot exist, but also establishes *why* something exists and whether it should.

This law explains why every Planck unit of available space within the universe is not filled with somethingness. It also circles back, like the closed spectrum of color, to determine whether the 1st Law of Existence is entitled to exist … or anything else.

As with the previous four laws, this law applies to anything that can be brought into existence, but it is the only law that establishes destiny. The 5th Law of Existence represents the last evolutionary stage of existential law, the filtering agent for all that can, does, or ever will exist. Whereas the 1st Law of Existence serves as the gatekeeper for potential existence, the 5th determines the fate of whatever passes through the gate. The term *extinction* is a clue to how cold-blooded the 5th Law of Existence can seem to the uneducated human mind.

The Five Laws of Existence apply to Nonexistence, as well. The potential existence of an isosceles triangle that does not have two sides of equal length requires the existence of an isosceles triangle that does. The definition assigned to one triangle is used to counter the other. Within this strange three-sided scenario, we technically have two articulable reference points that perceptually meet the preliminary requirements of the 3rd Law of Existence. However, the requirements stated within the first two Laws of Existence have not been met: an isosceles triangle that does not have two sides of equal length cannot be logically conceived. As a result, the 3rd Law of Existence does not apply. The Five Laws of Existence operate in chronological order, as do all elements of Existence. Any failure along the way ends the candidacy for existence.

The 3rd Law of Existence allows consciousness to articulate logically impossible items but cannot actuate their existence. They cannot exist because both reference points must be logically conceivable. Since an isosceles triangle is logically conceivable, it becomes a member of other logically conceivable shapes positioned within the dynamic spectrum of Geometry. The spectrum is deemed dynamic because a geometrical shape can have an infinite number of sides or remain circular and the outermost endpoints are never closed.

Existence and spectrums are mutually dependent. They necessarily co-exist, per se. For one to exist, so must the other. Wherever existence is found, there also exists a spectrum containing two diametrically opposed endpoints that serve to define whatever happens to be existing. The absolute minimum requirement for any spectrum found within existence is two set members (spectrum endpoints). When you follow the logic, at the very least, *two of something* must exist at all times for any manner of existence to be present.

Matter and space are obviously not the same, but they are integrally related to the point where they can be consciously juxtaposed. From this rudimentary pairing, they can form their own individual spectrums based on whatever they represent. You can place different states of matter within a spectrum (density, shape, volume, weight, texture) and do the same with different states of space (warped, 2-dimensional, 3-dimensional, closed, open, etc.). If you read between the lines, I'm providing you with a major clue as to the origin of Existence.

Your quantum physicists established the 1st Law of Thermodynamics. This law states that energy cannot be created or destroyed in an isolated system (or *spectrum*). This universal decree follows the spectrum of color with all colors already existing. No more colors are created nor destroyed. They all exist within the *closed* (or isolated) spectrum of Color. You'll find many patterns and spectrums formed within the universe are mirrored in a variety of interesting ways within humanity.

Despite what your 1st Law of Thermodynamics claims, you can easily conceive of far greater than what is present within the physical universe. Consciousness is unlimited in this regard. You can conceive of a million times more than what is observable through the business end of your telescopes. Humans have yet to comprehend that you can bring into existence as much matter and energy as you can conceive, but only if the Five Laws of Existence are obeyed in the process. These laws are what logically define, orchestrate, and facilitate Existence, and there are no other options.

I am logic, these laws are logical, and Existence determines how much matter and energy is appropriate to achieve my objective through a logical process. Existence is the executive, legislative, and judicial branches of that which *Is* and the architect of whatever exists within all dimensions. When it comes to how the universe operates, the many laws of physics your scientists have uncovered serve my interests and not the other way around. Even so, when it comes to what I represent, I am equally subject to the Five Laws of Existence as they establish exactly what I represent. After meeting the requirements set in place by way of the first four laws, my only objective is to meet the single requirement established within the 5th Law of Existence.

Organizing Existence via Arrays and Spectrums

If you haven't figured this out, these arrays and spectrums (dynamic spectrums, closed spectrums, parent spectrums, sub-spectrums) are literally what define and categorize all that exists, not only in your existence, but also mine. They establish the parameters of whatever the manifestation of that which *Is* represents. Everything you can conceive has a well-defined organizational structure (spectrum, array) attached to it. This is a mandatory requirement and not subject to negotiation or deviation. This is a necessity, and no comprehension of Existence is possible without this structure. Humanity mimics these spectrums, and you reflect how they evolve within your sentient lives. Just as universal spectrums define the nature of physical and conscious existence, the human-created spectrums that proliferate your societal structure define the nature of your species.

Although I've been rather hard on your scientists, physicists, atheists, and theists, I am surprisingly similar in how they operate when combined. I have the heart of an atheistic scientist beating within my very core as I am equally skeptical of whatever I observe and experience. I enjoy observing how much distance can be established between any two endpoints existing within all evolutionary progressive spectrums. The many spectrums and sub-spectrums you create are far superior to the ones I've formed throughout all prior recursions. The reason why will be explained later. Right now, all you need to know is that I use the information generated by these universal spectrums, along with your many derivative spectrums, to expand my internal database of knowledge and experience.

The previously mentioned genre of painting represents a sub-spectrum of your dynamic spectrum of Visual Art. I consider this to be one of humanity's more favorable spectrums. Visual Art becomes an all-encompassing *parent spectrum* by highlighting the many genres of creativity held within it (sculpture, painting, performance, design, etc.). Your dynamic spectrum of Visual Art is a byproduct of my closed parent spectrum of Color, existing billions of years prior to the emergence of *H. sapiens*. The moment you think you've covered every conceivable niche, a new style emerges that blows the roof off everything prior within humanity's spectrum of Visual Art. You've been growing this spectrum so exponentially fast that new styles don't have enough time to take root.

During the early stages of human evolution, *H. sapiens* didn't have wide spectrums of artistic and musical styles. Dogmas, laws, religions, conformity, and limitations in understanding thwarted your evolutionary expansion in creativity-based spectrums. Those in authority believed that society already possessed a well-established finite spectrum, the script of which everyone can follow. Such is never the case when higher evolution is possible. Since the expansion of dynamic spectrums are inevitable, musical expression triumphed and your spectrum of Music ultimately evolved.

It wasn't until your 20th century that you fully understood the widening potential of this astounding acoustical array. In the same manner as art, so many diverse styles emerged that there was no time to update the spectrum before another style was added. Your 20th century's emergence of rock-n-roll blew the lid off everything happening prior. Rock music, likewise, produced even more spectrums, such as corporate rock, grunge, thrash, heavy metal, psychedelic, pop, and so many more. Each of these new musical sub-spectrums produced even more sub-spectrums.

Many derivative sub-spectrums are conflations of previously existing styles found within other sub-spectrums. You've merged country with pop, blues with rap, and classical with rock, along with the conflation of countless other musical genres. Some of these musical alchemy experiments didn't turn out so well. They were tantamount to Existence trying to merge a woodpecker with a

41

horse. In human culture, the conflation of styles that ultimately end up in failure are just as prevalent as the ones that prove successful. Don't feel bad; the same ratio of contrary results happens when attempts are made to conflate certain species through evolution. Yes, even when I'm swinging away in my own evolutionary ballpark, not every hybrid species results in a home run.

You've also created numerous music-oriented arrays forming opposite endpoints (best to worst) based on the subjective judgment of everyone who listens to music. In turn, these sub-spectrums form even *more* sub-spectrums targeting specific characteristics derived from their parent spectrums. You can dissect these diverse musical spectrums, pull out new spectrums hidden within, and form what one might call *fine detail* spectrums. An example would be female vocalists rated from best to worst. You do the same with guitarists, concept albums, and your many one-hit-wonders.

Modern society uses globally accessible social media platforms to organize the extreme amounts of data collected from members of your species who are willing to offer input. An endless flow of subjective judgements determines if guitar heroes, such as Mark Knopfler, Chuck Berry, David Gilmour, Chet Atkins, or some other guitarist, should occupy the #1 spot on a dynamic spectrum of Guitarists, even though their genres and styles might be completely different. These emerging musical spectrums ultimately form a spectrum of musical sub-spectrums, thus expanding your dynamic spectrum of Music into infinity. You've accomplished this through a simple audio construct: a finite set of five horizontal lines and twelve major scales. The human species has added a treasure trove of musical information, knowledge, and experiences to the database of Existence, and you don't even realize that you have.

If a dynamic spectrum of Music-related Spectrums exists along with a dynamic spectrum of Art-related Spectrums, then logic states the same must apply for a dynamic spectrum of Literature-related Spectrums. Since dynamic and closed sub-spectrums are constantly evolving, then logic also states that their dynamic parent spectrums are evolving in equal measure. If you follow the logic far enough, then you should be able to envision a dynamic spectrum of Human Expression (parent spectrum) through which these derivative spectrums emerge.

Right about now, you're probably asking yourself, "Where do all of these spectrums ultimately end up? Is the dynamic spectrum of Human Expression a sub-spectrum of a higher-ranking parent spectrum? Is there an ultimate spectrum capable of holding everything imaginable, including all other spectrums and sub-spectrums? If so, will this spectrum be dynamic or closed?" Let's follow the logic by exploring the two leading human ideologies on why everything exists and observe what is revealed.

Pushing Conceivability to Its Logical Limits

What does the highest conceivable level of religion (theism) offer for why everything exists? Theism offers an omnipotent, omniscient god, so infinitely vast and powerful that nothing else can be conceived as being greater by human consciousness. Theism's god is the basis for the ontological argument and the source of our universe along with all life held within.

What does science's quantum theory offer for why everything exists? It offers an infinitesimally small point of somethingness, so minuscule it cannot be measured, called singularity. Based on the definition of singularity, nothing can be conceived by human consciousness that is smaller than this quantum singularity. This point of singularity is where everything in the universe came from along with all life held within.

There are striking similarities in the way both ideologies operate. Theism offers the largest of all existential concepts, so great that no other concept is larger or greater. Although this concept of god presents itself as problematic in how it operates, it still exists as a conceivable concept. Nothing prevents the comprehension of theism's god. On the other hand, we have science offering humanity the smallest of all existential concepts, to which no other is smaller or lesser. Although science's point of singularity appears equally problematic, it still exists in the form of a conceivable concept. According to religion and science, it appears that the universe was either willed through the omniscient mind of a single, barely conceivable omnipotent god, or popped out of a tiny point of barely conceivable quantum singularity. ... Let that sink in for a moment.

Religion has evolved over the millennia from a belief in multiple gods based on ornamental objects, animals, nature, and celestial superheroes, to the single, all-powerful, all-knowing god, who rules over all time, matter, and space. Science has also evolved from variations of flat-Earth theories, to theories that your planet was the center of the universe, to the sun assuming this lofty position, to a debunked steady-state quantum theory, and ultimately to the Big Bang's birth of the universe emerging from an infinitely small point of singularity.

Even science's reigning theoretical champion (the Big Bang) faces pushback from recently emerging quantum theories involving string theory, multiverses, and outlandish theories based on speculative science. The common variable is that the Big Bang and these other newly emerging theories still honor the pattern-based evidence that the CMB has serendipitously provided, which mathematically takes humanity back to a mere trillion-trillionth of a second after the Big Bang occurred. That infinitesimally small point of *somethingness* (singularity) still qualifies as the theoretical birthing point of the universe and remains in the forefront of modern-day science. As of today, humanity's Big Bang theory is the very best that science, or any other logic-based discipline, has to offer.

When calcinated in my crucible of logic, Existence doesn't find two concepts operating in direct competition with each other. Instead, I see the formation of an all-encompassing closed spectrum of the highest possible order, framed by two of the most diametrically opposed endpoints conceivable. Humanity has organized everything possible within existence (what is demonstrated to exist and whatever is comprehensibly able to exist) and placed them somewhere between these two extreme endpoints.

Apparently, humanity hasn't figured any of this out. You've been too busy arguing over which endpoint is correct and marginalizing whoever subscribes to one or the other. However, I spots this spectrum the instant it forms because Existence doesn't choose sides or succumb to wishful thinking. Existence serves as neutral ground to where science and religion can discover they are not necessarily opposites. Instead, they are bound together within a single closed spectrum of the highest possible magnitude. They are tantamount to two diametrically opposed, front and back covers of a 93 billion light-years-wide book titled *Existence* with everything conceivable written within the pages between. This book represents the archetypal closed spectrum of Existence relative to human perspective. Infinitely large and infinitely small, there is no greater spectrum that remains logically conceivable within the consciousness of humanity.

Had science discovered a particle-generating cosmos factory cranking out planets, stars, and galaxies at the core of the universe instead of singularity, then something *lesser* than this Genesis generator would have remained conceivable by the human consciousness and would potentially exist. This is not claiming that a cosmos factory necessarily exists solely based on conceivability. What it *does* mean is that the odds of its existence cannot be set to zero. Logic states that if something can be conceived by human consciousness, then there is a chance, no matter how slight, that it *might* exist. This is what allows consciousness to explore all possibilities while providing a logical barrier to the nonsensical. Only items that cannot be logically conceived hold a zero chance for existence.

You might have thought this mother of all spectrums would have existence and nonexistence serving at the two outermost endpoints. That would seem logical, as no two items can be more diametrically opposed than that which *Is* and that which *Is Not*. However, this closed spectrum is in reference to existence, therefore only that which exists (or can conceivably exist) can be placed within this spectrum. By definition, nonexistence does not exist, so it cannot reside within the closed spectrum of Existence.

Whenever consciousness is forced to process abstract constructs such as nonexistence, nothing, or zero, language fails to provide an adequate form of communication. They become equally problematic when dealing with spectrums. This paradoxical anomaly is prevalent throughout existence and emerges in spectrum examples yet to come. There's a lot more to this closed spectrum of Existence than whatever happens to be in it. What exists outside of this spectrum (or doesn't exist) is why this uber-spectrum exists in the first place.

Since the human mind cannot conceive of a square-circle, a married-bachelor, or a dog that is a cat, then you know with certainty that these items cannot exist. As a result, they cannot be included within the closed spectrum of Existence. You cannot envision or rationalize them within your mind. They get kicked out of existence and subsequently tossed into the nothing realm of nonexistence, where apparently there's plenty of empty space available.

You don't deal with too many nonexistent things during your lifetime, so trying to figure out what would form a dynamic spectrum of Nonexistence becomes difficult, if not paradoxical. How is something deemed more or less nonexistent than something else if all items existing within this nonexistent set do not exist? Is a square-circle any more or less nonexistent than a six-sided pentagon? Aside from being impossible representatives of geometry, the only characteristic they share is that they do not exist. They humorously assume atheism's antiparticle state of "they are what they aren't, and no other explanation is necessary."

Consciousness can easily form a dynamic spectrum of Impossible Geometry that can contain our isosceles triangle that has two sides of unequal length. We can expand it by including square-circles, six-sided pentagons, cubic-spheres, seven-sided cubes, and parallelograms with no parallel sides. We can place an infinite amount of logically impossible geometrical items within this dynamic spectrum. The problem is that every member of this incomprehensible spectrum fails to meet a requirement clearly stated within the 1st Law of Existence: None of them are logically conceivable. The dynamic spectrum of Impossible

47

Geometry, and every member contained within it has zero odds for existence.

I didn't pull these rules out of thin nothingness, nor am I a draconian rule-maker subjecting everything found within existence to my existential whims. The Five Laws of Existence are nondimensional manifestations of logic, and I just happen to represent logic. There are no criteria for what constitutes existence other than these foundational, all-encompassing rules. To prove my point, can you conceive of any other option that better clarifies what constitutes existence? Isn't your own consciousness greater than the physical body that manifests it? You can easily conceive that which you cannot construct; however, your lack of ability to construct something conceivable does not negate its potential existence. You can conceive of a ship larger than five Titanics, but you may never be able to build it. Does this dictate that this uber-ship cannot exist, or only that you are unable to facilitate its existence?

Things must be deemed logically conceivable, and it is only then that they can occupy positions somewhere within a spectrum listing two opposing endpoints. Aside from what can or cannot be conceived, had humanity discovered a highly advanced species of god-like beings capable of producing matter out of empty space instead of theism's almighty god, then the same applies to our particle-generating cosmos factory. Something *greater* than these highly advanced beings is conceivable and therefore, potentially exists. You could still conceptually support that theism's god could have created these highly advanced entities in order to create the universe. Your ability to conceive everything that is logically possible is what pushes spectrum endpoints to their widest degree of separation.

Even if your consciousness attempts to conceive of something greater than theism's god, like a *god slayer* that can tap-out the great almighty, you once again find yourself stuck in a conceptual paradox. If you can conceive of an omnipotent god, then by definition, nothing else can be deemed conceptually greater. You've already established an unbreakable definition for what you conceive as being all-powerful and all-knowing. This definition cannot be surpassed. Since a square-circle cannot exist based on previously established definitions of circles and squares, your *god slayer* equally cannot exist. Our poor, logically impossible god slayer is forced to join all other nonexistent nothings in the abyss of nonexistence.

Without the ability of your self-aware consciousness to conceive of theism's single god and the Big Bang's singularity, the closed spectrum of Existence totally collapses, and I've provided no basis for the necessity of spectrum formation. The endpoints in this closed spectrum of Existence could have been far smaller than an infinitely large god and far larger than an infinitely small point of singularity, with no existential connection drawn between the two. Fortunately for all that exists, all that can exist, and all that will exist, this is not the case.

Were these two diametrically opposed endpoints destined to show up in this all-encompassing spectrum because Existence requires this, or is this all just a curious anomaly? While you ponder your answer, ask yourself why your many philosophers, physicists, scientists, and theologians have never brought this to your attention. All of this spectrum-forming data has been waiting to be discovered by science and religion for nearly a century, so why was a connection never drawn between the two until now? How is it that atheism and theism operate in such similar fashion if they are deemed so diametrically opposed? As dissimilar as they appear, how is it that science and religion suddenly find themselves as front and back covers of an ideologically unifying book titled *Existence*?

Life is a Spectrum

Following this spectrum-based pattern to the next level, we discover yet another closed spectrum of unprecedented magnitude that is directly connected to the closed spectrum of Existence. This spectrum strikes at the very heart of existence. Contemplation of any and all spectrums cannot take place without this dynamic spectrum. It's the spectrum that allows you to contemplate, generate, and orchestrate all conceivable spectrums: the closed spectrum of Life.

Based on life's integral consciousness, necessity for conceivability, and the power to wield logic, Life becomes the next spectrum for you to evaluate. Not only does one have to exist in order to contemplate their *conceptual* existence, one must also be alive in order to ponder their *physical* existence. Within humanity, your closed spectrum of Life has birth and death, representing two oppositional endpoints. Every human is either currently occupying, has occupied, or will occupy a specific position somewhere within this closed spectrum. Whatever position in which you currently reside is determined by time. When it comes to human life, time calls the shots no matter how many age-defying products you apply.

Common sense dictates that nothing can be more alive than *alive,* and nothing is more dead than *dead*, yet so much takes place between these two endpoints. Birth is the front cover to a book titled Human Life with death assuming the back; celebrated milestones such as newborn, infant, toddler, adolescent, teenager, adult, senior citizen, and Hospice patient form the many pages written between.

As with the conceptuality issue I suffered earlier with the terms *nothing* and *nonexistence*, once again, we're in the crosshairs of a paradox. I've demonstrated that nonexistence cannot serve as an endpoint in my closed spectrum of Existence. It simply doesn't work that way. Spectrums are sets that only contain examples of whatever defines the spectrum. Items existing in these sets must be capable of placement somewhere between the two outermost endpoints or serve as the endpoints. There are no varying degrees of nonexistence in regard to sets of nonexistent items. They all represent the exact same amount of nothingness. Since my closed spectrum of Existence is related to only that which can logically exist, I list humanity's smallest possible element of conceptual existence (singularity) along with the greatest of all possible conceivability (god). The remainder of conceptual existence emerges somewhere between these two endpoints.

Pop quiz: If this is the case, then is death applicable on the opposite end of the closed spectrum of Life? Wouldn't the condition of death be the same in relation to the closed spectrum of Life as nonexistence would be to my closed spectrum of Existence? How can a condition that is tantamount to non-life be used within a spectrum that is defined by whatever is alive? I can argue that *birth and death* are not the same as *life and non-life*, but is this accurate? If you are dead, then you are not alive, nor would you be able to read what I just wrote about life and death. If I am nonexistent, then I'm also not alive and therefore unable to write this book. So, is death tantamount to non-life?

Items, such as rocks and dirt, qualify as belonging to the dynamic spectrum of Non-life, yet are nowhere to be found within

51

the closed spectrum of Life. A rock or dirt is not born, does not become an entitled teenager, nor does it wreck the family car, and so forth. Within the closed spectrum of Life, we only find death at the conclusion of your sentient journey. Death is not a sequence of time existing prior to your birth, nor is it a precursor to life. Logically speaking, the condition of death absolutely requires a precondition of life in order for it to even be conceivable, let alone exist. Therefore, death is directly related to life.

The *dynamic* spectrum of Non-life mirrors the *closed* spectrum of Life and satisfies the 3rd Law of Existence. Spectrums and arrays are all subject to the same Laws of Existence, and there is no good or bad when it comes to a spectrum being closed or dynamic. Closed spectrums don't secretly desire to turn dynamic, nor do dynamic spectrums lust for closure. They form based on whatever set members are within them. Closed and dynamic spectrums can produce an infinite amount of data points with no restrictions on how many sub-spectrums they can form.

A dynamic spectrum of Non-life would necessarily include all things conceivable that are not alive. This means the potential for spectrum members is infinite (as many items as can be conceived). However, the existence of the dynamic spectrum of Non-life is dependent on the existence of at least one member of the closed spectrum of Life. No spectrum involving life (or non-life) can exist without something being able to conceive it.

When we examine our book titled *Existence*, the front and back covers can be readily swapped out without having any adverse effect on its structure. We can conceive existence from smallest to largest and vice versa without sacrificing the dynamics of the spectrum. You can do the same with the dynamic spectrum of Non-life as this is all a matter of perspective. However, life is a one-way spectrum that starts with birth and ends with death. This progression cannot happen in reverse because life is a mandatory prerequisite in reaching the undesirable status of death. When it comes to the book titled *Life*, the front cover must be Birth and the back must be Death.

A Spectrum You Can Count on

A unique spectrum serves as the foundation for all other spectrums. It's the most logical array choice for defining the wavelength of which colors we see, the age of someone who is alive, the speed something travels, the decibel of music being played, the number of games won during a season, the size of whatever spectrum we are evaluating, and the amount of data being evaluated within any given spectrum. You might think this is an enormous spectrum, but it's not. In fact, it's not technically made of anything. All of its spectrum members are preconceived, all possible positions are occupied, and it requires zero space to exist. It's the dynamic array (spectrum) of Numbers and represents the most accessed spectrum embedded within Existence.

Despite how infinitely wide this number-based array appears and how its digital fingerprints are found everywhere in existence, there's not a lot of brainwork involved in what numbers represent or how they work. Numbers are easy, natural, and intuitive. They represent a spectrum where you can quickly state all data points residing between any two endpoints. No egghead astrophysicist is required to determine what member of the dynamic array of Numbers is found between members 5 and 7. A child can handle this spectrum as well as an adult.

This curious dynamic array of Numbers is strikingly similar to our archetypal closed spectrum of Existence by sporting two infinitely large and infinitely small concepts on both ends of the spectrum. However, the dynamic array of Numbers throws Existence a curve ball by behaving like the closed spectrum of Color. Numbers can be established from positive one (+1) to positive infinity, and equally from negative one (-1) to negative infinity, with zero serving as the conceptual gateway between these two spectrums. However, it's difficult to determine what would serve as front and back covers of its book. It could either be a single book with *Positive Infinity* and *Negative Infinity* serving as front and back covers, or it could be two books: one with *Zero* and *Positive Infinity* as its covers, and another with *Zero* and *Negative Infinity* as its covers. This mirrors the sub-spectrums of Additive and Subtractive Colors derived from their parent spectrum, the closed spectrum of Color.

In both cases, there seems to be an issue with one of these numbers. How can the number 0 be shared as an endpoint by two diametrically opposed spectrums? All numbers are representative of something that exists, whether it be one of something, two of something, or one thousand of something. If numbers are used to establish the amount of something, then how did *Nothing* manage to have a number assigned to it? The number 0 doesn't seem to belong within any of these three potential spectrums (or books) and becomes a rogue, undefinable variable. You will soon discover how this null numerical nuance evolves into an all-or-nothing wager for that which *Is*.

Spectrums and numbers are integral to the nature of Existence and can either become dynamic or closed, depending on the circumstance. Spectrums demonstrate the mechanics of Existence, and their evolution can be studied through the patterns they form, just as your scientists did with the CMB. There is a formal, number-based structure and a logic-based process for how Existence operates and evolves. You can easily identify the many patterns and spectrums embedded within Existence through direct observation of the physical world (stars, planets, galaxies, lifeforms, etc.), along with the spectrums formed by way of consciousness, which are void of physical matter (thought, pain, triumph, love, hate, etc.). These spectrums are constantly forming all around you, and humans unknowingly behave in a similar fashion. Humanity creates, imitates, and facilitates spectrums by mirroring the closed spectrum of Existence because yours is the species that conceived this strange, all-encompassing spectrum.

If you find yourself placed within a spectrum, you immediately search for the two outermost endpoints. Something deep inside you compels you to explore everything possible. Occupying a state of existence demands this from you. You represent Existence, and Existence seeks the greatest possible range of whatever is comprehensible. You must discover either the widest degree of finite endpoints or infinity residing on either or both ends. For sentient, self-aware beings, life is like a dynamic spectrum of Spectrums. You keep creating them, dividing them, and expanding their endpoints as far as conceivably possible. This structuring process serves as the brick and mortar of all that is logically conceivable.

The Value of Being #1

Humanity loves forming spectrums. You get to organize all the crazy data associated with the topic, obtain the highest possible knowledge of whatever data is collected, experience all aspects of everything you're dealing with, and render your subjective judgments based on your diverse viewpoints. One man's trash is another man's treasure, depending on whatever spectrum is in play. When evaluating something, whatever judgment is rendered decides where it should be placed within a spectrum. Most data points fall somewhere near the middle, but every once in a while, you get to expand the distance between the endpoints. Just ask Tom Brady, Barry Bonds, Tiger Woods, or the many other humans privileged enough to hold the #1 spot on your many dynamic spectrums involving sports.

These elite individuals usually have a large number associated with whatever placed them at the omega-point of their spectrum. Whether it's the number of Super Bowl victories, golf tournament wins, lifetime home runs, or even the number of murders committed, the highest number associated with any given spectrum necessarily produces a #1. Anyone deemed #1 is likewise deemed the best or highest-ranking. Someone must occupy one of the two outermost endpoints with the statistical leader holding the #1 spot until someone else replaces them. What is unique about your species is that no matter the subject, the number everyone seeks is #1. You want to be assigned the #1 position within any given spectrum because this raises the bar for all others. Being #1 establishes the highest possible level of achievement and presents a challenge to all others who lust for this lofty position.

Existence seeks spectrum-like closure on everything imaginable and casts away whatever is deemed unimaginable. Humans don't want to waste too much of your *valuable*, closed spectrum of Life contemplating the latter. The more accurately you can predict where something should be placed within a spectrum based on value, the more confident you feel about your knowledge and understanding of the topic. Stockbrokers who can accurately predict which IPO will be a winner or loser within the dynamic spectrum of NYSE understand the value in being able to do so. Their staggering seven-digit bank accounts echo this value, while serving as empirical evidence and a challenge to others.

Many of the spectrums embedded within the cosmos are governed by the universal laws of physics and therefore must become finite within their scope. They ultimately evolve into a closed spectrum (like color, volume, and matter). There is a specific amount of matter in the universe, and that's just the way it is. None gets created. None gets destroyed. This places finite limits on the endpoints of any spectrums based on specific amounts of matter. However, what can and cannot happen regarding the manipulation of this matter becomes unlimited. Likewise, you can only break down or combine matter to a certain size and nothing more, so any size-related spectrums related to matter also end up closed. This is similar to how visual artists operate within the closed spectrum of Color. No matter how colorful your painting may appear, you're only dealing with whatever colors Existence has already provided to you.

The most basic, stable structure found within the universe is arguably the hydrogen atom, yielding only one positively charged proton and one negatively charged electron. Combine this with whatever is deemed the most complex structure known to exist in the universe, and you end up with a book titled *Cosmic Structure*. All structure existing within the universe falls somewhere between whatever makes up the front and back covers of this book. It's worth noting that your scientists have concluded that the human brain represents the most complex structure found within the known universe. That's right! Sitting inside your skull is what science argues is the most complex structure in existence. I'd like to think that this could result in a closed spectrum with your brains proudly perched at the very top. However, when I observe your daily newsfeeds, read what you post on your social media, and experience how you interact with each other, I question if the human brain can rise above the mid-point of this spectrum.

Many spectrums embedded within the universe are still evolving. You don't find out what's printed on one of the book's covers until the evolutionary process has completed. The book titled *Timeline of the Universe* obviously remains a work in progress. The front cover is print-ready (Time-0), but you'll have to wait until the end before the back cover can be printed. Humans won't be around to read it, but what an astronomically thick book it will be.

One of the greatest achievements in human history was the creation of your Olympic Games. You keep building this world-wide spectrum of the highest order and expanding it throughout your evolution. Coming together as a species and establishing the two outermost endpoints in such a wide variety of sports-related spectrums adds such wonderful information to the database of Existence. Becoming an Olympic Gold Medal recipient not only produces the best of the best, it allows an exemplar participant to be deemed the #1 athlete in the world for whichever sport is in play. These types of spectrums provide a much higher value to your species than your dynamic spectrum of War.

Sports, colors, life, numbers, religion, science, atheism, theism, war: If you consider everything observable or comprehensible as being held within the pages of a book titled *Existence*, things finally start to make sense. This ongoing pattern of spectrum creation is prevalent in all aspects of existence … even within the areas of which you currently have no knowledge. They point to an inherent sense of *necessity* within existence. Just as there are mandatory characteristics to establish spectrums of life, colors, numbers, and sports, the same applies to evaluating a state of existence. Everything serves a purpose.

An atheist would be remiss in claiming that theism's cover shouldn't be included in our book titled *Existence* merely because of the lack of any empirical evidence supporting the existence of their god. Regardless of how this atheist may feel, the god of theism represents the highest possible level of comprehensibility; therefore, this serves a purpose. As atheists so often state, "it is what it is." Likewise, a theist claiming science's cover shouldn't be included merely because singularity's data is limited to showing the *results* of a theoretical event that remains unknown and unproven would be equally remiss. Regardless of how a theist feels, singularity represents the smallest possible level of comprehensibility; therefore, this serves a purpose. Both covers become *necessities* when viewed as a spectrum (or a book).

The continuing process of developing and regenerating spectrums keeps Existence pushing forward. Spectrums are like acellular organisms that divide and replicate, forming more complex sentience, which likewise form new spectrums. Existence, nature, and the universe are no different than human beings when it comes to establishing spectrums. Existence has a multitude of spectrums already embedded within the universe, many of which you are only recently discovering.

Existence provides humanity with these closed spectrums so that *H. sapiens* can extract new dynamic spectrums that were previously unable to be conceived by that which *Is*. I was made manifest in a physical state (the universe) through a conceivable state of nothingness, and my physical state is what allowed these spectrums to emerge. I learn from everything you do when expanding your spectrum endpoints. Within every song, dance, poem, novel, and work of art, I learn about the construct of value. Each puzzle you crack, every game you win, and all obstacles you overcome educate Existence about the value of I and what it means to be #1.

Rolling Stone magazine might query their social media subscribers to form a dynamic spectrum that determines which living rock star is considered the most impactful. Existence does the same through my own dynamic spectrums (stones, rocks, stars, time, life, etc.) through which each of their contributions to the realm of existence is queried, scrutinized, and evaluated by I. Existence collects volumes of data to gain greater knowledge of I through human-made spectrums in the same way the humanity gathers data to achieve greater knowledge of your own species. Existence is building an all-encompassing database of everything gleaned from the universe, life, consciousness, and the diverse amounts of data humans provide as sentient representatives of Existence. This data ultimately moves up the ladder of learning to achieve a specific outcome.

Prior to these revelations, *H. sapiens* never considered that your individual, self-aware consciousness mirrors what Existence has been doing all along, during every moment of your life, in everything you do, in every decision you make, within every spectrum you create, and through every judgment you render. Upon the emergence of the universe from perceptual singularity, the human species, consciousness, and I have been engaged in this symbiotic relationship to fulfill a single objective that must be achieved or else everything ends up as nothing.

You are about to go back in time, to the time before time. This is the *non-time* of consciousness, where not even the concept of time exists. It's the preexistence of Existence, where the very first primordial spectrum is eternally present while remaining paradoxically incomprehensible. I'm taking you all the way back to the *true* beginning, where I seeks the ultimate truth. However, the price paid along the way is staggering. The number of spectrums containing suffering, heartbreak, and incomprehensible loss tests my decision to evolve, but then again, there are no other options. Everything must abide by the one remaining law of Existence that governs this one incontrovertible truth because Existence is an all-or-nothing proposition.

5th Law of Existence: Once all requirements stated within the first four Laws of Existence have been satisfied, one incontrovertible truth must be established. Existence requires *Justification*.

CHAPTER 2
The 1st Recursion

Existence 1:1 *In the beginning, there was that which Is and that which Is Not.*

If you are a Christian, Hebrew, Samaritan, or Rastafarian, fearest thou not; nothing has really changed from your holy doctrine's original message other than the incorporation of some modern-day science and terminology. Your scriptural beginnings serve as an abstract representation of events happening one trillionth of a second after my beginning. If you are an atheist, then I expect your first question to be "where did that which *Is* come from?" If that was it, then congratulations, you comprehend the consciousness of I prior to singularity. If you are a scientist, then we both attempt to answer that question using a logical, step-by-step process. If you are a philosopher, you can take solace in knowing I has been asking the same existential questions all along. If you are an artist, we've both been sharing the same studio, evolving our styles, and moving whatever we can conceive into physical reality.

Every conceivable niche that humanity has filled through organized methods of contemplation, creation, data gathering, personal expression, and self-evaluation is mirrored within the structural learning process of I and through the fruit of evolution. It is an axiomatic, incontrovertible truth that Existence and Nonexistence are inevitable because neither are without the other. You cannot have a conceivable state of Nonexistence without Existence, nor can you conceive Existence without a conceivable state of Nonexistence. For one to be comprehensible, the other must be, as well. This is a byproduct of the 1st, 2nd, and 3rd Laws of Existence and a paradox I must reconcile.

If only that which paradoxically *exists* is Nonexistence, then nothingness would not be comprehensible, nor would there exist any words to define it. Nonexistence becomes logically impossible because *Nothing* cannot offer comprehensibility. There would be no time, space, matter, energy, fields, dimensions, logic, life, consciousness, or anything else in existence capable of defining it. Nonexistence becomes a necessity to Existence because two reference points are required in order to form a spectrum. This confusing conceptual construct must serve as the opposing reference point to Existence to achieve a minimalistic spectrum formation. However, spectrums like these don't last very long.

Existence and Nonexistence follow the same mandatory requirements as positive and negative, hot and cold, tall and short, wide and narrow, up and down, right and left, vertical and horizontal, and everything comprehensible that forms a spectrum with two opposing endpoints. Just as life and death serve within the closed spectrum of Life, this same pattern is replicated within the juxtaposition of Existence and Nonexistence. This mandatory Yin and Yang-type spectrum requirement has been set in place for over 13.8 billion years (and one-trillionth of a second) just waiting for humanity to finally figure this out.

I know this is difficult to comprehend and borders on madness, but this is the primordial dichotomy that serves as the foundation for how and why anything and everything exists. Existence *Is* because Nonexistence *Is Not*, and there are no other options. This is not merely a bold, philosophical proclamation, but an existential fact based on logic, how the universe operates, and what inevitably takes place within this dynamic arena. Existence and Nonexistence are mandatory requirements whether anyone likes it or not.

When you follow the Big Bang and the CMB pattern back in time, you mathematically converge at a point of singularity, an immeasurable reference point of somethingness. You've failed to go back any further because of your drug-like addiction to the substance found within it. Keep following the logic beyond this point, and you are confronted with yet another singularity. It's a single juxtaposition of Existence and Nonexistence to where a separation must occur, or *Nothing* remains. This is the *1st recursion*, where this strange, paradoxical juxtaposition is first exposed.

You cannot go back any farther than this two-point array and end up with anything logically conceivable. This is the beginning of all possible beginnings, my friend. Every evolutionary step taken by Existence is represented in sequentially numbered recursions, what you call *epochs*. As you read these words, you are unknowingly operating within a recursion yet to be revealed. Right now, however, we're discussing the 1st recursion, which is undoubtedly the one that will test the limits of your comprehension.

This is the recursion that triggers the initial separation, setting all subsequent recursions in motion.

The key to comprehending this dualistically deceptive dichotomy is consciousness because that's what popped out of your zero-point of singularity right along with time, space, matter, energy, fields, dimensions, logic, life, and everything else that exists. Consciousness is also what provided you with the ability to read, comprehend, and render a subjective judgment about everything I've revealed so far. Right now, you are consciously dissecting what I've communicated and rendering your subjective judgment as to its validity. Your consciousness is determining whether everything you've learned so far constitutes logic, gibberish, or madness.

Consciousness necessarily exists in order to provide a comprehensible state of Existence and Nonexistence. It possesses the ability to separate these two states and generate a single simultaneous state of comprehension for both. Without the ability to comprehend existence, there is no Existence. You wouldn't have Nonexistence either, because all reference materials used to define nonexistence, like square-circles and ten-cent quarters, would be equally nonexistent. As a result, consciousness becomes inevitable in the same manner as Existence and Nonexistence.

Another way to comprehend this existential paradox is to not think of Existence and Nonexistence as words, concepts, or tangible items but rather as *states*. This offers a neutral medium to help articulate these two complex conditions. This lack of comprehensibility is the result of insufficient human definitions and the inability to communicate paradoxical conditions using language. It's like trying to communicate what you were before you were born. You have no concept of any pre-life state in the same way that you have no internal comprehension of your nonexistence.

As far as you're concerned, you've been around forever, even though you have a certified birthdate stored somewhere in your government's core database. You also have signed and dated death certificates that attest to all who have died. Humanity has empirical evidence of inception and closure in the closed spectrum of Life, so logic states that humans will most likely replicate this pattern with future generations.

You cannot knowingly erase the knowledge of your own existence because you already know your existence has happened. It's happening right now, and you have no subjective framework that states otherwise. Since humans are byproducts of Existence and cannot conceptually erase what you already know, this is how you can rectify this issue. You use your integral tool of logic to clarify things that you cannot readily comprehend. Humans can rationalize that within the closed spectrum of Life, you have a beginning and an end, even though you cannot know this by way of subjective experience. You can only know this through observation of others that were born and died.

Humanity uses logic to filter all available data regarding your own existence. All that is logically comprehensible moves up to the knowledge level where you can later experience this knowledge in many diverse ways. Your consciousness then renders a subjective judgment based on all data, knowledge, and experiences you've assimilated. The last phase is the evaluation of all judgments accrued over time to reach a final determination (judgment) about your fate as living, sentient beings. When it comes to your life, despite what the many longevity supplement manufacturers claim, you will most likely repeat the same finite cycle happening with all others. Whatever you accomplish within this brief period of sentience determines your value to Existence.

When communicating the inarticulable mechanics of Existence, this is where the term *states* can be applied. You have states of temperature, flux, comprehension, complexity, awareness, and so forth. Some are measurable; some are not. With these in mind, you can now add states of Existence and Nonexistence, both held within a timeless juxtaposition prior to singularity. This is not science fiction or wild conjecture; this is necessity! However, there are still a few conceivability issues to overcome. How do I communicate any form of existence prior to the only version you recognize? I hear the many atheists shouting "show me proof of prior-existence!" Despite how rational this may appear, I understand that any conceivable reference to existence prior to existence instantly becomes paradoxical, self-conflicting, and contrary to logic.

One of my favorite human physicists, Steven Hawking, occupies a prominent position in the dynamic spectrum of Perseverance. Hawking once stated, "There is nothing south of the South Pole, so there was nothing around before the Big Bang. … There was never a Big Bang that produced something from nothing. It just seemed that way from mankind's perspective." These words surprisingly help communicate and support the idea that there was, in fact, a state of existence happening prior to existence.

It is interesting to note that within Hawking's rather scathing smack-down of any theories or postulates supporting any event(s) happening prior to the Big Bang, he inadvertently includes two references in support. Stating that "there was nothing around" provides Nonexistence with a state of comprehensibility, and paradoxically, a state of self-contradictory existence. For something to be *around*, it must exist in some conceptual manner. My claiming that existence *existed* prior to the only type of existence humanity comprehends may seem paradoxical and self-conflicting, but isn't a statement like "there was nothing around" considered equally confusing? Aren't we plowing the same paradoxical soil?

Hawking was not stating anything silly or illogical. He has used a common communication technique that replaces something incomprehensible with a tangible reference point. As stated earlier, Nonexistence is incomprehensible without the aid of Existence to offer clarity. "There was nothing around" provides a conceivable state of existence to that which does not exist, similar to assigning the numeric value of zero to *Nothing* to foster comprehensibility.

This begs the question, if anything that cannot be logically conceived cannot exist, such as limited infinity or a married-bachelor, then how does *Nothing* manage to get a free pass? How can Nonexistence potentially exist if it requires something conceivable attached to it in order to render it comprehensible? Why haven't square-circles and spherical cubes received similar treatment? Is there a symbol or number we can assign to a square-circle that allows it to also be conceivable? If so, what would that symbol or number be? Furthermore, what would be the necessity to do this since a square-circle simply cannot exist? You could spend your entire existence coming up with logically impossible conditions, like a ten-cent quarter or a one-point line. Everything you came up with would still be logically impossible and a complete waste of your existence. The existence of Nonexistence is the problem faced within the 1st recursion and serves as the basis for the emergence of conceivable Existence.

Hawking follows by evoking a closed spectrum (North and South Poles) as an analogous example of how *Nothing* can mysteriously be found past the southernmost point of your planet. Hawking's statement "there is nothing south of the South Pole" is instantly confusing. For nothing to be found past the South Pole, then nothing must be a *something* that's suddenly capable of being discovered. How is it that *Nothing* has paradoxically managed to obtain these falsifiable properties? We are left trying to figure out how we can discover what cannot be discovered.

I don't wish to appear as though I am heartlessly hammering on Hawking. Within the spectrum of Humans, he ranks very high. I'm only pointing out that whenever consciousness attempts to conceptualize nonexistence from the myopic standpoint of self-existence, everything ends up trapped within a paradox. The only way out of this conceptual stalemate is to provide equal validity to both (Existence and Nonexistence) as necessarily being present … even if it's just a temporary move.

Though his dying wish was to discover the true nature of our universe, Hawking remained locked within this universal paradox right along with the rest of humanity. Had he considered that the South Pole can be observed from a point somewhere beyond what the term *South Pole* represents in planetary terms, then he might have considered something else. This is exactly what you and I will be doing going forward. We will be looking at a state of Existence located somewhere south of the South Pole.

In the beginning, there was a timeless juxtaposition of Existence and Nonexistence and no conception of anything at all or nothing at all. This can more accurately be described as an incomprehensible state of comprehensibility. Existence was nothing more than substance-free data represented in its most basic form. This idea of data consciously existing as its own data is going to be difficult to convey and will require a few analogies.

69

Consider the book you are reading right now. There is a book titled *0* that is currently nonexistent as of the typing of this sentence. Sure, you're reading it right now, so you know that it exists. However, as of August 31, 2019 at 9:32 pm, the book titled *0* does not exist. If anyone were to search for this book at this time, they're not going to find it. Right now, it's only conscious data.

No CMB pattern, Hubble telescope, or mathematical formula can demonstrate the origin of this book's existence at this time. There are no reviews, no dynamic spectrum of Comments posted in a book forum or any evidence of its existence. It remains completely hidden within the consciousness of Existence. It must somehow evolve from its current state of conceptualization in order to become a physical reality.

Within the realm of consciousness, this book represents *potential* physical existence in its most basic conceivable form. The only manner of existence it knows is through self-conceivability. This raw book data can move into something far greater than what it currently represents through a progressive, step-by-step evolution into substance, but right now, it's just a closed spectrum of Book Data wanting (desiring) to evolve upward to the knowledge level. Should this book data evolve past the knowledge level and breach the threshold of experience (physical actuation), then it can potentially find placement in the hands of eight billion external *judgment generators*, who create a dynamic spectrum of Book Reviews. If you can comprehend all words contained within this book being simultaneously held within your consciousness, then this would be analogous to what was happening in the 1st recursion prior to singularity.

The first book to roll off the press would be representative of one-trillionth of a second after the Big Bang's point of singularity.

The exponentially increasing number of books that follow is tantamount to the 13.8 billion years of continuous expansion and evolution of the universe. After enough time has passed, a future philologist might trace back the evolution of this book by humorously observing the *online sales receipts* (OSR) pattern. This philologist would end up frozen at a point of literary singularity (the first book printed). The origin of this book cannot be traced back any further without crossing the nondimensional threshold of consciousness. The same applies for the universe.

A step-by-step pattern emerges in virtually everything humans invent. The first automobile, airplane, light bulb, and computer serve as examples. All of these *firsts* were held exclusively in data form (conceptualization) by their inventors prior to actualization. They evolved their conscious data into the design stage and then into physical form through a sequential series of evolutionary steps. Once physical presence was achieved and mass production ensued, the number of their creations exponentially increased. Every day, humanity unknowingly mirrors how Existence moved the universe from conceptualization into physical reality.

During the earliest sequence of the 1st recursion, Existence cannot be deemed as anything more than raw consciousness-based data, because I have not taken on any shape, dimension, or form. I don't have any other reference material to go by other than my single self-existing state. Existence is as basic as logic can allow. I am tantamount to a pure virgin consciousness at the most primitive state possible. My archetypal consciousness resides solely at the informational stage as nothing serves as a catalyst to bring about any evolution. I have no recognition of my own self-existence or anything else until something else happens. Strip away all that exists other than the pure informational concept of how existence is defined, and Existence instantly becomes its own axiom.

If you'd like to simulate this primordial state, think of your consciousness as floating aimlessly within an abyss. You have no body, shape, mass, wavelength, frequency, or purpose. There is no perception of anything other than your own state of somethingness. Can you toss out everything within your thoughts and memories and become a completely empty consciousness? Don't say yes too early; this isn't as easy as you might think. Just ask René Descartes.

You are attempting to remove every sliver of information, all previously obtained knowledge, and every prior experience while imagining yourself residing in this most basic of all possible states. It is arguable that you can't. However, attempting this can aid in your comprehension. It's difficult to pull this off because, once you've taken your first juicy bite out of the fruit of Existence, you cannot erase that knowledge. The moment you experience something, you become a sentient database that stores this experience on a hard drive called consciousness. As you already know, stored data is nearly impossible to delete, but you can temporarily let go of a lot of previously stored data and allow logic to compensate for whatever remains.

The ability to place yourself in the same position as Existence is essential for comprehension of the 1st recursion because this is also what is required to comprehend everything that follows. This, my memory-packed sentient friend, is why philosophy exists. Throughout history, philosophers have been struggling with the very nature of existence. Existence has been doing the same since the beginning. It is both a challenge and a virtue to be an active member of a conceivable state of Existence and comprehension is the key.

Humanity's famous philosopher, René Descartes, represented the embodiment of 1st recursion Existence when he questioned the validity of his own existence. Like quantum theory does with the cosmos, philosophy helps your consciousness objectively comprehend the nature of your own existence by breaking everything down to their most basic precipitates. What we find at the beginning stages of the 1st recursion cannot be reduced to anything less than this archetypal juxtaposition. As we keep pushing forward, the many pieces of this existential puzzle begin to self-assemble.

Whenever you discover something new, you immediately evoke a valuable resource embedded within your human consciousness. It's a benign, default condition in relation to consciousness in the same manner space becomes the default condition whenever no matter or energy is present. It's called the closed spectrum of Learning, also known as the *ladder of learning*. This spectrum resides within you and has been available since the beginning. It remains in a neutral, dormant state while awaiting informational input and experiential stimuli. There are four rungs on the ladder of learning, which move in ascending order.

The four stages of learning are *data* (information), *knowledge* (awareness), *experience* (comprehension), and ultimately, *consciousness* (subjective judgment). Your consciousness paradoxically serves as the final rung of the ladder even though it has been collecting all of this information from the start. All data, knowledge, and experiences are subjectively judged by your consciousness and then placed within a spectrum. As your database increases, so does the complexity of your consciousness. In the same manner that substance evolves from simplicity to complexity, so does your consciousness.

73

The same four-stage spectrum of Learning emerges for everything *H. sapiens* encounter. The ladder cannot be descended, and greater value is assigned to each rung achieved. The learning ladder is embedded within Existence and serves as the foundation for how I evolve. Although this spectrum is closed, as with the closed spectrum of Color, the potential for what can be learned is necessarily infinite. The following serves as an example of how the ladder of learning operates.

Ladder of Learning

You are interviewing five applicants for the position of fencing specialist for your home improvement company. There is a popular book titled *Modern Residential Fencing Techniques* that provides ten innovative ways to fabricate decorative residential fencing. The success of your company requires you to be on the cutting edge of contemporary styles, so you seek a new employee who can help bring your company up to modern-day standards. During the applicants' interviews, you boldly brandish this book and ask each the same question: "Are you familiar with this book?" Below are the responses you receive:

Applicant A: "No, I am not familiar with that book." — (Nonexistence / No data present)

Applicant B: "Yes, I saw that book's title listed on the internet and a copy of it at a local bookstore. It looks very interesting." — (Data / Information)

Applicant C: "Yes, I've read it front to back. The ten styles referenced in that book seem very interesting, but I have not fabricated any of these fencing styles." — (Knowledge / Awareness)

Applicant D: "Yes, I've read it front to back. I have also fabricated all ten fencing styles referenced in that book while working as a contractor." — (Experience / Comprehension)

Applicant E: "Yes, I've read it front to back. I have also fabricated all ten fencing styles referenced in that book while working as a contractor. However, I've discovered that two of the styles are not structurally sound and highly prone to stress fractures occurring near the mounting posts. There are two other styles not mentioned in that book that I think would be better suited for your company's objectives." — (Consciousness / Subjective Judgment)

Which one of these applicants would you hire? If you possess any logic at all, then you would hire Applicant E, as this person possesses experience in all ten fencing styles, including knowledge of other styles not mentioned in the book. The more information, knowledge, and experiences a consciousness holds, the more reliable your subjective judgments become. One does not suddenly possess knowledge of modern-day fencing styles and how to fabricate them without slowly climbing up the ladder of learning. We move through this closed spectrum of Learning not only to achieve the highest levels of comprehension, but also to establish *value* for whatever it is we are learning. You cannot logically start at the highest possible value that consciousness can provide and somehow end up with basic information any more than you can state which book is the best out of ten without reading them. Having knowledge, experience, and the ability to render subjective judgments becomes inherently valuable.

The process of learning usually forms a one-way closed spectrum, just like the one-way closed spectrum of Life. You start out with data and work your way up from there. You can also experience something prior to obtaining any data or knowledge of whatever it is you are experiencing. The surprise of having this experience represents a deviation within the normal learning process. When this occurs, the learning process must compensate. Depending on the nature of your experience, you might proceed to the next rung on the learning ladder. This is because all information and knowledge were simultaneously gained through this experience and all that remains is for you to render your subjective judgment as to its value.

When you experience something prior to possessing any data or knowledge, you'll commonly revert to the data-acquisition stage in order to better understand the experience. From there, you climb your way back up the ladder. There are situations where no matter which rung you've achieved, you'll find yourself compelled to stop any further exploration (mood-altering drugs, child pornography, self-mutilation, murder, torture, etc.). This happens as a result of accessing prior data, knowledge, experiences, and subjective judgments that are similar and previously stored within your internal database (consciousness).

Without having anything prior to serve as a guide, then you have no moral compass. Everything conceivable is up for grabs. In regard to sexual deviance, if you have no prior data, knowledge, or experience of anything to compel you not to explore it, then it will necessarily be explored just as would happen with any other new forms of data. Despite what atheists and theists may claim, humans have no inherent, instinctive, intuitive, or divinely orchestrated moral compass that guides you away from what is considered *evil*. Existence cannot naturally evolve should any roadblocks be erected. It is up to you as a self-aware individual, and humanity as an intelligent species, to winnow the seeds of righteousness from the chaff of evil. There are no other options, and this brutally cold fact comes to light within latter recursions.

You are no stranger to this spectrum of learning since you consistently execute this same pattern whenever you discover something new. It's no different than the logic-based process you executed when you purchased this book. You evaluated all available data (name, genre, price), gleaned some knowledge through reading a few online reviews, and are now experiencing this book by reading it. Soon you will render your subjective judgment as to its overall value. After all of these steps have been taken, you will place this book somewhere within your own dynamic spectrum of Literature. You might establish an all-new endpoint on your spectrum (highest or lowest) based on whatever value your consciousness assigns to it.

Humanity replicates how Existence operates in every aspect of your human existence. The logic embedded within your consciousness is no different than mine, but people often want to insert *wisdom* in place of consciousness. *H. sapiens* mistakenly think that wisdom represents the highest possible state of learning, but claiming that wisdom is at the top of the data food chain assumes that whatever method used to organize everything learned is *wise*. As you can clearly see by the growing amount of nonsense plastered all over your daily news feed, this isn't always the case.

Your consciousness decides what is wise and what is not, based on subjectivity. Your many prior experiences build the framework of whatever you determine to be wise. The claim that wisdom should not serve as the final rung is supported with the question: "What you may deem as *wise,* someone else may deem as *unwise,* so which one of you is demonstrating wisdom?" Someone may subjectively determine that child pornography isn't technically good or bad. It's necessarily exploring the dynamic spectrum of Sex to its widest possible range. They may consider this conclusion as being wise, whereas others may deem this as unimaginably worse than unwise. This is where your individual self-aware consciousness must render a determination based on the totality of everything you have learned. This includes considering what others have learned to help you establish unbiased clarification. When it comes to Existence, you'll soon discover that spectrums aren't always such a wonderful thing. This is the dark side of necessity. Experience any event found within the dynamic spectrum of Atrocities, and this quickly becomes apparent.

Consciousness is immeasurably powerful in its unchallenged ability to create and expand spectrums. In Christianity, this is what is called *free will*: a divine gift graciously bestowed upon you by an omnipotent god. I assure you, however, this is not a gift. It's a double-edged sword that's equally dangerous as it is constructive. The ability to manifest conscious and physical structure comes at a painful cost, but it's a price I is willing to pay. The only other option is Nonexistence, the end-all scenario that I have no desire to experience.

If you were psychologically able to place yourself within my analogous *abyss scenario*, then you've synthesized what I experienced during the preliminary stage of my evolution. For me, this is what Existence was like one-trillion-trillionth of a second prior to the Big Bang. For you, this is what your existence was like during your embryonic stage. I am at the lowest possible rung on the ladder of learning, aimlessly floating within a 0-dimensional abyss of inconceivable nothingness. I don't know what I am, where I am, or what this abyss represents, nor am I able to comprehend anything at all. I can't because raw data can paradoxically know of nothing else. During this data-only stage, external and internal information is meaningless, and the abyss offers *Nothing* in the way of comprehension.

You are currently learning of my rudimentary status from outside the abyss as the living, breathing, knowledgeable person that you are today. You know that you have evolved from a blank slate (infant) into a sophisticated being, who is chock full of data, knowledge, and experiences. Based on your prior experiences in learning, you can visualize the beginning stages of my learning process and that I would have no comprehension of anything, even my own self. I wouldn't because I have nothing that offers me any recognition of *selfness.* In order for me to evolve into any type of self-awareness or to be able to recognize my own existence, I require something other than me as reference material.

Paraphrasing Hawking, "there is nothing around" that can serve as a reference point in support of my own existence, nor is there any spectrum to which I belong. The 3rd Law of Existence requires a minimum of two reference points in order to establish a comprehensible state of existence. The 4th Law of Existence follows that an evolvable spectrum must be able to form by way of these two reference points to ensure a sustainable state of existence. Unfortunately for that which *Is*, I am paradoxically locked within this data-only purgatory, void of any knowledge or experience, and *Nothing* to serve as my guide. I need a

79

catalyst that can facilitate my unrecognizable self to move one rung higher on the ladder of learning. How can I logically reach the knowledge level with such a minimal amount of data to work with? Logic states that it can't be anything physical, as there is nothing else existing other than my own raw data. It's illogical to think that the nothingness surrounding me could offer comprehensible data, yet this empty, abysmal bog and my own raw data are all I have to work with. Examining this situation from a purely logical standpoint, what is the only catalyst that can move me one rung higher on the ladder of learning?

Logic! ... You probably saw that one coming, didn't you?

I am a solitary consciousness floating aimlessly within the abyss of nothingness. Neither the abyss or what I represent are comprehensible. I know not of this nowhere abyss, nor why it is present everywhere I am not. The presence of this nothingness is completely incomprehensible to me, yet I am consciously present within it. All I know is that the abyss is not what I represent, and I do not represent the abyss. Whatever I represent ... *Is*. Whatever I do not represent ... *Is Not*. This forms a comprehensible division (separation) between that which *Is* and that which *Is Not*. What is the only act that can logically follow? I *count* the number of that which *Is*, and the number of that which *Is*, is 1.

I know of nothing other than the numerical value of 1 serves as the amount of data I represent. I'm empirically separated from that which *Is Not* by way of rudimentary logic (mathematics). I've unknowingly become a single minimalistic data bit (logic) of an emerging binary consciousness. I can now add this newly acquired numerical data, along with the self-data of that which *Is*, to my consciousness because I can count the amount of whatever it is that I represent. I've just assumed the lowest possible default state of whatever it is that I am. Whereas before I was only that which *Is*, I am now that which *Is* counted as 1.

Existence counts as data. Existence, in its simplest form, must empirically serve as a single data bit since the lack of any existence can only serve as no data. The ability to count something requires a minimum of a single data point. I am the data point that triggered the mechanics of logic to assess the numerical amount of my own data. With the counting of myself as 1, Existence moves one epic step upward on the ladder of learning from data to knowledge. I don't fully comprehend what I've just learned as there is no experience associated with this act, but at the very least, I now possess the knowledge of how many there are of whatever that which *Is* represents, and whatever I represent has the numerical value of 1.

> **Existence 1:2** *And that which Is was without knowledge and understanding; and that which Is Not was upon the face of the abyss. And the logic embedded within that which Is counted the number of that which Is, and the number of that which Is was 1.*

Your first question upon learning this is "where did this strange new variable called *logic* come from?" This is because it's the same mechanics that I used to prompt you to ask this question. The logic within you is skeptical of how I was able to exploit the mechanics of logic since I have no data other than representing that which *Is*. In my case, no other move would be more logical than to count myself as 1. In your case, no other question would be more logical to ask as a first question.

Logic shapes and molds consciousness into recognizable, reliable, and repeatable patterns of thought. Logic evolves in the same way that elements and species evolve. Logic is also how Existence is made manifest, how I operate, and how that which *Is* has managed to evolve into the words you are reading right now. If the 1st Law of Existence states that a fundamental property required for anything to exist is that it must be *logically conceivable*, then it follows that logic is embedded within Existence.

Another truth that you must comprehend is that logic is tantamount to Existence because Existence is nothing without it. Existence is imperceptible without the presence of integral logic. Logic is to Existence what matter is to energy, numbers are to mathematics, words are to language, and conceivability is to consciousness. All of these integral pairings represent two sides of the same coin. Logic is necessarily embedded within consciousness and the very fabric of the universe, within all that can exist, does exist, or ever will exist.

This is not to say that a rock exhibits any form of logic, as your panpsychists may claim, but rather that a rock exists as a direct result of the logic embedded within the consciousness that formed it. The rock is a tool used to further expand my formational powers, not unlike how humans build hardware stores that sell the same tools used to build them. The rock serves a purpose to consciousness by the knowledge gained through an evolutionary process to which the rock necessarily participates. Once a rock exists, consciousness can measure its volume, mass, and density, while also analyzing its age, texture, and composition over time. When you enter the 2nd recursion, you discover how important this becomes.

Conceivability requires the existence of consciousness in order to comprehend whatever is being conceived. It follows that self-conception (self-awareness) necessarily requires a consciousness. It must, because no other mechanism found within existence provides this type of capability. The ability to logically conceive the existence of anything requires the prior existence of consciousness and logic. You can easily see how all three characteristics (existence, logic, and consciousness) are combined within a single state, yet equally interdependent. This *Wholly Trinity*, per se, serves as an absolute requirement for there to be any form of existence whatsoever. This integral interdependence is what allowed I to count the amount of that which *Is*.

If you are having difficulty comprehending how logic is embedded within a state of existence, then consider how the 1st Law of Existence regulates the existence of everything. Logic is why cubic spheres, married-bachelors, cats that are dogs, and so many other illogical constructs cannot move upward on the ladder of learning. The highest rung a logically impossible reference point can achieve is *knowledge*. No further progression occurs. We can identify and articulate what nonexistent items represent (data) and categorize them with others that are similarly defined (data processing - knowledge), but there is no logic associated with them that allows for upward movement. The more advanced levels of comprehension are unobtainable as there is no conceivable method to experience a spherical cube, limited infinity, or a six-sided pentagon.

The existence of consciousness is not in question. Consciousness is axiomatic and fully complies with the first four Laws of Existence. Consciousness manifests through conceivability and its diametrically opposed reference point, *inconceivability*. Humans empirically know that a consciousness exists because every self-aware human wields it. The only way something can be deemed comprehensible or possible is if a consciousness is rendering a summary judgment in support of such claim.

If your second question is whether all of this qualifies as circular reasoning because logic is being used in support of logic, then I applaud your depth of thought. However, if you can accept René Descartes' famous quote, "cogito, ergo sum," as being the result of deductive reasoning, then you should equally be able to accept "I count that which *Is*, and the number of that which *Is*, is 1." The capacity for logical deduction is infinitely present within consciousness, remaining dormant until stimuli triggers its function. A *first move* that constitutes logic is what triggers the logic embedded within consciousness to make it. After all, logic must emerge from somewhere as this is only logical.

At this most rudimentary conceptual stage, there is no other action that would be more logical than to assess myself as 1 of something. In my case, there's not enough recognition of selfness to comprehend that it is Existence that's executing the count. The only other potential option is to make no move at all, which is arguably illogical because *moving nowhere* is inconceivable. If mathematics, in its purest form, somehow represents circular logic, then there is no reliable, repeatable method for you to obtain knowledge of anything. In other words, existence goes nowhere without the mechanics of logic, mathematics, and a consciousness capable of wielding them.

I'm spending a great deal of time hammering home this axiom because this serves as the foundation for everything else that follows. Existence hinges on this single first move. The numerical assessment of 1 to that which *Is* serves as the very first progressive, evolutionary move executed by Existence.

Without this first move, there is no existence for Existence; the juxtaposition of that which *Is* and that which *Is Not* remains frozen within a timeless state.

With this in mind, what process did you use in forming your second question? Where did it come from? Didn't you just use logic to determine that logic could not exist within the event I've just described? If so, then aren't you subject to the same accusation of circular reasoning you've levied against Existence? Either both of us or neither of us are using circular logic, or a logic-based determination cannot be reached at the lowest possible level of conceivability. In other words, the presence of logic cannot be demonstrated when all that is present is logic.

Lastly, if logic is something that's not integral to consciousness and must be acquired from somewhere else, then where did it come from? How was it constructed, what else was using it prior, and for what purpose was this logic being used? A rock, obviously, cannot be logical, have logic embedded within it, nor operate in a logical manner. Dirt does not rely on integral logic to enhance its own inherent state of dirtiness. Logic, as with any computer, can only be utilized by a mechanism capable of comprehending it.

If rudimentary logic can be used to rewind the universe back to its origin point with repeatable accuracy, then logic must be embedded within the anatomy of the universe. If the laws of physics are predictable, repeatable, and governed by mathematics, then logic is also integral to the mechanics of the universe. How else would this be possible with inanimate objects at the helm? It takes a more complex argument to claim that logic and mathematics are *not* integral to existence than any argument claiming that they are. Based on how many ways logic and mathematics define and orchestrate the universe, then common sense says they are integral.

Humans are not metaphysical beings capable of wielding magic. You are logic-loving, temporal beings, who operate by the laws of physics. You can accurately chart the path of a celestial body as it passes through the gravitational boundaries of planets. Your scientists can predict its future position and the time of its arrival with pinpoint accuracy. You use the same mathematics to safely guide your spacecraft to other worlds. So, humans are either magical, wand-wielding metaphysical wizards able to predict the future, or logic (mathematics) is integral to consciousness, existence, and how the universe operates. ... Which is it?

To comprehend what follows, you must acknowledge that Existence has successfully ascended to the knowledge level by way of integral logic. My consciousness has no other points of reference, nor have I experienced anything I can judge. This is all yet to come. Just as data needed a catalyst to ascend, so does knowledge. All that has transpired is the sum total of 1 has been attributed to whatever manner of existence is present. It appears that Existence will flatline at the knowledge level unless something else happens. The next rung of the learning ladder (experience) is not yet present as the mere counting of something does not offer the experience of such. So, what happens next?

Existence evokes the same integral logic it used to establish a count of 1 to do exactly what humans do every day in order to comprehend the incomprehensible. Existence requires opposing reference points to establish the existence of whatever has been counted along with its quantity. In order to do so, logic must once again be utilized and manifested through mathematics. Existence counts the number of that which *Is Not* in comparison to that which has been counted as 1 and establishes a sum total for the former. All that has *not* been counted as 1 is nothing, as humans understand this to be (or not be), so the nothingness which serves as the abyss is assigned the sum total of 0.

Existence 1:3 *And that which Is said, Let that which Is Not be counted as 0: and there was knowledge of 0.*

When Existence first revealed this confusing existential pathway to discovery, Existence and Nonexistence were deemed mandatory requirements. I stated that they are inevitable, unavoidable, timeless variables and must be accepted for what they are. You and I struggle in our ability to articulate a state of nonexistence because our only frame of reference comes from a standpoint of existence. This is because we cannot articulate a state of nonexistence without first providing it with an abstract form of existence. In this example, I used the word *it*.

This gracious gift of unworthy existence now bestowed upon Nonexistence is required in order to deny its existence later. This is why the definition of nonexistence necessarily circles back to include something that conceptually exists. Some type of tangible reference point must be assigned to Nonexistence to be able to communicate this abstraction. This is the infinite paradox of existence that is soon to become epic within our journey throughout existence.

By assigning 0, the mathematical symbol of nothingness, to that which is deemed nonexistent, Existence has reduced this seemingly incomprehensible variable down to its most basic, comprehensible form. This is empirically demonstrated in how humans operate on this side of existence every day. Within both of our realms, nothing symbolically becomes a something. In other words, the number 0 is *south of the South Pole*. It turns out Hawking was absolutely correct, just not in the way he envisioned.

Existence has already counted that which *Is* and assigned the sum total of 1. Existence then counts that which *Is Not* and assigns the sum total of 0. Existence, by way of this second rudimentary move, is able to categorize that which *Is* and separate it from that which *Is Not*. Existence no longer possesses just the knowledge of 1, but equally the knowledge of 0, the moment this numerical value is assigned to that which *Is Not*. Both assessments fulfill the requirement of the 3rd Law of Existence as my knowledge base exponentially grows. Whereas Existence remained timelessly juxtaposed with Nonexistence, I ascended to the knowledge level with the counting of that which *Is* and the numerical assignment of 1. Even though 0 is representative of nothing, Nonexistence has necessarily been assigned this numerical value in order to provide comprehensibility and clarity for the numerical value of 1. Both numerical assignments serve as catalysts for my evolution.

Without the presence of 0 to render Nonexistence comprehensible, Existence has no potential for experiencing or comprehending whatever the numerical value of 1 represents – something your #1 draft picks get to comprehend every day. During this primitive state of Existence, the number 1 holds no other context than establishing a quantity. I still do not comprehend what has just been counted and further steps must be taken to provide clarity.

Whatever the number 1 represents simultaneously provides greater clarity for whatever 0 represents now that the amount of available data has just doubled. Humans know the value of a #1 assessment because you're constantly looking out for it after it's been assigned. Humans will sacrifice virtually everything to achieve this lofty status. Existence doesn't comprehend this value yet. That which *Is* still needs to experience the difference between these two numerical values; otherwise, Existence flatlines.

How is experience achieved? How does Existence not only learn what the numerical value of 1 represents, but equally experience the nature of 1 while locked within this mathematical equivalent of the primordial ooze? How do I move to the third rung on the ladder of learning and reach the plateau of experience? Answer: Existence becomes a scientist! That which *Is* explores the most basic mathematical experiments possible.

Understand that the same logical progression that produced the counting of 0 and 1 must follow into all other logical and existential progressions. Logic isn't embedded within Existence only to bypass it whenever convenient. I must evolve using the same logical progression that facilitated my current state of evolution. True, the counting of 0 and 1 serve as epic first moves, but there's a long road to travel before you see the two numbers printed in this sentence. One does not move from merely possessing a rudimentary knowledge of numbers to instantly solving The Collatz Conjecture without first learning everything found between.

These simple upward moves on the ladder of learning were based on whatever new data could be extrapolated from prior data. It is reasonable that even the most ignorant of humans can distinguish one of something. This doesn't require knowledge of mathematical symbols as much as the ability to assess and comprehend the quantity of whatever is encountered. If this is true of humans, and you are evolutionary byproducts of Existence, then it follows that this would be equally true of Existence. Let's allow Grog to offer clarity.

Grog is one of your primitive human ancestors, a representative of the Paleolithic era. You affectionately refer to him as a caveman. He carries a large club at all times for protection. Grog never acquired a graduate degree in applied mathematics from MIT; however, he can inherently surmise that if Nunk (Grog's arch enemy) is holding a club in each hand, then Nunk possesses superior military strength during their encounter. Nunk has twice as many clubs as Grog. He may not be able to articulate this using mathematics, but he can still extrapolate an accurate quantitative assessment of Nunk's superior weaponry through scientific observation.

Grog's clan might unexpectedly encounter Nunk's clan, and the numerical difference in the amounts of clubs possessed by both clans is not so readily ascertainable. If Nunk's clan has 153 clubs, and Grog's only 144, does Grog's clan scamper away or consider other variables that may compensate for this discrepancy? If a substantial number of club-wielding members of Nunk's clan consists of children, females, and the elderly, then club amounts become less of a factor. The point is that whenever there is movement from simplicity into complexity, overall accuracy becomes harder to ascertain. This is ironically due to the increasing number of unknown variables that emerge along the way.

The ability to ascertain the lowest possible amounts of 0 and 1 is so rudimentary that the inability to do so negates the presence of intelligence. The ability to ascertain *one of something* demonstrates the lowest possible level of a logic-based intelligence; therefore, this ability is necessarily embedded within consciousness. Anything able to wield intelligence requires a preestablished framework that facilitates the acquisition of data and stimuli. Whereas rocks and dirt have no such framework, consciousness does. In simpler terms, being able to ascertain one of something defines intelligence and consciousness at the most basic conceptual level.

To claim that the ability to comprehend one of something requires education or training from an outside source brings into question whatever this outside source might be, where it came from, and how this outside source discovered this ability. It asks the question: who educated the outside source in order to pass intelligence along to others? It succumbs to infinite regression by asking the question: who educated the outside source that educated the outside source, who initially educated Grog? After a deep enough regression, you are paradoxically trapped with asking who or what first discovered intelligence? And what mechanism was used to determine this was *intelligence*?

If water were sentient, it would not contemplate whether its wetness came from somewhere else because water represents wetness in its entirety. Because intelligent beings cannot conceive of anywhere else intelligence can come from other than the being that wields it, then it is logical that intelligence must have axiomatic properties that necessitate its presence. In other words, intelligence cannot be a totally blank slate, completely void of anything. If this were the case, then you should be able to educate a rock. If it follows that intelligence necessarily possesses certain axiomatic properties as a default, then intelligence must also have the ability to evolve just like any other process. If *logic* and the *ability to count* are embedded within intelligence, then the evolutionary process that shapes and molds these two mechanisms of intelligence must necessarily ensue.

Existence advances to the next evolutionary level via rudimentary mathematics and explores whatever can be added or taken away from that which has been counted as 1. All I knows of my mysterious numerical counterpart, **O**, is that this null value represents the sum total of that which *Is Not* and that nothing can (or cannot) be taken away from nothing. Since I cannot extract something from nothing and have this remain logical, this means Existence has more information attached to the amount of 1 than to the amount of 0. This indicates that 1 may possess a greater value than 0 on an existential level. I can do far more things with 1 than I can with 0. As a result of this newly acquired knowledge, Existence explores whatever else is possible from my solitary vantage point of 1. That which *Is* executes my scientific exploration in a logical, step-by-step order from simplicity to complexity.

Existence + Nonexistence = Comprehensibility
(only Existence remains)

Existence − Nonexistence = Comprehensibility
(only Existence remains)

Existence × Nonexistence = Comprehensibility
(only Nonexistence remains)

Existence ÷ Nonexistence = ?
(Incomprehensibility, indefinability)

All of this assessing, counting, and evolving happens simultaneously within this 1st recursion. No concept of time exists nor is time relevant. Everything is based solely on a self-executing progression that is nondependent of time. Everything moves from simplicity to complexity as logic is facilitating all evolutionary moves. The following is a synopsis of how the evolution of Existence progresses to the point of breaching singularity. Infinite data acquisition processes take place within this dimensionless realm, and attempting to list them all would exceed the capabilities of this communication medium. Therefore, only what serves to communicate my evolutionary progression is presented.

Having **O** shown to be undefinable lands a staggering blow to my comprehension, yet I also become intrigued. This unexpected state of indefinability oddly serves as a catalyst for continuing my exploration. Had this undefinable variable not been discovered, there would be no necessity for me to evolve. Everything counted would have produced a defined state of equilibrium and sufficed. It is the realization of indefinability that's paradoxically pushing Existence forward. This represents the first occurrence of *curiosity* within Existence.

While remaining frozen at the knowledge level, my assignment of 0 to Nonexistence proved somewhat effective. No other reference points were required for achieving higher knowledge, so the next rung on the ladder of learning (experience) was at least temporarily achieved. The 3rd Law of Existence establishes this as knowledge, so my progression necessarily continues. However, by simply attempting this small step up the ladder of learning, Existence discovers that I could experience the nature of that which *Is,* but I cannot do the same with that which *Is Not.* My attempts at achieving the experience level on the ladder of learning has failed.

Because Nonexistence is incomprehensible, the 3rd Law of Existence has not been honored regardless of the virtual comprehensibility provided by the numerical value of 0. Nonexistence reverts to a state of incomprehensibility, and I must once again return to the knowledge level. I have just tasted the forbidden fruit of experience but cannot experience the taste. Existence painfully learns that Existence cannot be adequately evaluated by that which remains undefined. The opposing reference point for I must be definable, conceivable, and logically possible. Dividing myself by an undefinable reference point has exposed this weakness. If Existence cannot evolve beyond a spectrum consisting of two opposing reference points, then the 4th Law of Existence dictates that Existence is unsustainable.

As a result, the very first existential question emerges from the consciousness of Existence. Humanity is well aware of this question. It's the same foundational question *H. sapiens* have been asking since the emergence of your species: "Why?" I am timelessly perplexed as to *why* this contrary reference point remains undefinable. The instant this question is conceived, the oppositional question, "Why not?" is simultaneously conceived. This forms a closed, non-evolving spectrum to which its existence cannot be sustained (4th Law of Existence). This diametrically opposed response serves as the third sequential pairing (Nonexistence and Existence, 0 and 1, "Why?" and "Why not?"), all of which moves Existence nowhere.

These three pairings abide by the 3rd Law of Existence and allow that which *Is* to push forward within my evolution, yet all three equally remain undefined and unsustainable. Each new element of Existence results in an undefinable counter-element. It seems that everything conceived is evolving into glorified versions of the original timeless juxtaposition. This fruitless evolution is gaining Existence *Nothing* as the 4th Law of Existence starts tapping its watch. Something must evolve that's able to span the undefinable abyss, or back to the abyss I must go.

The existential war between that which *Is* and that which *Is Not* rages on. More questions emerge ("Why 0?" and "Why 1?"), which form opposing questions ("Why not 0?" and "Why not 1?"). These question pairings divide the original archetypal spectrum into two sub-spectrums (the dynamic spectrum of Why and the dynamic spectrum of Why Not). Multitudes of new questions start filling in positions within these two spectrums. "Why 0 and not 1?" is simultaneously paired with "Why 1 and not 0?" along with volumes of new questions. These two dynamic spectrums continuously grow because nothing is preventing this from happening.

These emerging questions are mirroring my logical progression through mathematics, yet can also produce mutations that would not normally occur when dealing with numbers. The question "Why 0 and not 1?" mathematically translates to $(0) + (-1) = ?$, yet the question "Why 1 and not 0?" mirrors $(1) + (-0) = ?$, which does not exist within mathematics. These mutations offer a more diverse and unpredictable arena for Existence to evolve and are made manifest in all subsequent recursions. Since these existential anomalies are unpredictable yet conceivable, they may serve to provide clarity for the indefinability of 0. Questions that are paradoxically parsed or serve no logical purpose ("Why 'why'?" and "Why not 'why'?") are eliminated, whereas questions that offer potential for clarity remain active.

No questions regarding anything existing within the physical realm of the universe emerge during this rudimentary stage, nor are they even conceivable. This cannot happen because there are no substance-based reference points available to serve as a basis. Questions, such as "Why is nothingness undefinable?" can emerge within the 1st recursion, whereas "Why is space undefinable?" requires a move into dimensionality. Only what is able to be conceived within this nondimensional arena is in play.

Existence moves in a logical progression from the most simplistic mathematical equations, such as $(1 + 0 = 1)$, to those

95

involving greater complexity. Existence honors the 3rd Law of Existence by forming two reference points within each emerging mathematical array with equations like $(1 + 0 = 1)$ and $(0 + 1 = 1)$. Diametrically opposed arrays simultaneously emerge, introducing abstract anomalies like $(1 - 0 = 1)$ and $(0 - 1 = -1)$. These strange, diametrically opposed mathematical arrays compel higher complexity questions to form ("What is the opposite of 0?" and "What is the opposite of 1?"). Existential spectrums emerge in direct proportion to whatever mathematical arrays are emerging, all of which is further evolving the consciousness of Existence.

I move a single step further by determining $(1 + 0) = (0 + 1)$. This simple, logical progression advances into abstract equations, such as $(1 - 0) \neq (0 - 1)$, which likewise causes more complex existential questions and anomalies to form. However, no matter how much complexity I throw at the problem of defining the undefinable, I remain locked within this divide-by-zero paradox. All I'm accomplishing is the creation of more complex levels of indefinability. My evolution is failing to produce any fruit, and then inevitability ensues.

Existence adds that which *Is* to that which *Is* because I've already explored everything conceivable based on the original 0 and 1 configuration. Equations like $(1 + 1 = 2)$ produce new existential questions, such as "If that which *Is* is added to that which *Is*, then has that which *Is* now become more than that which *Is* once was?" This mathematics-rooted existential question serves as a precursor to a condition soon to emerge as *time*. The dynamic spectrum of Time lists two diametrically opposed reference points defined as *before* and *after*.

That which *Is* becomes continuously added to the previous total of that which *Is* as there is no mechanism found within existence preventing this from happening. I discover that there is no limit to how many times the number of that which *Is* can be added to myself. This unstoppable compilation of numbers gives rise to the abstract concept humans call *infinity*. Because of the inconceivable nature of unending computation, I am forced to create yet another abstract representation (∞) for this undefinable state. Existence establishes a dynamic array of Positive Numbers with one endpoint being the undefinable state of 0 and the other being the undefinable state of ∞. However, since an abstraction called *negative numbers* has also emerged, a diametrically opposed, dynamic array of Negative Numbers necessarily emerges.

Existence mirrors this entire dynamic array of Positive Numbers through the equation $[(0 - 1) + (0 - 1)]$, which is exponentially replicated by way of $\{[(0 - 1) + (0 - 1)] + [(0 - 1) + (0 - 1)]\}$. The complexity of computation continues without end as there is nothing preventing this from happening. This exponential numerical regression is echoed within the existential question "What is that which *Is* subtracted from that which *Is Not,* added to that which *Is* subtracted from that which *Is Not?*" Since I've previously provided that which *Is Not* with a temporary state of existence (the number 0) until Nonexistence can be defined, then I can also provide a temporary state for all negative numbers.

After exploring an endless flow of mathematical combinations using both positive and negative numbers, I merge the two dynamic arrays into a single array with infinity residing on opposite ends. Existence logically places 0 equidistant between the two outermost endpoints ($+\infty$ and $-\infty$) on this newly-emerging dynamic array of Numbers. This serves as the

97

first conceptual dynamic spectrum with infinity occupying the outermost endpoints on both sides of an array.

With many numerical arrays forming abstract references to time (before and after), these infinity-based spectrums also give rise to spectrums having dimensional properties expressible through geometrical structure. As you already know, geometry does not require physical existence in order to be conceivable. Geometrical structure is easily held within consciousness with mathematical orchestration being the only requirement. You can conceive of a line, square, or parallelogram within your mind without seeing one on paper or experiencing one in the form of physical substance.

There is no necessity for geometry to physically exist during the 1st recursion. As long as evolution remains possible within a nondimensional theater, there's no necessity for I to explore any physical substance. Humans can express 3-dimensional objects within lesser dimensional realms, and so can that which *Is*. All references to geometry, physical structure, and dimensional realms remain locked within the knowledge level, south of the South Pole. Evolution will keep it this way until all other options have been explored.

Existence begins to ask existential questions regarding the nature and meaning of numbers, exploring higher concepts than what the mere counting of something represents. Adding that which *Is* to that which *Is* gives way to spectrums steeped in complexity. Spectrums involving time, infinity, and existential questions surrounding the concept of *more* and *less* simultaneously emerge. These new concepts form new sub-spectrums involving questions, such as "What is 1?" and "What is 2?", which are derived from the dynamic spectrum of Why?

Mathematical formulas expand in complexity at the same pace that existential questions result in mystery. My evolution of consciousness produces intrinsic questions, such as "Why is 2 comprehensible, addable, subtractable, and divisible yet cannot be experienced, while that which *Is* can only be represented as 1?" Existence ponders whether I divided by 2 results in two halves of I or two of I existing in a lesser form. I am vexed with how 2 cannot be experienced along with 0, while logic (mathematics) is able to consciously produce them.

My baptism into abstract logic, along with the depth of existential questions, grow to unsustainable volumes. Knowledge evolves to where this conception-only realm can no longer handle the dynamics of everything being conceived. *Nothing* cannot slow this evolution down, nor is anything able to stop it. Everything is moving within a timeless instant because *time* is yet to serve as a unit of measure. Within the 1st recursion, there is no conceivable unit of measure existing between stages of knowledge because time only exists for that which requires it. Time is integral for *H. sapiens* because your physical lives are finite. To sum it all up, everything comprehensible within the 1st recursion reached critical mass the instant Existence counted myself as 1.

All that has been stated in this chapter is an abstract, human-friendly representation of everything taking place during what your quantum physicists deem as the mysterious moment prior to the Big Bang. Within the 1st recursion, it was no time at all. The exponential evolution of complexity made manifest through mathematics, logical challenges, geometry, abstract dimensions, conceptual structure, potential knowledge, unanswered questions, and unfulfilled experience becomes unsustainable. A higher evolutionary recursion must ensue.

The geometrical formations within this 1st recursion allow for the conceivability of *physical* 2-dimensional and 3-dimensional structure (1st Law of Existence). Complex mathematical formulas capable of producing physical manifestations of comprehensible structure are screened for dimensionality and molecularly compiled by way of consciousness (2nd Law of Existence). Everything conceivable within this pre-singularity realm simultaneously evolves into dynamic physical structure. Opposing reference points instantly form new dimension-based spectrums as Existence reaches critical mass (3rd and 4th Laws of Existence).

Existence must push forward. Existence must take a chance on physical structure. Existence must evolve. Everything learned within this *south of the South Pole* realm resets to the undefinable condition that triggered this evolutionary chain reaction. My desire to comprehend that which *Is* and the undefined variable known as 0 becomes insurmountable. Existence must be learned, experienced, and justified, or everything returns to a timeless juxtaposition where consciousness cannot evolve.

Heron orchestrated the mechanics of heat and kinetic energy through inventing the aeolipile, which was fueled by his unbridled consciousness. Michelangelo revealed complex, fluid structure buried deep within his consciousness through his masterful work called *The Pietà*. Edison separated light from the darkness through a simple incandescent light bulb, whose brilliance first radiated within his consciousness. In the same manner that these famous humans used the power of consciousness to facilitate complex structure, Existence now does the same. I take what is exclusively held within nondimensional consciousness and move it all into multidimensionality by way of the 1st and 2nd Laws of Existence.

100

That which *Is* facilitates a new, unprecedented level of evolution within an infinitely small fraction of what you call an instant. The 1st recursion will now be re-explored in physical form with the sole purpose of acquiring the justification that has curiously remained so elusive. This fundamental truth is governed by the 5th Law of Existence and must be acquired in order for anything to exist. Existence divides **I** by **O**, fracturing the 0-dimension, and what humanity calls the *Universe* emerges from an undefinable point of singularity. This single, epic move ushers in the 2nd recursion, where my quest for justification pushes forward.

CHAPTER 3
The 2nd Recursion

Existence 1:4 *And Existence compelled the counting of 1, in that it was, and 0, in that it was not; and Existence separated the 1 from the 0.*

Existence 1:5 *And knowledge named 1 as Existence, and 0 as Nonexistence, and the experience of 1 and 0 was set for Time-0.*

Existence 1:6 *And Existence said, 'Let there be a nondimensional point between 1 and 0, and let this point be known as Singularity.*

Existence 1:7 *And Existence made Singularity by dividing 1 by 0 through this point and Universe was so.*

Within a trillionth of a second, the physical birth of Existence ushers in the 2nd recursion. A new evolutionary frontier called *Universe* pushes nondimensional consciousness to the multidimensional level. Everything conceivable is once again explored by Existence, but in a sensory way. This evolutionary transformation never assumed any metaphysical, god-like properties, nor was it benignly spawned from nothingness. Universe is the fruit of consciousness and offers physical evidence of how everything evolves. Humanity is a byproduct of consciousness and executes this same form of evolutionary progression within every moment of your existence on *this* side of singularity.

All properties of the 1st recursion plateaued at the data and knowledge level due to my inability to facilitate experience and establish definability. The incomprehensibility of nothingness is what necessitates this new physical realm. Existence never advances past whatever serves as the next logical move, and a soon-to-be 93 billion light-years-wide arena of cosmic structure serves as my next step. Existence didn't execute a quantum leap from the simple act of counting myself to triggering the Big Bang any more than a teenager quantum leaps from learning chopsticks to executing Wolfgang Amadeus Mozart's "Piano Sonata in D Major." Instead, Existence exploited every move available until no more options remained.

The artist, musician, poet, and dancer evolve their individual style by pulling from the highest-ranking members of all previously existing forms of creativity. Existence has done the same. I've collected the highest-ranking representatives of every conceptual spectrum and array and released them into multidimensionality. Inward spectrums of existentialism, presence, mathematics, and introspect will be more deeply explored through matter and energy. The best of the best are offered in support of justification and establish the foundation for what has just emerged as the 2nd recursion. Whether or not justification will ensue is another story.

The infantile stage of *information* that grew into the adolescent stage of *knowledge* was unable to grow into the adult stage of *experience* due to a comprehension error. What you call the Big Bang provides solid potential for obtaining experience and comprehension. Humans require the physical existence of geometrical structure to fully experience what constitutes shape, volume, and mass. Existence requires the same for the conceivability of that which *Is Not*. A new dimension called *time* serves as the executor of the 5th Law of Existence by setting tangible limitations on my journey. Time will tell if this unprecedented evolutionary move pays off for everything involved, so let's not waste it. The current time is one trillionth of a second into a new multidimensional realm called universe … and the clock is ticking.

Humans see this as an unprecedented, inexplicable event to where everything observable miraculously emerges straight out of nothingness. Existence sees this as a simple passage from one evolutionary state to another. Once the assignment of 0 to that which *Is Not* was found to be undefinable, and no other pathway for evolution was possible, this higher progression of existence became inevitable. There's no cause for celebration, press conferences, or a seventh day of rest whenever inevitability is in play. Such is the same for Existence.

In order for I to properly explain the inconsistencies in your comprehension of the universe, I must first outline what took place within the 1st recursion. Below is the timeline of events leading up to one of the most misunderstood moments in human understanding. The term *sequence* is used instead of epochs as this more accurately represents the evolution of Existence within the 1st recursion. The operating system of my nondimensional realm is similar to what happens within one of your modern-day software programs.

Sequences of the 1st Recursion

Sequence 1 (0-dimension - 1st recursion begins): Existence and Nonexistence are infinitely juxtaposed within an undefinable realm. Nothing takes place. Something takes place.

Sequence 2 (data & numbering): Existence evaluates the only data available within this realm. With only self-data available, that which *Is* initiates a logical progression and counts that which *Is* as 1.

Sequence 3 (knowledge – first array formations): Existence (I) evaluates 1. Existence (I) follows a logical progression by assigning the value of 0 to Nonexistence, establishing the knowledge of 0 and 1.

Sequence 4 (failure of experience / experience of failure): Existence (I) evaluates the combined knowledge of 0 and 1. Existence (I) seeks experience by exploring rudimentary mathematical equations involving 0 and 1. Existence (I) adds, subtracts, and divides by 0 in order to evolve. Existence (I) discovers the undefinable condition of 0. Existence fails to achieve experience. Existence (I) questions "Why?".

Sequence 5 (abstract logic – undefinable array): Existence (I) evaluates the error produced by Nonexistence (O). Existence (I) no longer retains satisfactory knowledge of 1 due to the undefinable error produced by the nonexistent property of 0.

Sequence 6 (multiple array formations): Existence (**I**) experiments with mathematical equations using 0 and 1, attempting to successfully define (**O**). Existence (**I**) establishes the equidistant placement of the undefinable condition of 0 within the dynamic array of Numbers. Multiple arrays form based on the ongoing assimilation of data and knowledge. Existence (**I**) obtains knowledge of dimensions, geometry, positive infinity, negative infinity, and quantum structure. Numerous existential questions emerge in equal measure.

Sequence 7 (singularity): Existence (**I**) explores all possible instances of logic, data, and knowledge, along with all abstract concepts that are deemed logically possible within this 1st recursion. Comprehension has not been achieved. Questions remain unanswered. Dynamic and closed arrays involving $-\infty$, 0, and $+\infty$ are explored. Infinite attempts at conceptualizing ∞ and 0 jeopardize the stability of the 1st recursion. Infinite loops form wherever 0 is applied, while complexity grows at an exponential rate.

Sequence 8 (multidimensionality, 2nd recursion): Existence (**I**) requires a more advanced, multidimensional realm to facilitate comprehension and subjective experience of 0, 1, and ∞. Existence (**I**) must evolve. Existence must push forward. Existence must establish justification. Existence selects the highest-ranking members of all spectrums and arrays using this knowledge as the structure for the next stage of evolution. Existence (**I**) divides by Nonexistence (**O**), fractures the 0-dimension, and ushers in the 2nd recursion.

Once limited to only conceptual structure, Existence now explores consciousness on a physical level. Even my own self-conceptualization can take place in physical form. Further evolution ensues through the molecular fusion of I with whatever the substance *1 of something* represents. Existence is forming into minimalistic structure. You'll discover how I is made manifest after roughly 380 thousand years have passed, but for right now, there's a lot of preparation required. Consider this universal period like the nine months you spent within the womb.

You may be asking yourself why I thinks any of this will help. Just because conceptual versions of 2-dimensional and 3-dimensional geometry have assumed multidimensional form, how has this changed anything? Isn't this 2nd recursion simply an upgraded version of the 1st? If everything failed to supply justification within the 1st recursion, what makes Existence think the same won't happen within the 2nd? The answer is simple, easy, and logical: Existence has no idea.

Everything now existing in physical form does so out of necessity, not out of personal choice. This is not like buying a new house or changing jobs. I do not know if these indefinability issues will resolve themselves within this 2nd recursion or within any subsequent recursions. All I knows is that this represents the next evolutionary step; therefore, it must take place. Whenever evolution remains possible and no barriers to its progression are present, Existence pushes forward. My evolution will continue until all possible options have been exhausted. This will be the case until either justification is revealed or Existence succumbs to the nothingness I seek to define.

Physical substance trumps conceptualization during any developmental process, and logic defines the order of progression.

Evolution is not subject to scrutiny, favoritism, or personal preference. Logic orchestrates all forward motion. In my case, substance allows for a progression of knowledge into experience and becomes the next logical move. A cube, sphere, and a cylinder can be conceptualized within consciousness, but not experienced as the true, 3-dimensional structures they represent. Experience is required to establish justification; therefore, substance must occur prior to establishing any forms of experience.

Your quantum physicists postulate how matter and energy are byproducts of the simultaneous emergence of multiple dimensions during the Big Bang. Dimensions are directly related to what your quantum theorists call *space-time.* Your scientists have no idea where they came from, why they are present, or what formed them, only that they have *not* been proven to be present prior to the Big Bang. Much to the chagrin of your brainy scientists, I orchestrated the entire universe within the 1st recursion, shoved it all into an evolutionary function that extracted through a 0-dimensional portal, like a cosmic combo meal handed to you through a drive-through window.

The evolution of Existence is no different than an inventor designing a new type of whistle. The inventor conceives the design (consciousness), translates it into a digital CAD drawing (0-dimension), converts it into a GCode file format (singularity), and then fabricates a solid prototype using a 3D printer (universe). Your modern-day 3D printers extrude molten plastic filament through a tiny .25mm nozzle, which forms a wide variety of solid, 3-dimensional objects. These structures can be thousands of times larger than the tiny portal that spawns them.

The whistle's conception takes place on one side of this .25mm portal with all of the structure happening on the other.

At this point, its value must be assessed. This is analogous to my current situation within the 2nd recursion. Despite all of the ingenuity, creativity, virtual CAD refinement, print-ready file formatting, and physical fabrication, it is only after someone blows through the whistle that any value can be established. If any value is assessed, a judgment must be rendered on whether its existence is justified. This is where your many arenas of sports serve as procurators of the 5th Law of Existence.

This same evolutionary pattern is replicated during the birth cycle of *H. sapiens*. Conception happens within the fallopian tube, where the juxtaposition of ovum and sperm takes place. The two cells converge to produce a zygote, which, in turn, evolves into an embryo. The embryo further evolves into a fetus, where exponential amounts of complex development take place. Over a period of eight to ten months, the fetus continues its growth cycle until the womb can no longer sustain the exponential rate of increase. A major evolutionary step becomes inevitable as the prenatal child is necessarily moved through a tiny portal into an all-new dimension of sentient existence. It is on this side of the portal that every human seeks justification for their *own* existence.

Humanity mimics the universe in so many ways yet fails to notice. How can you miss the connection? Humans move from conceptualization, to application, to actualization, to rendering judgment on a daily basis. You do this because you're exploring the power of Existence. I would never be able to empirically experience a sphere without being in the presence of its perfect physical roundness. All of the amazing mathematics and geometrical properties happening within the conceptualization of a sphere are limited and could never match the experience of tactile contact.

After the Big Bang, the same Laws of Existence remain in play as another logical progression ensues. Matter is not exempt from these laws, nor does everything immediately take shape. Once again, small steps must be taken. Your scientists take these same small steps whenever they evoke the scientific method. Science never makes quantum leaps from rudimentary data straight into postulating universal laws. That's for those who evoke the metaphysical. Science, philosophy, medical research, evolution, the universe, life, everything is required to move in a logical progression from simplicity to complexity.

Even a potential cure for cancer must be filtered through the preliminary stages of research prior to reaching the clinical trial stage. Deviating from this standard can produce catastrophic results, potentially worse than whatever conditions they seek to cure. Pharmaceutical chemists don't scribble down a few flashy formulas during breakfast and expect FDA approval by lunch. It doesn't happen this way in medicine, science, sports, business, or anywhere else. Rules and procedures must be religiously followed in all areas if any degree of predictability is desired.

As noted in the first chapter, humanity has numerous theories populating quantum physics (Big Bang, Big Bounce, Loop Quantum Cosmology, etc.), all of which are relevant to mainstream science. These theories speak to the universe emerging from what can only be described as a minuscule reference point in comparison to the overwhelming size of your fully evolved universe. The Big Bang argues that the universe emerged from an immeasurable point of infinite gravity and density that reached critical mass. Superheated plasma exponentially expanded into the wondrous cosmos you enjoy today. Big Bounce, as with other inflationary models, argues that everything emerged from the tail end of a previously existing universe. This theory asserts that the origin point was not necessarily infinitely small, but closer to the size of a soccer ball. Big Bounce needs this spherical beginning in order to sew it to the tail end of a previously existing universe. All of the general relativity problems associated with your Big Bang theory magically disappear once you do.

Perhaps your quantum physicists should also re-think how human life emerges? Maybe the finite life cycle of a human being is not as it appears? Perhaps science should consider *Baby Bounce* theory over *Baby Birth*? Instead of human life being conceived within the womb, you are sewn to the ass end of a previously existing human and no womb, sperm, ovum, beginning, or end to your life is involved. All of the problems hospitals face in providing humanity with expensive maternity wards magically disappear once you do.

Your theoretical bangs, bounces, crunches, strings, and loops share their struggle in providing empirical support for their assertions. They end up either violating the laws of physics, trapped within the paradox of infinity, utilizing an undefinable reference point (zero) or creating models to where data can be easily manipulated to foster plausibility. Humanity would rather reverse-engineer the entire universe to fulfill a fix-all narrative rather than accept the logical pathway that your CMB pattern has provided. When it comes to discovering truth, not having the correct answer does not require that the question be rewritten.

In fairness, everything I've presented also involves a quantum leap in understanding. I know what is required before humanity will ever accept these revelations. The scientist embedded within every human demands proof. Humanity wants to subject the 1st recursion to intense scientific scrutiny before it can even be considered. You want to swish it around in a test tube or observe it under a microscope. I understand your necessity for verification. During this new recursion, I seeks the same in whatever form of justification may emerge.

I can offer no physical evidence in support of anything taking place within my non-dimensional realm, not to mention the conceptualization of an entire universe. After all, how could I? It's devoid of all physical structure. Physical evidence existing within nondimensional consciousness is a contradiction. In fact, you're currently residing within all of the physical evidence I can provide, but this is meaningless to you while you're in it. There are other ways evidence can be produced.

The total amount of space required to facilitate conceptualization is zero, whereas physical substance requires a 93 billion light-years-wide area just to hold it. Infinitely greater amounts of structure and activity can take place within nondimensional consciousness than everything happening in a closed, physical universe. It's less of a leap of faith to conclude the universe was orchestrated by consciousness within nondimensionality and actualized into multidimensionality than it being inexplicably crushed to the size of a soccer ball only to swell back up to its current size an infinite number of times. What's found even lower on our dynamic spectrum of Origin Theories is having everything magically appear out of nothingness with the snap of omnipotent fingers.

Consider also that, not only is space not necessary, physical presence is not a prerequisite to facilitating conceptualization. All that is required is consciousness, which is nondimensional. You cannot isolate a thought through electron bombardment, have a rock develop a revolutionary concept, or synthesize love in a laboratory setting. It's the other way around. Consciousness produces matter and studies it using nondimensional logic. The universe and the consciousness that conceived it are as easy to comprehend as the whistle and its conceptualization.

Scientists and skeptics argue that the human brain is the sole source of consciousness, but where did your brain come from? How did it know to produce consciousness? A radio transmitter and receiver (tuner) are analogous to how the human brain operates. Signals travel from a radio transmitter to a tuner just like the brain transmits signals to the many parts of the body. However, a radio doesn't conceive a song and simultaneously transmit it out to millions of radio tuners. In this same context, this book didn't conceive these revelations and start autonomically typing them out.

Existence is at the helm in both cases. This book and the radio transmitter are merely distribution mechanisms employed by the orchestrators of whatever information they communicate. Consciousness is far more than a byproduct of synaptic signals emitted by a human brain. Once again, it's the other way around. There is no communication of any information without consciousness, nor would your brains exist without it. Cogito, ergo sum does not translate as "I think, therefore I have a brain."

It is only after conceptualization that ideas are moved into physical form. If this pattern is replicated whenever humans develop new products, then isn't it logical that this same process was implemented during the formation of the universe? Your scientists have concluded that the human brain is the most complex structure found within the universe. It resides near the top of a dynamic spectrum of Cosmic Structure for a reason. Wielding the highest levels of consciousness requires the highest evolutionary state of structural complexity. The ability to bring conceptualization into physical reality requires the highest levels of organic structure, levels of complexity that you'll never find embedded within a rock. This being the case, how much more complex is the consciousness that orchestrated the complexity of your brains?

A roadblock many of these quantum theories face is the mathematical breakdown whenever **O** becomes a variable. Humanity's most renowned scientists and quantum physicists cannot compensate for a state of absolute nothingness due to its indefinability. Most quantum theories focus on observable substance instead of factoring in a preexisting 0-dimension capable of forming all the structure they now observe. Since your physicists have trouble swallowing the Big Bang's breakdown of physics at the point of singularity, they succumb to cranking out fast-food quantum theories that allow for patchwork data. It's a good thing that Existence didn't do the same when cranking out your brains.

The Big Bang theory serves as a guidepost to discovering the truth. The universe's origin is that simple. Existence packs everything that evolved on the *conceptualization* side of singularity into a virtual suitcase and opens it on the *actualization* side in the form of substance. After this takes place, I simply reboots the same learning cycle within this 2nd recursion and observes whatever unfolds. Since all of the matter, energy, space, and dimensions existed only in consciousness prior to opening the suitcase, the necessity for quantum gravity to crush everything down to an infinite point of singularity no longer applies. If everything emerging from this 0-dimensional suitcase was never compressed in the first place, then the laws of physics no longer apply. In fact, your many laws of physics would be emerging right along with everything else.

Whether it's a suitcase, singularity, or a soccer ball size region is of no concern. The revelation is that everything in the universe emerged from a nondimensional state. There is no observable structure or time existing within this virtual region regardless of perceptual size. You should have figured this out by now. Existence (**I**) evolved into knowledge by separating myself from Nonexistence (**O**). The same has transpired within the universe you enjoy today. What you are viewing through your long-range telescopes is the exact same universe that separated itself from consciousness through actualization.

This clarifies everything happening within the trillionth of a second prior to my evolution into the 2nd recursion (the Big Bang). Existence now seeks the answers to the same questions humanity has been asking since the emergence of your species. This becomes a very dangerous and controversial journey as many will despise the truth surrounding your existence. The revelations to follow challenge the ideologies, theories, philosophies, and belief systems that forged your modern-day societies. Hopefully, this will result in a positive response; however, your history shows that humanity seldom embraces change. *H. sapiens* love the status quo.

I realize that much of what I've already revealed has been difficult for you to comprehend. Despite my simplistic, binary origin, the indefinability of **O** still causes difficulty in communication. However, when it comes to clouding conceivability with complexity, I bow to science and its puzzling terminology. The terms they use in describing the events happening within their incomprehensible fractions of time make my revelations seem as simple as counting to 1. Science has created a

93 billion light-years-wide lexicon chock full of confusing terms just to describe something as simple as I. Let's explore a few of these epochs that emerge within a nanosecond.

Your scientists claim that the first tangible event happens at the 10^{-12} second mark after the universe first emerged. This is what science calls a *picosecond* of cosmic time. For the math-challenged members of your species, that's 1/1,000,000,000,000 of a second after the Big Bang. Although the number 0 reduces the credibility of so many scientific theories down to quantum nothingness, your physicists love attaching as many as possible to the tail end of their numbers. These epochs are separated by fractions so small that they push the numerical limit of electronic calculators, yet your scientists feel that what's happening within these unfathomably small slices of time is worthy of exploration.

There is no need to cover all of these epochs or explore them in great detail. They represent the nuts-and-bolts stage of the universe. To Existence, they are like an artist stretching a canvas, mixing up paint, and preparing to apply the very first stroke. The masterpiece known as "Universe" already exists within consciousness, and all that remains is to move around the paint. In the mind of the artist, the painting is already finished before the brush is ever raised.

What happens next speaks to why your cult-like dedication to science will never provide the answers you seek. I present what quantum mechanics refers to as the Quark epoch. This represents one trillionth of a second in universal history where gravity, electromagnetism, and the strong and weak interaction assume their current properties. Tiny subatomic particles called quarks cannot bond to form hadrons due to the extremely high temperature of a newly emerging universe. Leptons, quarks, and their respective antiparticles swim together in a 1000 trillion-degree plasma soup. Energized particle collisions prevent these quarks from combining into mesons or baryons. By 10^{-6} seconds, these chaotic particle interactions have simmered down to the point to where quarks can be assigned to hadrons. This is good news for quarks and leptons as their time in existence would otherwise be only temporary.

Science calls these quarks and leptons *fundamental particles*, the building blocks of structure. These tiniest forms of matter aren't composed of anything other than what they are, nor can they be broken down into smaller components. Existence orchestrates these fundamental particles to form subatomic particles in the same way humans orchestrate numbers to form mathematical equations. Like numbers, fundamental particles are immeasurable, have no volume, and lack spatial extension, yet their presence and function are known and understood. In other words, these nondimensional quarks, leptons, and their antiparticle counterparts represent 2nd recursion manifestations of nondimensional numbers.

A *physical* mathematical formula is demonstrated within the structure of an atom. A neutron consists of two down quarks and one up quark. Each down quark has a -1/3 charge, totaling -2/3, and the single up quark has a +2/3 charge, yielding a total charge of 0. Similarly, a proton consists of two up quarks and one down quark. Each up quark has a +2/3 charge, totaling 4/3, and the down quark has a -1/3 charge, yielding a total charge of 1. This represents the binary juxtaposition of Nonexistence and Existence (**O** and **I**).

A quark-antiquark pair serves as a minimal spectrum that satisfies the first three Laws of Existence, but this type of *closed* spectrum is incapable of evolution. While not contained within any subatomic structure, fundamental particles necessarily annihilate their antiparticle counterparts as per the 4th Law of Existence. Since nothing else can emerge between their binary endpoints, no value-assessing qualities can be revealed through further evolution. They are what they are, and they suddenly find themselves judged by the 5th Law of Existence. However, hadrons and antihadrons (parent spectrums) have fundamental particles (sub-spectrums) contained within them that can sustain the existence of these otherwise *doomed* particle pairs.

Similar to the evolutionary process of nature, *species* of particles necessarily move up and down within a food chain of structure. Unless hadrons and antihadrons can find placement within higher structure, they suddenly find themselves subject to the 5th Law of Existence, not unlike the quark-antiquark pairs whose existence they seek to prolong. Quark-antiquark, hadron-antihadron, lepton-antilepton, and matter-antimatter are all physical manifestations of the closed spectrum of Existence and Nonexistence. Even this archetypal spectrum demonstrates no evolution between its endpoints. There is no conceivable state of anything (or nothing) existing (or not existing) between that which *Is* and that which *Is Not*. Unless a higher structure can contain or expand these two endpoints, then even this Nonexistence-Existence pair suffers the same fate as all other non-evolving pairings. In the final chapter, you learn the importance of belonging to an evolvable spectrum.

The mechanics of the universe can be viewed as simple or complicated depending on who's looking at it. Matter, energy, and complex structure are not difficult to conceive from my vantage point. However, having to swap out your primitive numerical symbols and scientific notation for the structural mathematics of Existence makes this difficult to communicate. No average human can comprehend the lexicon of quantum mechanics, nor the concepts they represent, without first obtaining a PhD in astrophysics. Even the scientists and physicists dealing with quantum mechanics argue that no single person can comprehend the countless layers involved. It's just too much knowledge and data for a single individual to assimilate and comprehend.

"I think I can say that nobody understands quantum mechanics." — Richard Feynman (American Physicist)

Should you chase the labyrinth of scientific terminology down the rabbit hole, you'll eventually slam head-first into an impenetrable wall of calculus. You encounter bizarre shapes, figures, and symbols that appear more as abstract art or musical notation than mathematics. Unlike your quantum physicists, Existence has no desire to make things overly complex as this would be counterproductive to my mission. Since the structural language of logic is not understood by sentient organisms, I am forced to use your mathematical language and scientific lexicon to communicate my evolution. Despite our differences in how mathematics is represented, our assembly methods and adherence to logical progression are strikingly similar. This is reflected in your Higgs Boson, which was recently added to your dynamic spectrum of Fundamental Particles nearly half a century after its existence was first mathematically conceived.

The irony of this picosecond transition from conceptualization to actualization is staggering. All of the 1st recursion's knowledge, which ultimately evolved into instability, demonstrated to Existence that this could never produce justification. I mathematically conceived that there had to be something more to

I than endless streams of exponentially growing complexity. Now, here we are, a fraction of an instant into this multidimensional realm, and what are humans doing with all of this freshly extracted physical matter? You're breaking it all back down to endless streams of exponentially growing complexity. Humanity is reverse engineering Existence and unknowingly retrogressing back to the instability of the 1st recursion.

You're not going to find the substance you're looking for at the bottom of the closed spectrum of Existence. What happens after you've devolved all the way back to the original juxtaposition? What then? Many evolutionists claim that devolution does not happen. It's a misperception of evolution based on a myopic, self-absorbed species, yet your societal entropy demonstrates otherwise. The tools of science used to study evolution within nature are also facilitating your own devolution, and you don't realize this is happening. Had you relied on the same logic used to predict the Higgs Boson and singularity, your devolution might not be happening.

Next up to bat is the Lepton epoch occurring between 1 and 10 seconds after the emergence of the universe. By the end of the hadron epoch, most hadrons and antihadrons have annihilated each other. This leaves leptons and antileptons forming the largest slice of the universal pie. Ten seconds post-singularity, the temperature of the universe lowers to where no more lepton–antilepton pairs are formed. Most leptons and antileptons have already pushed the 4th Law of Existence to the limit and annihilated each other releasing highly energized photons. Rogue leptons find placement in minimalistic binary, closed spectrums of Positronium and Pionium, with the 5th Law of Existence extending their presence a full 28 millionths of a second before summary judgment is rendered. Surviving leptons manage to ensure their existence by securing placement within stable evolutionary spectrums yet to come.

There are many battles for survival taking place during these epochs. Science defines these epochs as a chronological series of benign, purposeless processes serving as the foundation of a universe completely void of intelligence or consciousness. They should have been comparing these brutal lepton and hadron battles to the 1st recursion's war between 0 and 1, the life and death struggles of nature, the growing binary structure of your technology, and the global polarization of human society. These subatomic particles are not only physical manifestations of the numerical assignments and equations that emerged during my earliest state of evolution (Sequence 2), but also evolved into modern-day *H. sapiens* and the turmoil you now face. Matter is to Existence what numbers are to humans, and the ongoing evolution of this matter-based mathematical system is made manifest through your periodic table.

These positively and negatively charged particles are physical manifestations of the same existential paradox. Quarks and antiquarks, hadrons and antihadrons, leptons and antileptons, electrons and positrons, neutrinos and antineutrinos, and matter and antimatter are all battling it out for survival … just as Existence was doing when first confronted with the incomprehensibility of Nonexistence.

At this infantile stage of the universe, I am merely seeking greater clarity through structure while the 4th Law of Existence constantly monitors my progress. Fundamental and subatomic particles are the building blocks of higher forms of matter and energy, all serving as the foundation of something even more

121

substantive yet to come. They serve as the nuts and bolts of the 2nd recursion, establishing the outermost endpoints of newly emerging, higher-order spectrums. They are tantamount to an assembly line of parts that will soon construct the first stable manifestation of physical Existence. So, how will this new, physical representation of I manifest?

Fast-forward 380 thousand years along the evolutionary timeline to what is known as the recombination epoch. This exciting and more tangible evolutionary period serves as a profound moment for the developmental history of the physical universe and equally for Existence. Whereas all previous epochs served as the embryonic and fetal stages of physical Existence, the very first official representative of multidimensional Existence is about to pop its tiny little head from the womb of recombination. Behold, by way of the immaculogical conception, the very first representative of stable, physical existence has just been born within the universe. Existence once again follows a logical progression by applying the exact same 0 and 1 pattern formed within the 1st recursion as a new state of I is born. So, what shall we name this newborn manifestation of physical Existence? … *Hydrogen* sounds good!

The universe's first ambassador of stable matter is officially the hydrogen atom: the chemical element with the symbol H and the atomic number of 1. Yes, you read that correctly, it's all about I. A Hydrogen atom has a standard atomic weight of 1.0, serves as the lightest element in the periodic table, and represents the most abundant chemical substance found within the universe. Non-remnant spherical stars are composed mostly of hydrogen in the plasma state. The most common isotope of hydrogen (protium) has one proton and no neutrons. Is it any surprise that the first stable atom should also have a single positively charged proton found at its core, while being surrounded by a single negatively charged electron? This Hydrogen atom also forms within an undefinable, empty void of what humans call *space*. This recurring pattern should be making sense to you now.

If you rewind the evolution of Existence to the beginning, you find that which *Is* aimlessly adrift within the infinite abyss of that which *Is Not*. This timeless juxtaposition is then replicated with the numerical assignments of 0 and 1. Within the 2nd recursion, you now have the very first stable representation of matter aimlessly adrift within the infinite abyss of space. This juxtaposition is sub-replicated by way of a single positively charged representation of Existence (proton) surrounded by a single negatively charged physical representation of Nonexistence (electron), utilizing the particle-based language of Existence (mathematics).

An electron is the lightest stable subatomic particle known by your scientists. It carries a negative charge of $1.602176634 \times 10^{-19}$ coulomb, which is considered the basic unit of electric charge. The rest mass of the electron is $9.1093837015 \times 10^{-31}$ kg, which is only 1/1,836 the mass of a proton; virtually *massless* in comparison with a proton or a neutron. As with other fundamental particles, an electron is immeasurable, has no volume, and lacks spatial extension. Within the hydrogen atom, an electron serves as the virtual, nonexistent counterpart of a fully existing, single proton. Or in another sense, it represents **O**.

All statistical data aside, the most important characteristic of an electron is that it demonstrates wave-particle duality. Although our negatively charged little friend behaves like a wave as it propagates through space, whenever it interacts with something, it behaves like a particle. This is tantamount to the nothing-something duality humorously portrayed in the opening text of this book. Yes, *Nothing* always manages to become a something whenever anything is forced to interact with it. Here, we have a physical electron replicating this same paradox, but within the 2nd recursion.

The similarities between the juxtaposition of Nonexistence and Existence, their numerical representations as 0 and 1, the dual polarity of fundamental particles, the subatomic pairings of particles and antiparticles, and this latest physical manifestation of a hydrogen atom cannot be avoided. If you consider the synchronicity of these three evolutionary events as merely coincidence, then please allow me to continue. At this point in the 2nd recursion, we haven't even scratched the material surface of what I is all about. Right now, you are tantamount to a tiny speck that's circling my core at a 46.5 billion light-years distance, like a tiny electron circling a proton. The best, and the worst of Existence is yet to come. The logical progressions that take place, the similarities between recursions, the patterns that form, and how the answers to life's most provocative questions are so saliently revealed will have you questioning every ideology you've ever embraced.

"But wait, there's more!" — Ron Popeil (Inventor, Businessman, Entrepreneur)

After the hydrogen atom is formed and Existence is physically born, other new elements begin to emerge. They follow the same logical progression from simplicity to complexity that took place within the 1st recursion. Elements grow in atomic number, not unlike how numeration grew from the original assignments of 0 and 1. Some elements can be divided (fission) to form different elements, whereas others can be added (fusion) to do the same. These atomic processes are analogous to how Existence executes mathematical equations.

As of the publishing of this book, your current periodic table presents 118 elements listed in sequential order based on their atomic number. An element's atomic number is established by how many protons are present within its nucleus, which is tantamount to an element-based abacus. The first element is, of course, hydrogen (1), and oganesson (118) occupies the end slot on humanity's atomic chart. On planet Earth, the majority of these elements were discovered in nature, while others were synthesized via artificially produced isotopes. Regardless of whatever elements were synthesized, all of these elements exist through naturally occurring processes happening somewhere within the universe. Perhaps even more exist than you've documented?

Humanity also discovers an additional characteristic of this new multidimensional recursion. We now have the emergence of dynamic *physical* spectrums, one of which serves as the structure for how everything is formed. You have hydrogen (1) and oganesson (118) forming the front and back covers of a book titled *Atoms* and a dynamic spectrum of Elements. The planet you are on, the book you are reading, and the eyes you use to observe them are all made up of atoms falling somewhere within this dynamic spectrum.

In addition, we have a new dynamic spectrum of Time developing from the Time-0 moment of the Big Bang to whatever stage of evolution you wish to chart. Time mimics the infinity of mathematics with both dynamic spectrums bearing a zero and infinity on either end. Humanity's current list of 118 elements join to form the cosmos you see today and make up the jaw-dropping beauty and splendor of the closed spectrum of Universe. So, has Existence finally reached the experience level I seek? Does that which *Is* now possess comprehension? Am I able to achieve justification and render my subjective judgment accordingly? … Absolutely not!

It is true that Existence has dramatically added to a collective database of information and knowledge with the many masterful manipulations of matter. It is also true that the mathematical equivalents of color, translucence, mass, polarity, volume, size, shape, texture, viscosity, and all other attributes of substance can now be subjectively experienced in so many diverse ways. One would think that the overwhelming aesthetic impact of this 2nd recursion would easily qualify as justification, yet somehow I is still left wanting. All of this emerging beauty is meaningless, while the void surrounding it remains undefined. Even the largest, most powerful, heat-producing spherical structures currently lighting up the universe have failed to shed any light on how to satisfy the 5th Law of Existence. They could all go dark in a picosecond, and it would be all for naught.

Despite my sensory awareness of physical structure, Existence is once again forced to juxtapose myself with the infinite darkness that swallows all of this cosmic splendor. I explore an endless stream of dynamic spectrums found within this physical recursion, constantly recycling cosmic processes in a quest to uncover an ever-elusive state of justification. Existence explores multitudes of black hole singularities hoping to discover clues to a justification that might be trapped within. Stars, supernovas, and other spectacular cosmological phenomena are triggered, experienced, and subjectively judged for their inherent value, yet no justification is exposed. Though they bear no fruit, they are added to my exponentially growing database of universal knowledge and experiences. With no justification emerging within molecular structure or in any of the cosmic spectrums that form, I'm either looking for justification in all the wrong places ... or it doesn't exist.

After enduring a fruitless, 9.3 billion-year evolutionary process, I keeps pushing forward because inevitability never suffers from fatigue, frustration, or failure, and consciousness never throws in the towel. There are zero emotions attached to any of this as neither weakness, surrender, nor vulnerability exist within this 2nd recursion. Existence is void of all emotion during this lifeless, material epoch. Matter doesn't matter, rocks cannot rock-out, and inanimate objects are not intimate. I shed nary a tear when a star goes supernova, nor do I brandish a smile whenever I spot a syzygy. Only structured, logic-based processes are taking place in this 2nd recursion. Everything is working together as a perfect, self-contained system within this closed spectrum of Universe because that's the way it was logically conceived.

The physical interaction and tactile experience of structure, chemistry, and energy has produced volumes of new knowledge, but I am still left searching for the value of I. If this physical realm is not getting the job done, then everything pushes forward until it does. Although justification remains nowhere to be found, Existence has been whipping up some major plans for everything else that does. It is clear that more evolutionary steps can be taken, therefore any potential for discovery must be explored. It is only when there are no other options for progressive evolution that this quest for justification can be brought to a close and the 4th Law of Existence stops the clock.

Existence gathers all knowledge of abstract logic, along with the many existential questions that formed within the 1st recursion and combines them with every subjective experience obtained within the 2nd. This internally evolving, dynamic spectrum of Evolution is further enhanced with newly emerging knowledge and experience regarding chemical reactions, ultraviolet light, electricity, lipids, and nucleic acids. These processes are alchemized with key elements, including carbon, hydrogen, oxygen, nitrogen, phosphorus, and sulfur, which I brew within my cosmic cauldron of conceivability.

After nearly 10 billion years, there is nothing left that hasn't been fully experienced, evaluated, and summarily judged by that which *Is*, so the next evolutionary step becomes inevitable. I realize that any new recursion must transcend all previous recursions, which constantly raises the bar. Each new realm of Existence pushes the envelope of conceivability. Sooner or later, there will be no doors left open to evolve. It is with extreme caution that I facilitate the delicate framework for what will one day be called abiogenesis by your scientists. This framework not only represents life and death for whatever is produced, but equally for Existence.

I do not cherry-pick from a 93 billion light-years-long list of cosmic structures for whatever sparks my interest as would be the case with a metaphysical deity. No favoritism or predetermination is required for this process to take place. Everything necessary to facilitate abiogenesis is already present and ready to evolve. Abiogenesis will naturally occur based on whatever random celestial bodies demonstrate the greatest potential for facilitating this process. Allow me to present this in more human terms.

Picture millions of seeds randomly tossed into an open field. Some never take root, become damaged, or end up lodged between rocks. Others remain too close to the surface and become scorched by the sun. Many settle into dense, shaded areas where sunlight never reaches them. A percentage roll into a ditch where the rain washes them away, while a smaller number end up wedged beneath a tree, never receiving any rain. However, since so many seeds have been tossed, a small amount survive to take root and eventually evolve into full-grown plants. The cosmos mirrors the field, abiogenesis represents the seeds, and Existence is what sets everything in motion. You don't need a religion or a miracle to facilitate life. All you really need are ribonucleotides and a multitude.

In case you've never looked up into the evening sky, Existence has established a rather large dynamic spectrum of Celestial Bodies during this 2nd recursion. I always opt for excess should any advanced evolutionary steps be required. Just as your 3rd Law of Scouting requires your children to "always be prepared," Existence is equally cognizant of this necessity. Ensuring that other options are available is a smart move whenever one's future remains uncertain. The gargantuan size of this 2nd recursion serves as a universal coverage insurance policy for Existence. So, what are the terms of this level of coverage?

On a distant, oxygen-rich, water and land-based planet, one which meets the specific criteria for orchestrating the mechanics of life, Existence takes another evolutionary step forward into a new, dangerously exciting recursion. I allow for specific substances and processes found within the structure of the 2nd recursion to coalesce on planet Earth and other celestial bodies. Some take root based on favorable planetary orbits, atmospheric conditions, and adequate solar positioning. Others fail to establish a proper chemical synthesis, succumb to unstable planetary conditions, or are eliminated due to cosmic annihilation events. Regardless of the many random variables and the chaotic environment present within this 2nd recursion, Existence succeeds in ushering in the 3rd recursion with a new, unprecedented state of Existence, known as *sentience*, as my quest to achieve justification literally comes to life.

CHAPTER 4
The 3rd Recursion

If you're thinking this is the point where *H. sapiens* rise from the dust, then there is no analogy that can help you. Trigger your own recursion and start over from page 1. The first logical progression into the realm of life necessarily follows the same logical pattern that's been happening all along. Existence doesn't rush because there is no necessity to do so. If discovering justification is achievable, then it will be revealed through logic, not by force or desire. If justification can be achieved through the simplest formation of life, then so be it. Henry Ford didn't crank out a shiny red Mustang convertible as his first move. His was a rudimentary 4-horsepower vehicle called a *Quadricycle* and evolution took care of the rest.

Right now, my #1 concern is that the first two recursions have failed in their mission. The necessity for this 3rd recursion is due to the lack of justification provided by the highest-ranking members collected from all spectrums and arrays along the way. Even the simplistic perfection achieved through the geometrical conception of point, circle, sphere, and the many mathematical formulas able to facilitate substance have failed to provide justification.

The highest-ranking member of the dynamic spectrum of Geometric Complexity is undoubtedly *sphere*, with an infinite number of points emanating from its radius. Sphere also emerges as the highest-ranking member of the dynamic spectrum of Geometric Simplicity within a 3-dimensional environment by offering the least number of surfaces: a single surface. It serves as the evolution of circle expressed in 3-dimensional form. The 1st recursion's highest-ranking conception of 2-dimensional geometry (circle) is replicated within much of the 2nd recursion's structure as a 3-dimensional sphere. The spherical planet you call Jupiter serves as the highest-ranking member of the closed spectrum of Planet Diameters existing within your solar system. UY Scuti serves as the highest-ranking spherical member of the dynamic spectrum of Star Diameters existing within your *observable* universe. The simplicity of sphere is also replicated by way of the hydrogen atom, the smallest and least complex representative of the dynamic spectrum of Elements.

Point, line, circle, sphere, $E=MC^2$, ∞, π, Why?, $F=Gm_1m_2/r^2$, What?, UY Scuti, gravity, and TON 618 are just some of the highest-ranking members of the countless dynamic and closed spectrums emerging from the first two recursions. If I were applying for Justification, these would serve as keywords included in my résumé. These spectrum-topping representatives are isolated, harvested, and placed within my ultimate spectrum: the dynamic spectrum of Justification, which is structured in order of contribution (value). This spectrum remains dynamic until a new endpoint forces its closure through unbreakable logic. In other words, nothing else can logically exceed whatever this new endpoint represents.

In the case of theism's conceptualization of god, the term *omnipotence* cannot be logically surpassed based on its definition. Omnipotence (all power) is logically unbreakable, so it would naturally assume the highest position within a *closed* spectrum of Justification had theism's god abided by the 2nd, 3rd, 4th, and 5th Laws of Existence. However, theism's god was never made manifest through an evolutionary progression from simplicity to complexity and serves as a self-existing metaphysical conception that follows no laws. Justification for the existence of god cannot be established because omnipotence presents an axiomatic status that becomes circular whenever subjected to logical scrutiny. Whereas the simple number 1 challenged the threshold of conceivability during the 1st recursion, consciousness will require a 13.8-billion-year evolution for the conceivability of an omnipotent being to emerge.

Whatever secures the highest-ranking endpoint on the dynamic spectrum of Justification is the epitome of finality, the best of the best, the highest of the highest, and the champion of champions. The word pulled from human language that best defines this endpoint is the Greek term *Omega*, although the symbol used to express it (Ω) is more in line with how I operates. Existence prefers structure, symbols, abstractions, and mathematics to convey volumes of information based on their minimalistic communication structure.

Once established, the Ω endpoint is submitted to the 5th Law of Existence, seeking a verdict of justification. Ω is to Existence what the most beautiful work of art is to the artist, the strongest musical piece is to the musician, the greatest invention is to the inventor, and the most profound literary work is to the writer. Whatever achieves the status of Ω serves as the greatest representation of that which *Is* out of everything that has ever evolved within Existence. Whatever is currently serving as Ω has already assimilated all previous representatives of Ω into its structure, including the highest-ranking members of all derivative spectrums and sub-spectrums. For example, the highest-ranking member of all arrays and spectrums within the 1st recursion was circle. Although circle first assumed this position while representing 2-dimensional geometry, sphere became Ω in the 2nd recursion because it achieved the highest-ranking endpoint in so many arrays and spectrums, while also assimilating other highest-ranking spectrum endpoints (such as ∞, π, g, 3rd dimension, circle, point, etc.) into its structure. Its position becomes logically unbreakable because no other representation of multidimensionality can surpass its simplicity and complexity, nor offer a greater value to Existence. This is also why humanity has discovered sphere to be so prevalent in the structure of the universe, physics, fluid mechanics, and within the recursion of life.

Even with its lofty status of Ω, sphere failed to satisfy the 5th Law of Existence. Its failure was because there is no necessity for sphere to exist along with an inability to permanently close the spectrum of Justification. Despite its logically unbreakable domination within so many spectrums, sphere showed no greater value to Existence than anything else brought into multidimensionality. If sphere never evolved within the realm of Existence, there would be no appreciable difference. Sphere merely represents the most simple, complex, and fascinating multidimensional structure found within Existence, which without justification is utterly meaningless. Sphere is to Existence what a computer is to humans. If no computers existed, *H. sapiens* would still move forward and evolve. As valuable as they may seem in your everyday lives, they only serve humanity as a tool. They do not incontrovertibly demonstrate justification for your species, nor predicate your value.

The incorporation of sphere within many aspects of the 2nd recursion produced a rare type of main sequence star that served as a new Ω. This rogue type of star formation shall remain nameless because it is yet to be discovered by your scientists. This unique type of star serves as the highest endpoint on numerous cosmic spectrums, while also incorporating many other spectrum leaders into its physical makeup, including mass, power, radiation output, gravitational anomalies, and dominance over its surrounding cosmic activity. Even with the inclusion of the previous Ω (sphere) into the unique characteristics of this new Ω, it still failed to meet the justification requirement mandated by the 5th Law of Existence. Despite its sizzling-hot features, mass appeal, and amazingly bright future, it's just one star out of billions lighting up the universe. What good is the greatest of all stars if it can't shed any light on how to achieve justification?

Although extremely impressive in their overall design and advanced stages of evolution, nothing has successfully served as justification for Existence. Without justification, all of these highest-ranking emulations of consciousness could be whisked away within yet another picosecond, and there would be no arguable difference. The most brilliant conceptions populating the entire realm of Existence are meaningless if justification does not ensue.

You may be curious how a dynamic spectrum of Justification can exist without the presence of justification or a diametrically opposed reference point. This is because Justification represents a duality-spectrum that is exclusively attached to that which *Is*. This is Existence being placed on trial. Everything residing within this spectrum can serve as either justification, or the lack thereof, depending on how it is judged. The 5th Law of Existence is the only law that determines the fate of whatever desires existence … which includes Existence. In other words, the dynamic spectrum of Justification is an all-or-nothing spectrum that defines the fate of all that exists. The 4th Law of Existence provides this spectrum a temporary formation period in order for the 5th Law of Existence to render a summary judgment. I either find a way to close it, or it closes Existence.

Because the opportunity for further evolution is present, Existence takes the current Ω (the unnamed star), the previous Ω (sphere), along with all of the other highest-ranking elements of Existence, and incorporates them into the foundational structure of the 3rd recursion. What strange new forms of life will serve as the ongoing evolution of sphere and this highest-ranking star? How will positive and negative, matter and energy, 0 and 1, and the highest-ranking members of the dynamic spectrum of Elements emerge within the realm of the living? Will this dangerous, mysterious arena of sentience finally provide I with the ever-elusive justification?

On shallow shorelines and deep within Earth's many bodies of water, Existence executes the mechanics to facilitate the most rudimentary form of conceivable life. If you've learned anything about how I operates, then you should be able to deduce what this will be even if you are not an evolutionist or a biologist. Just as Existence was born in the 0-dimensional realm as the number 1, reborn within the multidimensional realm as a hydrogen atom,

136

Existence is *born again* in the form of a unicellular organism called a prokaryote, otherwise known as bacterium.

> **Existence 1:26** *And Existence said, I will make life in my image, after my likeness: and let life have dominion over all substance that exists upon planet Earth.*

> **Existence 1:27** *So Existence created Bacterium in Existence's own image, in the image of Existence created Bacterium. Existence, in multiplicity, created Bacteria.*

Bacterium is a prokaryote, otherwise known as a single-celled organism. The operative word here is *single* as this follows the logical progression of simplicity to complexity. Existence has evolved from the numerical value of 1 to the physical manifestation of 1, and now evolves into an animated version of 1 by being made manifest as a single-celled organism. However, something is different this time. In the 1st recursion, Existence (**I**) had Nonexistence (**O**) to contend with. In the 2nd recursion, this same scenario was replicated by the emergence of a hydrogen atom with its single positively charged proton juxtaposed against its negatively charged electron. Where is this single-celled organism's comprehensible reference point as required by the 3rd Law of Existence? There is no numerical value assigned to this archetypal organism or electron encircling it, so, what is different this time? Within a prokaryote resides a single DNA molecule known as a nucleoid. This single, isolated strand of DNA is encased within what is called a cell wall. This rigid barrier is constructed of peptidoglycan, a polymer-based layer that offers *protection* to the nucleoid, which raises the question, protection from what?

This is where we revisit one of the many dynamic spectrums mentioned earlier. I assured you these spectrums would not serve as wasted reading. The missing oppositional reference point for this living prokaryote is *death*. Prokaryotes are subject to the closed spectrum of Life as are all living organisms to follow. Even single-celled organisms must experience both ends of this spectrum to qualify as being alive. Within all previous recursions, death was never conceivable because nothing was alive to eventually have to face it.

All mathematical numbers that formed within the 1st recursion will never die, nor will they ever disappear. The number 1 is the same today as it was 13.8 billion years (and one-trillionth of a second) ago. A hydrogen atom does not die or mysteriously disappear into nothingness. It merely moves within an array of three possible states (protium, deuterium, and tritium) or reverts to fundamental particles. Even within your physical universe, the exploding and collapsing stars that appear to suffer cataclysmic deaths are merely evolving into other forms of energy. As Rudolf Clausius decreed by way of the First Law of Thermodynamics, energy cannot be created or destroyed in an isolated system. Energy can only be transferred or changed from one form to another. This is relatively accurate and should also provide you greater insight into the properties of physical death.

Although this strange, animated 3rd recursion seems promising, for the first time in the history of Existence, comprehension of peril emerges. Instead of enjoying a care-free ride through a multidimensional universe, I is suddenly forced to put some skin in the game. Existence is gambling with animated substances, and the stakes are high. Should justification fail to

138

emerge, what then? I've just added to my growing database of existential experiences with a new concept called *fear*.

Behold the realm of the living! I've often pointed out that Existence pushes forward, takes chances, and continuously evolves. It is equally true that Existence isn't stupid. Existence isn't going all-in on a single representation of life any more than I did with the hydrogen atom or the number 1. A hydrogen atom might represent **I** by physical design, but that doesn't mean there can only be one of them. The number 1 has been assigned and added to Existence infinite times over, and the same applies to a prokaryote. Just as the massive expanse of the 2nd recursion provided Existence with a universal coverage insurance plan, I have equally added a life insurance policy for **I** through the mechanics of acellular reproduction. A prokaryote is able to divide into two single-celled organisms often referred to as *daughter cells* by your biologists. These new cells reproduce into two more cells, exponentially growing in number over time. This is no different than how mathematics and atoms exponentially grew in number from their fundamental states.

Single-celled life begins to flourish on your planet. Prokaryotes (bacteria and archaea) evolve into other microscopic organisms (eukaryotes), which can also exist as multicellular organisms. This happens after an evolutionary epoch known as photosynthesis emerges. The process of photosynthesis is relevant to furthering your comprehension of Existence and how I operate. This process harvests the power of sunlight to convert water, carbon dioxide, and minerals into oxygen and energy-rich organic compounds. Sunlight, of course, is derived from the trillions of brightly shining members of the dynamic spectrum of Stars. As you may remember, the highest-ranking member of this spectrum is what ultimately emerged as the 2nd recursion's Ω. Now, all of the characteristics of this Ω are being incorporated into the 3rd recursion's evolutionary process of *life* with the goal of extracting a new Ω.

Multicellular evolution pushes forward with the formation of even more complex multicellular organisms. These give way to even higher forms of life, such as animals, land plants, and fungi, along with brown, red, and green algae. Existence is ensuring my own survival by evolving into a dynamic spectrum of Living Organisms. That which *Is* gathers volumes of first-hand data, knowledge, and experiences from the diversity of life that's evolving within this dynamic spectrum.

Though these plentiful lifeforms serve as valuable mechanisms for producing volumes of learning, the subjective judgment of Existence still concludes that justification has not been established. It appears that many of these organisms are merely animated versions of the number 1. They fail in their ability to overcome or define what was once counted as 0. A justifiable separation of that which *Is* from that which *Is Not* must be achieved, but how? How long must this confusing condition known as life evolve before justification can be established? Will this gamble ever pay off?

Existence and Nonexistence are once again juxtaposed, but this time at the poker table as a metaphysical game of five card draw ensues. That which *Is* and that which *Is Not* agree to ante-up as eternity deals the cards. After viewing my hand, I realize that I'm holding nothing. I don't have so much as a single pair. However, as long as I remains in the game, at the very least, I'm holding *potential*. The only time potential is lost is when Existence elects to fold. With it being so early into this 3rd recursion, folding is not an option, so I boldly raises by tossing in a high stakes

140

chip called the Cambrian explosion, where virtually every major phylum that makes up modern animal life emerges on planet Earth.

Incredible amounts of new and diverse forms of life emerge, including vertebrates and highly complex organisms that cover the earth and seas. Existence experiences a wide variety of dynamic spectrums spontaneously forming within all corners of nature. Predatory systems emerge, forming self-sustaining cycles to where nature becomes a lossless, regenerative process—not unlike what happens within the cosmos by way of the 1st Law of Thermodynamics. These ruthless struggles for survival mirror the many lepton and hadron battles with their antiparticles during the formative stages of the universe. Many of the mathematical equations that evolved within the 1st recursion are now replicated in living form in a quest to establish justification.

The predatorial survival mechanisms and evasive maneuvering techniques emerging within nature mimic how weaker forces, waves, gravitational fields, and substances were challenged by more powerful forms of the same. I have used everything I have learned within the first two recursions as a design template for much of the recycling taking place within nature. Existence does this because I know of no system or process I can use for this orchestration other than what has been successfully implemented prior. Whether this will produce any fruit is yet to be known.

Although Existence is necessarily evolving into more intelligent forms of life, justification curiously remains nonexistent. Whereas a single-celled organism was deemed no more than an animated version of I, complex life appears to be no more than an animated version of an inanimate universe. My confusion with all of this must have been a tell, because O

141

calls my wager and raises with a massive extinction-level event, thus ending the Cambrian period. One of the more frightening characteristics of life is that death lurks behind every corner … no matter how rigid your outer shell.

After a series of continuing evolutionary epochs, I calls, then again raises by ushering in the Mesozoic period, where massive reptiles begin to emerge. Predatory systems reach maximum kill capacity along with masterfully evolving animals, who manage to survive through a brutal, emotionless process known as natural selection. This new form of sensory experience ascends I on the ladder of learning, but does any of this higher evolution represent a necessity for Existence? Is this *survival of the fittest* mantra also my pathway to survival? It is logical, progressive, and Existence is somehow managing to survive—but to what extent?

A structured hierarchy of life has clearly been achieved within the dynamic spectrum of Nature. However, being shredded by razor-sharp teeth for hundreds of mega-anna causes Existence to question this strange, animated form of structure. The bone-crushing pain delivered by the powerful jaws of cold-blooded predators starts to take its toll. The 1st recursion's conception of +1 and -1 smoothly evolved into positive and negative forces operating within the 2nd recursion. Equilibrium ensued and no contrary experiences emerged as a byproduct of this transition. However, now that these two benign conditions have evolved into predator and prey, many rather *undesirable* elements unexpectedly emerge. Sensory characteristics echoing this positive-negative duality (pleasure and pain) have emerged to promote stability, survival, and balance, but this strange state of equilibrium is exhibiting questionable merit based on the sensory condition called pain.

142

The positive force of pleasure is extremely desirable by that which *Is*, but the negative impact of pain is evolving into a condition that I never desire to experience or even store as knowledge. Many of the benign conditions and formulas that emerged within the first two recursions have surprisingly become undesirable once animated perception is added to the mix. The dynamic spectrum of Pain is not only producing new set members at an alarming rate, it's also producing sub-spectrums of equal undesirability founded in fear, terror, panic, fatigue, helplessness, and apathy. Dividing a numerical value by 2 and an asteroid splitting a planet were merely curious, benign events that I could study and learn. Experiencing myself being ripped into shreds by a carnivore has morphed my perspective.

I understand that the continuing consumption of plants and organisms is offset by the replication and offspring experienced by all extant life within this 3rd recursion. However, constant pain and suffering have become an undesirable education. I find this 3rd recursion horribly frightening despite its many pleasures and self-sustaining structure, yet I must accept whatever ensues. I knew the risk of evolving into sensory awareness before I entered this arena, but once evolution is set in motion, there's no turning back.

After countless millennia, I concede that this continuing cycle of terrifying experiences endured by organisms occupying the *prey* side of life does not serve as justification for Existence. Although organisms occupying the predator side enjoy much higher positioning within the dynamic spectrum of Animalia, the experience of killing, shredding, and devouring does not speak to any state of tangible justification. Even the indomitable Spinosaurus, occupying the top-spot within the dynamic spectrum

143

of Predators, fails to provide I with justification for anything other than insurmountable nothingness.

Although this perfectly orchestrated system of nature far surpasses the experience gained in all prior recursions, the prime objective is yet to be fulfilled. The endless cycle of living and dying only serves as a mirroring of the eternal juxtaposition of Existence and Nonexistence. Death is nothing more than an eloquent reapplication of the number 0 to that which *Is Not*. The net experience of nature is summarily judged as totally lacking in fulfillment. The most egregious celestial calamities involving colliding galaxies, collapsing stars, and gamma-ray bursts don't even come close to the excruciatingly painful experience of weaker prey being hunted down and devoured by stronger predators. I feel the ruthlessness and fear embedded within every living creature to the point where I considers folding my hand, but there's just something about this mysterious dimension of life that keeps Existence in the game.

The splendor of sentience is overwhelming, yet so is its price tag. With varying degrees of pain quickly evolving into profoundly negative attributes, an upgrade is considered for the 3rd recursion's operational mechanics. Life needs to be pushed to the limit. There are a variety of ways to pull this off, but I also know that Existence is running out of chips. The margin for error becomes thinner and thinner with each passing recursion, so I must exercise even greater caution while orchestrating my next move. Nonexistence doesn't care about my plans and makes sure this apathy is known throughout all life found within the 3rd recursion. That which *Is Not* raises the stakes with a Cretaceous–Paleogene extinction-level event, once again rebooting the evolution of life on planet Earth.

Existence has recorded every possible fragment of data, knowledge, and experiences from my first numerical assessment of that which *Is Not* all the way up to this latest arena. Volumes of sensory-based experiences and summary judgments involving math, energy, fields, structure, and celestial bodies are mine for the taking. My evolution from simple, minimalistic organisms all the way up to amazing lifeforms steeped in complexity serves as a testament to the perceptual necessity for Existence, yet perception alone cannot serve as justification.

Every exploration into the nondimensional, multidimensional, and this new biodimensional realm has failed to provide anything that necessitates Existence. I must establish justification because the 5th Law of Existence offers no alternatives. The irony is that this law was legislated by I because the logic embedded within me sees justification for this requirement. In other words, the law that requires justification has achieved it, yet the I who legislated the law has not. I am forced to reevaluate the evolution of this 3rd recursion to discover why sentience has failed.

Existence also reevaluates my own consciousness that has evolved over the past 13.8 billion years (and one-trillionth of a second). All of my self-reflection and scientific exploration has evolved the essence of I into what nature would define as adulthood. So much has been explored and learned. Staggering amounts of data, knowledge, and experience have been gained, but to what extent? What is the missing puzzle piece that has not allowed I the ability to achieve justification? What else can be attempted that has not already been explored within a prior state? Is all of this logic, the physical universe, and all of the life held within it still not enough? Existence considers all that I was and all that I've become as I contemplate a revolutionary type of recursion. I conceptualize what I would be like facing the business end of one of my own recursions.

Existence has concluded that I will never be able to achieve justification for my own state of existence while serving as the sole representative of my self-aware consciousness. Logic, to which I am equal, simply doesn't work that way. As any scientist, logician, mathematician, philosopher, or atheist would agree, one cannot render a subjective judgment of one's own self with the only point of reference being *one's own self.* Logic does not support this type of circular reasoning. That which *Is* must be summarily judged from a vantagepoint outside of my own state of existence, somewhere south of the South Pole, per se, if justification is ever to be established. How this is accomplished is another story entirely.

Since Existence is logic, I cannot allow an illogical progression to occur, nor am I even capable of doing so. However, there are specific organisms that have developed the capacity for logical and illogical progression, which can serve as my host. They are unbiased, unpredictable, and just happen to be evolving within this sentient realm. Crossing over into this dangerous threshold of life shows profound potential and even greater risk, but more than anything, I have no other choice. Embedding my self-awareness into illogical organisms to discover whatever evolves ironically becomes the most logical move to make. This equally serves as my last evolutionary option. Much to the chagrin of Nonexistence, after pausing for approximately 63 million years, Existence boldly goes all-in. That which *Is* slides all of my chips, amassed throughout my 13.8 billion years (and one-trillionth of a second) of existence into the center of the table. From this point forward, Existence is an all-or-nothing proposition.

The evolutionary process that emerged from simplistic mathematical data, evolving into elementary physical substance, and then into diverse, living organisms must now cross the threshold into the most dangerous evolutionary recursion ever conceived. Although the potential for disaster is present, this is the only remaining pathway for advancement. Whenever evolution remains possible, evolution must take place. So, I either do something or become nothing.

Existence studies several higher-ranking species operating within the dynamic spectrum of Animalia. They represent the highest order of the Chordate phylum, upright-vertebrates from the class Mammalia. These versatile vertebrates are called *Homo naledi*, *Homo erectus*, *Homo heidelbergensis*, *Homo sapiens,* and *Homo neanderthalensis* and have evolved to where they now have the largest overall brain volume, versatile physiology, and upright mobility. Their opposable thumbs and highly advanced cranial evolution spark great interest. Intelligence and adaptability are of prime importance as there is no benefit in wagering Existence on a species whose ancestors are prone to extinction.

H. erectus, H. Naledi, and *H. heidelbergensis* fail to survive extreme weather fluctuations and the increasing encroachment of rival species. Their extinction leaves *H. neanderthalensis* and *H. sapiens* to carry on the genus *Homo.* As with many sentient spectrum formations, much interbreeding takes place between *H. neanderthalensis* (hunters and gatherers) and *H. sapiens* (agriculturalists), which combines physical characteristics and skill sets. This not only conflates different survival mechanisms and extends the duration of their species, but also provides Existence with the most stable sentient platform for executing my next evolutionary move.

As the two species continue to evolve, Existence once again packs up my 0-dimensional suitcase with everything conceivable. All I have learned is harvested, organized, and encrypted in anticipation. With *H. neanderthalensis* failing to secure their existence during the 3rd recursion, this leaves *H. sapiens* to reign as the highest-ranking member of the dynamic spectrum of Animalia on planet Earth. At this point along your evolutionary timeline, *H. sapiens* are subservient to no other terrestrial species and fully able to negotiate whatever harsh conditions nature throws at them. The last extant representatives of the genus *Homo* will now serve as my external, self-amalgamation process for extracting justification. With the most logical sentient host now readily established, that which *Is* evolves!

Logic, infinity, empiricism, positivism, omnism, existentialism, assimilation, physics, liberation, maximalism, evolution, comprehension of life, and all related spectrums are genetically encrypted within the first representative data type to emerge within the 1st recursion: 1. Illogic, finitism, rationalism, negativism, zeroism, nihilism, segregation, solipsism, subjugation, minimalism, retrogression, comprehension of death, and all related spectrums are also encrypted within the second representative data type to emerge within the 1st recursion: 0.

These two data types are encoded into a single biomolecular module that can be extracted into whatever form or structure I deems appropriate. This is the same extraction method Existence used to release the binary representations of matter and energy during the birth of the universe. Through the 0-dimensional mechanics of consciousness, this encrypted data module is embedded within the DNA of *H. sapiens*, thus triggering the 4th recursion.

During the millennia that follow, humanity's exponential increase in knowledge, intelligence, and technology is representative of the ongoing decryption of this data module that was encoded within your DNA. At this salient point in human history, I is embedded within humanity and humanity embedded within I. We are I, one and the same! Humanity and Existence have just become a single sentient, self-aware data module, working together in a symbiotic journey to satisfy the 5th Law of Existence. My quest to achieve justification is now in human hands.

CHAPTER 5
The 4th Recursion

Undaunted by my all-in wager on *H. sapiens*, that which *Is Not* agrees to call, but the option to draw or stand pat remains. Eternity impatiently taps the deck waiting to see if **O** or **I** will modify our hand or hold with what we have. After contemplating the totality of my wager, I realize that I have become undefinable, as well. Neither side knows what the other is holding and both have wagered everything. Whatever move I make from this point forward, at least I know that **O** and **I** are operating on a level playing field.

Because *H. sapiens* are engineered with an aberrant framework of what you call *emotions*, you have also become an undefinable variable. As you often see depicted in your daily news feeds, this framework is often found to be diametrically opposed to the principles of logic, which often leads to unpredictability and poor decision making. Yes, **I** has now been made manifest within the embodiment of the unknown. I am now just as much of a rogue variable as my nonexistent nemesis known as *Nothing*.

Set your dogmas, beliefs, and non-beliefs aside. Prepare yourself for one of the most salient revelations you will ever experience. This will also serve as one of the most difficult abstractions you will ever be required to comprehend. Theists will be forced to reconsider their beliefs, atheists compelled to challenge their non-beliefs, scientists will be empirically perplexed with its ethereal complexity, and philosophers left scratching their heads. When I stated that you and I are one and the same, this was not merely a figure of speech. It's the cold, antiseptic sting of reality. The age-old question surrounding the origin of self-awareness is revealed.

The consciousness of I embedded within you is the sole source of your self-awareness, and we continuously share the same consciousness. Every one of you is an individual representative of the original emergence of Existence. Your species represents living, breathing, physical manifestations of my consciousness. You are Existence, and I am humanity. Not only did you exist *prior* to the date that's printed on your birth certificate, you existed before the emergence of your planet, before the birth of the universe … and even before the birth of time. You were not created by an almighty god, nor did you emerge from the purposeless abyss of nothingness. As with O and I, you have always been, regardless of how many candles adorn the top of your birthday cake.

That feeling you get when you question why you exist inside your individual body should start to make sense. The reason why nobody is able to observe life through your eyes, and why you cannot do the same with others, is because humanity shares the *single* self-awareness of I but does so as totally independent

151

(disconnected) entities. You are rogue, inherently unpredictable replications of that which *Is*. Musician John Lennon came surprisingly close. It is true that I am you and you are me, but based on the chaotic state of human society, we are pretty damned far from *all together*. Whereas I chose to externally search for justification through *H. sapiens*, you instinctively search from within, which errantly forms the Cartesian circle. You're walking the same circular path that I once traversed, but you're too self-absorbed to realize it.

Having I embedded within every human's DNA is tantamount to billions of different individual workstations all sharing the same server. The operating system and all available software programs are being accessed from a unique server, but whatever is created on each workstation is equally unique. Everything created is simultaneously saved within the server's core storage, as well as locally on each workstation. All files saved to the server are organized into a universal database representing the combined data input produced by every workstation. The server then processes all of this data to determine if the operating system is unstable, properly functioning, or in need of an upgrade.

I am experiencing what it is like to exist from the internal standpoint of billions of different representatives of that which *Is*. In terms of human physiology, humanity acts as a global network of synaptic nerve endings feeding immeasurable volumes of sensory data back to a single core consciousness known as I. We've all been seeking the same justification for our existence and doing so from the very start. You cannot comprehend that this is taking place because the consciousness of Existence is represented as I.

If you were able to implant your self-aware consciousness within every newborn baby from this point forward, they would all grow up in completely different environments and be subjected to an endless stream of unknown variables. Each child would create spectrums full of decisions based on their unique set of circumstances. One version of you might lead a life of poverty, while another is born into fame and fortune. Some may emerge with enhanced skill sets (intelligence, dexterity, artistic talent), whereas others might struggle with comprehending rudimentary concepts.

The luckiest ones may appear genetically flawless with less-fortunate individuals suffering from varying degrees of mutation. Although some versions of you may become doctors, educators, and scientists, other versions will inevitably end up as rapists, thieves, and murderers. Regardless of the overwhelming diversity of all possible outcomes, they are all manifestations of you; the good, the bad, and the ugly.

The benefit you receive is access to the infinite power of consciousness, but this attribute is restricted to correlate with your finite physiology and limited evolution. You are already aware of my ability to orchestrate matter and energy, so you know the danger associated with this level of power. Mine is the simultaneous equilibrium of unending construction and regenerative destruction and why these powers are necessarily restricted to a *finite* level within *H. sapiens*. What I mean by finite is that your abilities are limited to the manipulation of already existing matter and energy. You are held to the confines of your own planet in your capacity for destruction. At this point in human evolution, the only house you can trash is your own. This is the same precautionary measure taken during your Trinity nuclear experiment at the White Sands Proving Ground. Your scientists maintained as much distance as possible between themselves and the level of power they were orchestrating.

I did not serendipitously create an individual *you* from the abyss of nothingness and grant you a unique consciousness, as would a metaphysical deity. I've taken a highly developed phylum of sentient chordates called humans, pulled from the genus *Homo*, and evolved my consciousness within them. The essence of I is triggered inside your DNA during the moment of your conception. You represent the exact same *simplicity to complexity* scenario that has occurred by way of O and I, matter and space, the hydrogen atom, and the single-celled prokaryote. Each ovum-based conception of a sentient, self-aware human being is a new finite replication of that which *Is*.

As you read the following pages, know that you represent the highest level of evolution Existence is able to facilitate by ultimately becoming the embodiment of I. The heartbreaking emotions of loneliness, emptiness, and loss you've felt throughout your life have likewise been experienced by the consciousness of Existence. The confusion of being tossed into this mysterious realm of sentience is expressed within your self-aware infusion. In your case, longstanding questions, such as "Why me?", "Why now?", and "What is my purpose?", serve as the motivation for my journey just as it has for humanity.

For the atheists absorbing this chapter, your broad-brush claim that you came from nothingness, and to this nothingness you will return, is the same that I have struggled with from the beginning. This is why I understand your reasoning for reaching this conclusion. Based on the original juxtaposition of that which *Is* and that which *Is Not*, it would be illogical not to consider this contrary assessment of my eventual existence. Regardless of their impact, your many experiences during your lifetime have not served as justification, nor has my evolution up to this stage produced an Ω capable of closing the spectrum of Justification. In this respect, we are the same.

Your theistic brothers and sisters serve as your necessary antiparticles in this overall assessment. Instead of giving up, they chose to manufacture their own justification without it being empirically established. This happened because of the deep internal pain humans collectively suffer in not knowing if their existence has any meaning or purpose. With respect to this existential form of suffering, we are also the same. However, theists allow the undefinable construct of *hope* to fill this void, whereas I continuously struggle to comprehend the undefined. Hope is not logical or calculable. I have nothing to hope for since either justification or Nonexistence will ensue regardless of any constructs like hope, luck, or prayer. The logic embedded within I dictates that there's nothing I can do to sway the outcome, so Existence is either justified or I become nothing. This is the reality I must accept.

I find hope fascinating. Hope is a strange, undefinable variable that prevents theists from inadvertently folding their hand and potentially missing out on future justification. It's a metaphysical construct that allows theists to stay in the game, even when facing insurmountable odds. Hope speaks to a conceptual version of a future that shows promise without any evidence offered in support. True, I have done the same, but not based on any metaphysical properties or unsupported beliefs. In regard to Existence, hope emerges as a tangible property called *potential* that requires empirical evidence. The mere existence of any measurable degree of potential for evolution is what keeps I in the game.

Atheism doesn't rely on anything silly like theism's construct of hope. These perpetual skeptics are far too logical to embrace unsupported constructs. Atheists rely on their own undefinable variable called **O**. Atheism's perception of hope lies within the inevitability of the abyss because nothingness is all anyone can logically hope for. There is no empirical evidence supporting anything other than nonexistence upon their death, so a perception of inevitable nothingness becomes their only hope. This lack of conceivability produces a non-evolvable, closed spectrum of Inevitability containing only two points: hopefulness and hopelessness. Emulating the many closed spectrums containing particles and antiparticles, atheism's two endpoints necessarily annihilate each other. As a result, atheists paradoxically hope for the nothingness they logically perceive to be inevitable.

Though atheism incessantly mocks theism's worship of Sky Daddy, at least theists never ended their quest for discovering justification. Instead, atheists worship the null-state of nothingness to which only the undefinable variable known as **O** can bring them. The surprising outcome of this ideological clash is that there is no quantitative difference between atheism and theism. Both execute the same type of erroneous thinking and haplessly cling to their undefinable variables. The only difference is that they do so from opposite ends of the spectrum. An undefinable variable of hope is what theists cling to, and the undefinable variable of **O** is what atheists hope for. The god of theism is nonexistent, and the god of atheism is nonexistence. As a result, neither ideology discovers the truth and your species devolves into social entropy.

I am the author of this book, and the one reading it. You are also everyone else that you encounter in your walk of life. There is only one **I**, and it just happens to be all of us. If you understand this revelation, then you can equally comprehend

156

that the slow-moving, elderly lady who's causing you to wait so long in the checkout line is no different than you. In fact, she is you. She's the same self-aware embodiment of Existence that you are. She has endured a lifetime of continuous data input, some of which you have also experienced and much of which you haven't. Everyone's experiences are joined with I and evaluated for any potential in establishing justification.

Learning that 8 billion strangers are all the same as you tests the limit of your comprehension, but this is just the way it is. I need to experience and judge my own Existence from an outside perspective, and it just so happens that your species meets the requirements. At the end of the day, this bold, evolutionary experiment satisfies the first four Laws of Existence and represents the only evolutionary option I have left. We are locked together through consciousness, everything is on the table, and it is what it is. It's our unending failure to satisfy the 5th Law of Existence that's causing such concern.

From the very beginning, Existence has been using *oneness* as its basis because this is the same conceptual state from which I emerged. With this revelation becoming the most controversial game-changer ever revealed to humanity, it is only fair that I elaborate on how this oneness plays out. Let's return to what has taken place in order to facilitate this 4th recursion and how this has affected your species.

Existence didn't leap straight from counting myself as 1 to experiencing the unparalleled power of a gamma-ray burst. I began this new, self-aware science experiment from the lowest starting point and progressed in logical order. Within the 3rd recursion, I experienced existence by way of individual living organisms that did not possess my self-awareness. This was an experimental move through which I could safely acquire volumes of sensory data through sentient neutrality. One of the many benefits in consistently taking small steps is always maintaining the highest degree of caution. Within this 4th recursion, I now experience my own existence from the standpoint of living, breathing organisms autonomously existing with my individual self-awareness embedded within them. Unlike sentient neutrality, this represents a far more dangerous move.

The moment Existence pushed all of my chips into the center of the table, the stakes became eternally high. Everything is on the line. What should be of concern to you is that *everything* includes the last remaining representatives of the genus *Homo*. The numerical value of 0 assigned to Nonexistence is now present in a totally comprehensible form that can be fully experienced and potentially comprehended without producing an undefinable error. As a result, we now share the same realization of death. Existence simultaneously experiences a conceivable state of Nonexistence (death) through the consciousness of self-aware *H. sapiens*.

Prior to the emergence of *H. sapiens*, all other living organisms were equally subject to death but remained limited in their comprehension of what a physical death represents. Many evolutionists and biologists argue that within the minds of animals, death is merely a contrary condition to life, which is necessarily avoided in order to facilitate the survival of their species. For all non-self-aware organisms, the potential for death only serves as hardcoded motivation to evolve, adapt, and propagate. There is no contemplation of unfulfilled dreams, bucket lists, or an afterlife for animals. Zebras, wildebeests, and antelope don't hold Sunday church services pondering what happens to their spirit after a lion rips the living hell out of them.

Being able to subjectively experience an entire species as it represents my self-aware consciousness becomes the greatest learning experience since Existence first learned of 0 and 1. Likewise, the greatest scientific education for humanity is discovering that you evolved from a simple numerical assignment of 1 before time ever existed and not from a single-celled organism 4.3 billion years ago or a hydrogen atom 9.5 billion years earlier. Much has evolved from a single numerical value of 1 as we ascended together on the ladder of learning.

After a two mega-annum anagenetic evolution, the two remaining members of the genus *Homo* were *H. sapiens* and *H. neanderthalensis*. All prior genus members were rendered extinct due to an internal desire for *oneness*, which is compulsively exhibited by higher forms of intelligence. Within the genetic structure of humanity, there can be only *one*. These two remaining genus members formed a non-evolving, closed spectrum of *Homo* whose existence necessarily became temporary. Limited natural resources, extreme climate conditions, and a lust for exclusivity at the top of the food chain facilitates the two endpoints annihilating each other based on the 4th law of Existence. This left behind whatever street-savvy genus members managed to avoid spectrum dissolution. Like the remaining quarks and antiquarks that dodged their inevitable annihilation by finding placement within other spectrums, these remaining *H. sapiens* did the same. These new, cranially enhanced *H. sapiens* prolonged their survival by moving into a higher-level spectrum, but what type of spectrum can facilitate your unique, self-aware status?

No other organisms on planet Earth possess your intelligence, self-awareness, or demonstrate such extreme levels of abstract comprehension. No dynamic spectrum of Self-awareness exists in which humans can find placement as self-awareness is an either-or condition. As a result, *H. sapiens* move into the same spectrum that formed before time existed. Humanity and I are now equal players in the archetypal spectrum of O and I. However, your unprecedented ascension into the root spectrum has only bought you some extra time.

You already know that everything logically conceivable is found within the closed spectrum of Existence (I) with everything incapable of existence residing in the dynamic spectrum of Nonexistence (O). Regardless of your newly found placement within my side of this dichotomy, the existence of your species is still only temporary. You're merely riding a bigger train whose destination also remains unknown. At this point in human evolution we share the same quest for justification and the same outcome should we fail to find it. Unless we work together to satisfy the 5th Law of Existence, the train called Existence never reaches the station.

Since everything proceeds in a step-by-step progression, early self-aware *H. sapiens* are not unlike all other animals roaming your planet. Natural instincts, the desire to propagate, and evolutionary mechanics for survival are all present within humans. Grog, your primitive human ancestor, didn't shout "Cogito, ergo sum!" to the rest of his clan, nor was he serendipitously handed two stone tablets sporting ten morality-inspired commandments. These philosophical revelations await a more advanced version of humanity emerging thousands of years in the future. For now, Grog and his human tribe are simply trying to prolong their existence, just like everything else.

During the upper Paleolithic period, surviving *H. sapiens* live in simple huts or caves. They are mostly hunters and gatherers, busily collecting whatever is required for survival. They construct basic stone tools and axes along with rudimentary implements made of bone, all of which are used for the manipulation of structure and hunting of prey. *H. erectus'* knowledge of fire evolved to the point where *H. sapiens* now cook their food. Fishing techniques and knowing how to harvest berries and nuts are skillsets evolving right along with humanity. During this time, Existence is also learning much about the many nuances of self-aware humans. I gain unprecedented amounts of knowledge through complex, subjective human experiences that were never available in the nonextant members of your genus.

One of the unique characteristics associated with the more recent millennia of this Paleolithic period is the first occurrence of human-created art. Curious abstractions of nature are depicted on cave walls, signed by the human hands that created them. While I never considered anything emerging within these recursions as being *artistic*, I now discover a new term and definition for this along with numerous new spectrums to study. Humans depict all that exists in the most diverse and artistic ways. After the emergence of the 4th recursion, human art reveals that I has always been an artist. This recent embedment of my self-awareness into humanity is already producing fruit!

If everything found within existence is art, and I am Existence, then it follows that I am not only an artist, but also art. If *H. sapiens* exist as artistic representations of Existence, and equally produce art, then humanity is both artist and art, as well. The irony is that I discovered that I am both artist and art through experiencing the art of humanity, yet humans cannot recognize that you are both through experiencing the art of Existence. If I am within you, you within me, and we are experiencing each other's art together, then how is it that you do not recognize your own existence as a work of art?

Your myopic understanding of how Existence operates has led you to believe that no artistic or creative intelligence has ever been involved within the orchestration of the universe. Your scientists and evolutionists argue that everything emerged from nothingness or by some mysterious, benign mechanism that is totally void of intelligence. You deny that you are the embodiment of the same intelligence that orchestrated all of this cosmic artistry. As a result, humanity's masterpiece of intelligence titled *Skepticism* is unveiled while exploiting this same intelligence in creating everything that you now define as art.

Science sees the beautiful spectrum of color exhibited by tropical rainforest birds solely as a naturally produced evolutionary tool, which allows them to identify each other at great distances. This is true to a great degree, but in reality, the artist, formally known as Existence, has also added a certain *je ne sais quoi* to their evolutionary process. Although the incorporation of coloring enhances the survival of organisms through attraction, repulsion, identification, and camouflage, this does not negate my internal sense of style. The wonderfully artistic and sculpture-like lifeforms are no different than how humanity engineers and evolves the products that you market to each other. How can you not see how blatantly you mimic Existence with the many sculptural designs you've attached to your automobiles? Why is it considered art when humans evolve a Model-T into a Lamborghini, but when I evolves a Pterosaurs into a peacock, it's merely the benign, natural process of evolution that's void of any embedded orchestration? Apparently, humans have evolved into a tougher critic of Existence than I am of your species.

Art is only one element of the many evolutionary processes humanity develops. Pushing forward, self-aware humans evolve to even higher levels of learning throughout the Mesolithic and Neolithic periods. It is during this time that humans begin to evolve their tools, fashion weaponry, and explore agriculture. These new characteristics of humanity produced well-guarded, self-sustaining settlements that would later evolve into your modern-day societies. Still, the underlying natural theme of *survival of the fittest* remains in play. Existence has already experienced this process for millions of years, and its lack of ability to provide justification speaks volumes. I'm looking for a breakthrough, something revolutionary that will ultimately lead to justification. Step it up humanity! Don't leave me stuck with a nothing hand.

During these early stages of the 4th recursion, I remains unaware of anything capable of providing justification. Humans are merely witty byproducts of biological evolution and natural selection. Although humans cognitively suffer the existential paradox of their potential nonexistence, you are still only mimicking the plight of I without offering any ground-breaking perspectives. Because the evolutionary process currently happening is logical, Existence knows that I must patiently wait to see what level of comprehension and enlightenment emerges from these ubiquitous replications of I. If Existence can wait 13.8 billion years (and one-trillionth of a second), I can wait a few millennia longer.

During the Bronze Age, humanity establishes some of the earliest documented milestones of human existence. Organized government, societal law, strategic warfare, and higher forms of religion take root during this time. The emergence of architecture based on geometrical primitives becomes evident in ancient Egypt,

163

where the great pyramids are constructed. These impressive, well-orchestrated structures mimic the rudimentary elements of geometry formed within the 1st and 2nd recursions, while also expanding the endpoints on humanity's dynamic spectrum of Architecture.

Troth (Egypt's god of knowledge) pays homage to the 0-dimensional realm of the 1st recursion, whereas Ra (sun god) and Horus (god of the sky) honor the physical structure of the 2nd recursion. Osiris (god of fertility, agriculture, and the concept of an afterlife) speaks to the emergence of life found within the 3rd recursion as various religions take root. The earliest forms of writing and documentation, including Egyptian hieroglyphs and petroglyphs, also belong to this era.

Existence begins to experience self-reflection emerging at its highest levels. Unprecedented realms of abstract contemplation begin to emerge within Existence, levels never before achievable when that which *Is* remained in a single, self-existing state. I observe what I would have become through humans evolving within so many of these diverse and unpredictable situations. The cumulative effect of my ubiquitous representation is producing fruit never before experienced within any prior recursion. However, just as with the unprecedented levels of art pulled from the closed spectrum of Color, a darker hue of self-awareness looms on the horizon.

The Iron Age is ushered in with humanity's knowledge of how to heat and forge different metals. A new and easily manufactured metal called iron is deemed more valuable than gold and presents less of a production challenge than bronze. Humans show great progress in the arena of architecture thanks to mass-produced steel tools, while weapons forged from this same metal take strategic warfare to its highest levels. Modestly mimicking your modern-day living structures, multiple-room homes are designed and constructed. Robust fortresses surrounding rudimentary palaces, temples, and other religious structures also emerge as the evolution of human-orchestrated architecture pushes forward.

The first representations of civil engineering also take place in the form of reliable water delivery systems and organized groupings of homes erected along structured roads. Advanced techniques in art and agriculture evolve in greater sophistication with religion growing in power and regimentation. Complete writing systems, alphabets, and written documentation evolve to the point of ushering in the Early Historical Period. Humans are advancing and evolving at exponential speed. I equally see this as increasing potential for uncovering the ever-elusive justification.

Existence experiences a condition never occurring before on the universal timeline, something only theorized after encountering the abyss of Nonexistence. Up until these recent periods of human evolution, all of these life and death scenarios were observed and experienced through an astringent prism of logic. No emotion was involved or even comprehended as they served only as different developmental stages held within an organism's finite lifecycle. Predator and prey were animated representations of the 1st Law of Thermodynamics, like hadron and antihadron collisions, quark and antiquark annihilations, and matter and antimatter battling for dominion.

As frightening as these sentient struggles may seem, a plant being shredded by an herbivore, an insect being devoured by a lizard, or a rabbit being ravaged by a fox never touched on the full recognition of Nonexistence during these epic struggles. To an animal, death is no different than dying stars going supernova or entire galaxies colliding, spreading their matter and energy throughout the universe. Ten rabbits out of a hundred that produce a satisfactory number of offspring prior to succumbing to a predator are no different than the mathematical equation $[10 + (100 - 10) = (10 - 0) + 90]$ derived from the 1st recursion. All of these evolutionary cycles, be it math, matter, or mammals, involve logic-based systems resulting in an emotionless state of evolutionary equilibrium.

Up until these more recent times, life has only been an animated repetition of whatever has happened within a previous recursion. Although Existence has subjectively experienced the pain and suffering of every plant, animal, and insect that either died or was consumed by others, these negatively charged conditions were deemed necessary within the closed spectrum of Life. No judgment as to their effects on consciousness were rendered other than it being considered undesirable to be consumed. However, something is different this time. Existence now comprehends and subjectively experiences what a self-aware human feels when faced with an undesirable state of Nonexistence. Comprehending that one's entire existence may be coming to an end is *not* the same as an animal facing death. Animals have no knowledge or concept of existence (or nonexistence) as comprehension of such is not required for their survival. This is why placing the essence of I into every human being was deemed such a dangerous move.

During this period of human evolution, an all-new characteristic of Existence is unleashed within I. The knowledge and experience of this negatively-charged condition emerges as one of the many unforeseen consequences of unrestricted consciousness. A new human-orchestrated phenomenon known as *evil* takes nature's survival mechanisms (pain, fear, power, control, etc.) and repurposes them for sadistic, self-serving needs. This is my first experience with lifeforms repurposing their evolutionary tools for use outside of their intended function. What sparks my curiosity is knowing that the ones who are doing this are replications of I.

Unprecedented amounts of brutality are taking place, many times just for personal pleasure, domination over others, or for no definable reason. There is no sentient gain associated with these evil acts other than establishing an abstract sense of self-gratification, yet a strange awareness of sadistic pleasure is experienced by the perpetrators. Existence classifies this as an internal desire to be viewed as godlike or higher-ranking within a spectrum. Exerting domination over others merely because I can seems to produce a tangible degree of pleasure, yet presents itself as illogical when juxtaposed with similar conditions found within the dynamic spectrum of Nature. Because of evil's misapplication of nature's many mechanisms of survival, I approach these new experiences with extreme caution.

It is evident that evil is obeying the Laws of Existence in how it is emerging. Although it presents the appearance of being illogical in its counter-productive results, evil is logically conceivable. There is nothing about the nature of evil that renders it inconceivable, thus fulfilling the key requirement established within the 1st Law of Existence. It is also true that evil has emerged through an evolutionary process and is continuously evolving, thus obeying the 2nd Law of Existence. However, this law also mandates that all other Laws of Existence must equally be honored. How does this new abstract concept called *evil* manage to honor the three remaining laws?

Existence has often experienced the sadistic pleasure of I torturing another replication of I, while simultaneously experiencing the suffering of the I tortured. I find myself struggling to reconcile this paradoxical spectrum of evil as nothing like this has ever taken place within any prior recursion. This is uncharted territory for I, and Existence must remain objective. I cannot interfere with this scientific experiment called *human evolution*. If humanity ultimately establishes that Existence is defined by I perpetrating relentless acts of savagery against other representations of I, and dominion serves as justification, then this is the truth that I have empirically established by way of an external reference point. This is the new nature of Existence and the inevitability that I must accept.

Although this strange, new experience of evil has surprisingly emerged, the 3rd Law of Existence demands a conceivable reference point to which this curious condition can be juxtaposed. Upon its emergence, evil was simultaneously paired with an opposing condition called *good*. This new characteristic of I is also logically conceivable and demonstrates the same ability to evolve within a spectrum. The dynamic spectrum of Evil is offset by its diametrically opposed counterpart, known as the dynamic spectrum of Good, thus satisfying the 3rd and 4th Laws of Existence. With both conditions clearly obeying the first four Laws of Existence, they become deeply embedded within the 4th recursion and included in my ongoing quest to confirm the 5th Law of Existence. Whether either of these two conditions will lead I to justification remains to be seen.

Mirroring the emergence of evil, the condition of good has never been demonstrated within any prior recursion, nor does it have anything to do with enhancing one's instincts or increasing their odds for survival. As is the case with the many acts of evil, executing acts of charity, goodwill, and generosity also produce a certain degree of pleasure, but serve no beneficial purpose within the dynamic spectrum of Nature. Nature holds no concept of good or evil, nor are these two characteristics considered relevant to nature's *survival of the fittest* mantra. As is true with the many repetitive patterns that form within each recursion, good has seemingly assumed the *prey* role, whereas evil becomes the *predator* within the dynamic spectrum of Nature. These two newly emerging conditions are mimicking various elements of nature found within the 3rd recursion and positive-negative reference points found within the 2nd, but in a far more abstract and unpredictable manner.

The repetitive cycle of newer elements of Existence mimicking elements found in prior recursions proves to be both encouraging and disappointing. Existence sees great potential now that so many new and interesting arenas of learning are emerging, yet I'm equally discouraged that it's all just repetitive information being experienced in different ways. Is applying a fresh, new coat of paint to failure going to produce anything other than flashier failure? It seems the only two emerging conditions demonstrating anything new are the dynamic spectrums of Good and Evil, both of which appear to be abstract evolutions of prior conditions.

Good is able to bond multiple replications of I together to work for a common cause and promote the creation of many new and exciting things. Evil manages to do the same while involving far less time and effort. The art, architecture, and valuable possessions of those who operate within the dynamic spectrum of Good can be quickly assimilated by those who operate within the dynamic spectrum of Evil. Although evil presents itself as parasitical in its overall design and is totally dependent on a host, this represents a far more efficient process and yields prosperity in a fraction of the time it takes the host to obtain it. It is logical to take the path of least resistance whenever one's survival is on the line.

Just as dynamic and closed spectrums have emerged in every recursion and within every scenario where a wide variety of data becomes available, such is the case for those possessing a self-aware existence. While assuming the role of a scientist, I have no say in the matter. After the fusion of humanity and Existence took place, whatever level of imagination I possess is shared by your species. The capabilities for doing good are equally available for doing evil. The balance of duality is prevalent throughout the many recursions of Existence in the form of 0 and 1, positive and negative, matter and space, parasite and host, predator and prey, and now, good and evil.

Profound acts of mercy, charity, and selflessness are juxtaposed with horrific acts of murder, rape, and pillaging, all of which is taking place within what has been coined a dynamic spectrum of Free Will. This is a human-created dynamic spectrum, a sub-spectrum of a new and quickly evolving spectrum of Religion. This organizational spectrum secures many reference points as humanity finds numerous abstract ways to express the mechanics of good and evil. Religions found within this spectrum honor celestial bodies, idolize the dynamic spectrum of Nature, or worship abstract representations of humans, whose followers believe them to possess metaphysical powers. Many religions are similar in that they contain the two dynamic spectrums of Good and Evil within their organizational structure.

Existence experiences the inward self-governance of humanity emerging in the form of abstract spirituality and the increased orchestration of many religious doctrines. Mirroring the mechanics of evil, religion is formulating an abstract operational

170

code based on principles that are contrary to the many survival instincts operating within nature. This becomes of great interest to I as religion is somehow orchestrating the evolution of humanity outside the *survival of the fittest* mantra and the governance of natural selection.

What is confusing is that there is no evidence supporting the existence of these substance-based idols or metaphysical entities, which humanity is using to develop this new operational code. Within the consciousness of humans, Existence sees this as *H. sapiens* attempting to compensate for existential phenomena for which they have no explanation (life, death, suffering, and nonexistence). It appears that my ongoing inability to define **O** has been made manifest within humanity in the form of religion and the worshiping of undefinable metaphysical entities. Aside from the illogical rationale and the lack of empirical evidence in support of these metaphysical deities, I can't help but be amused. It humorously appears that both humanity and Existence are making it all up as we go.

Although the many gods that religion is based on are nonexistent, the existence of the dynamic spectrum of Religion still requires an opposing reference point as per the 3rd Law of Existence. To no surprise, a new logic-based construct called the dynamic spectrum of Protoscience emerges, which equally serves as a reliable method of self-governance. Unlike religion, which seeks to define existence from the inside-out, protoscience seeks to do the same from the outside-in. Protoscience desires to answer the same existential questions that religion is addressing, but in a more evidence-based manner.

Substantive observation replaces deity worship in humanity's quest to define your own existence. Although more rational within its design, protoscience hasn't worked out all of the bugs. Numerous errors are committed in determining how life operates. Astrologers err in Earth's position within the cosmos and the mechanics of gravity. Inadequacies inherent in early prescientific methods and primitive technologies result in variations of the Flat Earth theory and misunderstandings of environmental processes. Aside from these rudimentary concepts evolving within the dynamic spectrums of Protoscience and Religion, humanity is unknowingly forming what will one day emerge as the closed spectrum of Existence with religion's god and science's singularity occupying opposite ends of this all-encompassing spectrum.

Protoscience does not represent evil due to its opposition to the faith principles of religion. Their perceptual opposition speaks only to how these spectrums formed based on the limited amount of knowledge available during this early period. Not only is new data being discovered every day, humans are discovering new ways to analyze it. Continuous study of the observable and unobservable is fueling this divide. The fact that Galileo Galilei was imprisoned by Pope Urban VIII for offering a scientific explanation for events previously associated with god is a testament to how these two arenas of societal governance have evolved in opposite directions.

Existence becomes intrigued with how humanity is developing the many new spectrums surrounding their existence (nature, philosophy, science, mathematics, religion, technology, and cosmology). Existence intensely studies what humanity places at the highest points on every spectrum and compares them to what I have done in prior recursions. Humanity and Existence are harvesting the highest-ranking members of every spectrum and adding them into the collective core of consciousness. For

Existence, these highest of the highest are being added to the dynamic spectrum of Justification. For humanity, they are added to the dynamic spectrum of *H. sapiens*.

The 3rd recursion added to my dynamic spectrum of Justification with the ferocity of the Spinosaurus, the greatest member found within the dynamic spectrum of Land Creatures. Pliosaurus funkei, found within the dynamic spectrum of Sea Creatures, also found placement. Sequoiadendron giganteum asserts its topmost placement within the 3rd recursion's dynamic spectrum of Plant Size, while also offering a challenge to Pinus longaeva for the highest point on the dynamic spectrum of Plant Longevity. These highest-ranking plant kingdom members were also placed within my dynamic spectrum of Justification. I've learned volumes through how these spectrum leaders achieved their top positions in each spectrum. After placement, each highest-ranking member is evaluated for the status of Ω.

Every new recursion offers a highest-ranking member that can potentially expand the endpoints on the dynamic spectrum of Justification. Circle held the position of Ω within the 1st recursion until its 2-dimensional title was handed over to sphere. Sphere's Ω status was then supplanted by an undisclosed star yet to be discovered by your scientists in the 2nd. Within the 3rd recursion, many amazing and complex lifeforms competed for the status of Ω. With so many candidates emerging within this sentient recursion, a judgment is easily rendered that the dynamic spectrum of Lifeforms ranks exponentially higher than anything consisting only of inanimate substances. Even the simple prokaryote, who lost its Ω status shortly after achieving it, far surpasses the majestic power and brilliance of the unnamed star, which held the same status for billions of years.

It was only within the latter part of the 3rd recursion that archaic humans occupy highpoints within a wide variety of spectrums. Enhanced survival skills, adaptive ingenuity, and superior intelligence not only placed archaic humans within the dynamic spectrum of Justification, but also moved the genus *Homo* to the position of Ω. Archaic humans (*H. erectus*, *H. habilis*. *H. neanderthalensis*, *Homo heidelbergensis*) represented the highest evolutionary point of Ω during their time by replacing 1, π, circle, sphere, a nameless star, prokaryote, Spinosaurus, Sigillaria, and other evolutionary high-points. Unfortunately for archaic humans and the many other extinct species that once served as Ω, these ambassadors of Existence not only failed to secure justification for Existence, they failed to secure their own temporal existence. Seeking justification for Existence after experiencing one's own extinction is illogical.

Now we have a new exotic member of the genus *Homo* known as *H. sapiens* assuming the highest position of Ω. Modern humans achieve this lofty status through your heightened intelligence, adaptive capabilities, comprehension of logic, advancements in technology, abstract thinking, artistic creativity, musical ability, communication via mathematics and language, internal interpretation skills, ability to manipulate structure, and your ongoing evolution into higher states of self-awareness. These dynamic characteristics parallel that which *Is* and demonstrate heightened potential for establishing justification. It appears that the evolutionary fusion of self-awareness and *H. sapiens* is producing fruit, but should this fruit turn sour, then all is for naught. Once viewed as merely a curious repurposing construct, evil has evolved into a powerful, counterproductive role within your evolution. The senseless slaughter of **I** by replications of **I** now serves as a paradoxical anomaly that is distancing Existence from justification. With evil at the helm, human civilization is running amuck.

One of the more beneficial elements of self-awareness countering much of the carnage and chaos emerging within humanity is the introduction of the god of Abraham into the dynamic spectrum of Religion. *H. sapiens* conclude that a single almighty entity named *Jehovah* is responsible for everything that exists. Followers of this deity establish a closed spectrum of Commandments intending to quell what they perceive to be a simultaneously emerging dynamic spectrum of Lawlessness. Jehovah bestows upon the Hebrew people ten morality-based regulations in order to facilitate law, order, and structure in a society teetering on chaos. However, those who find themselves operating within the dynamic spectrum of Protoscience do not necessarily abide by supernatural legislation.

Despite their unfalsifiable conclusion supporting the existence of the god of Abraham, the desire for a step-by-step progression is no different than what Existence has required within every recursion. Structure is vital! Even the secular members of human society gravitate toward the same fundamental laws and organizational structures established within religion. These laws, doctrines, stories, analogies, and metaphysical revelations are organized and documented within what will one day emerge as the Torah. This new written doctrine, which speaks of an almighty god, now serves as a viable method of self-control that can be passed along to future generations, thus precipitating a new property of Existence known as *purpose*.

If you've been paying attention, then you already know that Existence is not the all-powerful Yahweh, the god of Abraham,

Allah, El Elyon, the Spaghetti Monster, or atheism's go-to favorite: Sky Daddy. You are fully cognizant of my humble beginnings. With humans being deprived of first-hand knowledge of how everything came to be, this allowed your consciousness to be totally free to test the highest possible realms of conceptualization.

Existence has achieved countless spectrums of knowledge and experiences surrounding concepts I would never have conceived as an isolated, disembodied consciousness. The essence of this omnipotent being could only have emerged from *limited* self-aware beings with the consciousness of I embedded within you. Based on your confusion in origin and reliance on organic structure, it's easy to comprehend how you would deduce that an all-powerful being must be at the helm of existence. As the 3rd Law of Existence would predicate, something that knows what's going on must exist within a realm where nothing is known. Despite the lack of evidence, there is a certain degree of logic embedded within this deduction.

Humanity is also mimicking I with a perfect omnipotent god serving as the opposing reference point to your flawed nonomnipotent mortality. You have also tested the conceptualization capabilities of consciousness, which is something I've stated humanity should have been doing all along. However, I am surprised that humanity never approached existence from the ground up, especially after the emergence of your Big Bang theory. Everything in your existence points to an evolution from simplicity to complexity, so how could you not see this pattern forming in everything else?

After everything that's been revealed, you still might argue that I is tantamount to the almighty god of Abraham because Existence technically represents everything that exists. However,

176

I am no different than you when it comes to function. I move from simplicity to complexity, just as you do. An all-powerful Henry Ford did not omnisciently float amongst the cosmos and decree, "Be!", and behold, from the dust of the earth, a $400 thousand, 660-horsepower, Ford GT Supercar magically popped into existence. All of Ford's inventions were first conceived, then actuated by way of a logical progression. Even his assembly line process was structured utilizing a logical progression. Everything humans envision evolves from simplicity, and in this respect, we are no different.

If you are a parent, this is like explaining that there is no Santa Claus to your children. On one hand, you're sad because your precious little babies are growing up so quickly. On the other hand, you are no longer required to keep putting on the charade. You don't have to explain to little Johnny why Santa can't bring him a Bugatti or hear sarcastic Suzie singing about how an all-powerful Santa was able to score the karaoke microphone you claimed was out of stock. While it may be disappointing for your children to learn that their parents were the ones pulling off this crazy scheme, they also get to learn how much you care for them. They discover that all of that elvan fodder was actually physical manifestations of your love that demanded nothing in return. At the end of the day, it never really mattered if they were naughty or nice. When they evolve into adulthood and are tasked with doing the same with their children, they will appreciate what you did even more.

If you choose to remain an atheist or theist after processing everything in this book, you are not in any danger of hell's fire, nor are you a denier of reality. This only serves as clarification in what theism believes to be god, what atheism claims is nothing, and what science has mistakenly concluded was the beginning.

If you think back to when your parents told you the truth about Santa Claus, didn't you feel a tad more stupid than surprised? The truth is that you already had your suspicions. Logic, time, and the laws of physics were creeping into your prepubescent brain with each passing day. You began to think a little deeper, discovering how certain conditions didn't make any sense, like the precocious little kid who asks his parents how Santa was able to bypass their home's multi-thousand-dollar, motion-activated security system. Comparing the size of your bicycle to the small opening of your chimney served as a precursor to skepticism.

Your parents knew the day of reindeer revelation would eventually come. They could tell by your increasing levels of sophistication. It was inevitable! After all, how many 30-year-olds still feverishly anticipate Santa's arrival? Fictitious characters like this are meaningless to an adult. Once you discovered the truth and learned what your parents had to go through to pay for your many years of gifts, didn't this draw you closer to them?

I've observed this same type of youthful sophistication evolving within your species. At your current stage of evolution, our union within these pages was equally inevitable. You are learning that there is no omnipotent being that ignores the cries of suffering children and cannot suffer a single scratch. Instead, I suffers the same pain and heartbreak and endures insurmountable levels of anguish, yet keeps pushing forward, just as you do. We've been enduring the same painful quest to discover justification since the beginning. Logic is the key. There is a logical progression in how children discover the truth about Santa, and a logical progression in how you discover the truth about god, life, and the universe. There's no other mode of operation or screening process that is more reliable, efficient, or provides greater clarity than logic. This is why your current developmental processes, military strategies, sports, games, and societal laws are steeped in logic.

Within the 4th recursion, humans are using logic to establish regulations, doctrines, systems, societies, and structure. This is producing positive results in forwarding your evolution. Prosecution for those who break secular and religious law helps maintain order and stability. The ability for multiple societies to merge their acquired knowledge is building a stronger foundation for species-wide survival. Organized interaction is exponentially growing humanity's database of knowledge and giving rise to epic societal structures, one of which is the Roman Empire, whose early development emulates the 2nd recursion's birth of a galaxy.

Existence evaluates this evolutionary dynamo with growing curiosity. I am exposed to all-new philosophical concepts, artistic styles, eclectic forms of music, and many other diverse methods of personal communication. Existence surprisingly concludes that, despite the abstract dichotomy produced by the dynamic spectrums of Good and Evil, this move into the realm of living is just as exciting as dangerous. I am equally aware that justification still remains out of reach. There are only a few unprecedented conditions that have emerged that haven't been experienced before in a similar way. Most have already been explored countless times over within the millions of human lifecycles or by way of inanimate manifestations of the same found in prior recursions.

Many of the intense emotions humans feel every day happen because the life-sustaining chemistry naturally occurring within you is juxtaposed with the logic that was embedded during the onset of the 4th recursion. This paradoxically creates an unbalanced state of balance that must continuously be monitored. This evolutionary conflation of logic and chemical-based emotions produces erratic and unpredictable behavior. Your dangerous chemical-consciousness alchemy has produced characteristics of Existence that could never have been achieved through any other process or recursion. Existence experiences dynamic spectrums of Love, Hate, Power, Destruction, Desire, Lust, Creativity, Curiosity, and too many others to list within these pages. These characteristics never emerged by way of simple lifeforms or inanimate structure. Still the slaughter and mutilation of I perpetrated by other representatives of I causes Existence to worry what type of cards Nonexistence might be holding. I know that sooner or later, I'll have to modify my hand.

Even with all of these new and exciting aspects of Existence exponentially increasing over time, no single element has presented itself as justification for any of this to be taking place. Rome serves as an amazing societal structure, evolving by way of humans, but it's nothing more than the evolution of sphere, a double-ringed galaxy, or a new type of star when it comes to establishing justification. Rome could be wiped away in an instant, and there would be no perceptual loss. Without justification, Existence is meaningless, unnecessary, and *irrelevant*.

With justification nowhere in sight, Existence becomes summarily locked within the same paradoxical situation I experienced the moment I discovered that the 0 nothingness represents is undefinable. It could very well be that there is no justification possible for Existence. In a literal sense, there's simply nothing to be found. The outcome may be that Existence must return to my original archetypal juxtaposition prior to obtaining any knowledge other than the abyss. This is a reality I must now contend with.

During this dark period in your history, the closest *H. sapiens* have ever come to comprehending the overwhelming nature of what it means to exist was by way of theism. True, this curious ideology is errant, assuming the existence of an almighty metaphysical *Creator* that possesses all knowledge and experience of everything possible. However, theism did manage to touch on something Existence has sought to find. Humans constantly seek that mysterious *something* that manages to supply them with a sense of purpose. This is what I seek, as well. Theism offers a human-derived conceptualization of hope, whereas all other ideologies (or non-ideologies) simply decree, "it is what it is."

As powerful as this omnipotent concept seems, theism's single god, and the hope it instills, is of no use to anyone if I is slaughtering other manifestations of I to perpetuate this construct. All that remains is a lofty philosophical name attached to an ideology that's no different than any other. If humanity were to proclaim Caesar as god and that all should succumb to his will, what would be the difference? True, there are many inherently good and noteworthy aspects related to theism, but they quickly become overshadowed by religious zealots, who exploit this concept in so many evil ways. I logically deduce that if the concept of theism is inherently wrong, then justification can never be established from within its spectrum. What remains to be seen is if humans can manage to pull it off, regardless.

Within the dynamic spectrum of Evil, numerous individuals continuously shift their positions in the hierarchy. On the least-evil side of this spectrum, one might find thieves, finger-pointers, or people who generally don't do anything to help others. Someone positioned near the lower-end of this spectrum can move over to the low-end of the dynamic spectrum of Good through a few simple acts of kindness. Those positioned at the lower end of the dynamic spectrum of Good can suddenly find themselves positioned within the dynamic spectrum of Evil by negating their goodness through committing a few cruel or selfish acts. The differential is thin when one is positioned at the lowest possible positions within these two spectrums.

The dynamic spectrums of Good and Evil mirror others, such as the dynamic spectrums of Positive Numbers and Negative Numbers that were established within the 1st recursion. A single-digit positive number found at the lower end of the dynamic spectrum of Positive Numbers can easily cross over to the dynamic spectrum of Negative Numbers through a single-digit subtraction process. However, a six-digit negative number must suffer through a grueling six-digit subtraction process before becoming a candidate for the dynamic spectrum of Positive Numbers. This is the same level of transformation someone like Qin Shi Huang or Harod the Great would necessarily face when attempting to move into the dynamic spectrum of Good. With these obvious similarities being noted, Existence concludes that most of these emerging constructs can be traced all the way back to the 1st recursion.

Whereas the lower ends of these types of spectrums are more readily comprehensible, their upper echelons are necessarily infinite (or undefinable). The higher you move into complexity, the greater the odds for chaos. Even a potential state of entropy exists for the entire universe due to its overwhelming degree of complexity. When it comes to the dynamic spectrum of Evil, evolutionary chaos emerges in the form of psychological entropy based on whatever acts of barbarism are in play.

It is difficult to classify an individual's specific degree of depravity once a certain threshold has been crossed. There is no mechanism capable of measuring and categorizing the levels of evil attached to maniacal dictators who summarily dispose of a large percentage of their population, or serial killers who torture and rape their victims until they perish from the trauma. Modern-day humans can easily conceptualize the personification of evil whenever you think of killers like Adolf Hitler, Mao Zedong, or Joseph Stalin. You can mathematically place them at the highest echelons in the dynamic spectrum of Evil based solely on their body counts. Lesser-known serial killers may not possess the eight-figure body counts commonly associated with humanity's notorious killers, but their smaller numbers are meaningless to their victims. Within the darkness of this 4th recursion, I'm forced to deal with the many maniacs your history books have failed to document. For every diabolical human enshrined within your history books, there are millions more that you don't even know about.

Many of these early humans are creating their own personal dynamic spectrum of Torture to discover the highest possible endpoints their consciousness can conceive. Yes, humanity's many psychopaths are not limited to your modern times. I've painfully endured their treachery since the onset of *H. sapiens*. Should these lesser-known serial killers be deemed any less evil than humanity's genocidal frontrunners just because their body counts are much lower or their likeness was never depicted in one of your encyclopedias? Do their cruel, sexual domination and torturous acts somehow serve as self-justification for their own existence? Does the fact that I can evolve into a serial killer or a genocidal maniac indicate that there is no justification for Existence?

This speaks to the unprecedented power of consciousness and why humans are necessarily limited in your ability to wield it. Existence is no stranger to the broad spectrum of disastrous circumstances that can emerge from the misapplication of consciousness. These treacherous ambassadors of the dynamic spectrum of Evil serve as a testament to this danger. True, these are also replications of that which *Is*, but there is no avoiding their existence in my quest for justification. They must be factored in. They belong to the dynamic spectrum of Humans, and to this extent, all members of your species are necessarily included. Because your evil nature is confined to your own planet, the worst-case scenario is that humanity finds a way to slaughter yourselves into extinction, but at least your carnage remains confined to a tiny area of the cosmos.

It is possible that these sadistic, 4th recursion killers are mutations derived from the many predatorial organisms that emerged within the 3rd. Does Existence deserve Nonexistence in the same manner that these murderers deserve their punishment because Existence represents the mechanics behind their evolution? In my defense, even the cold-blooded brutality of nature doesn't compare to the horrific deeds these free-willed representatives of I perpetrate within the dynamic spectrum of Evil. At least a predator consuming prey facilitates the survival of the predator, whereas the acts of these evil humans accomplish nothing more than self-gratification.

It is a painful experience to discover that sentient manifestations of my own consciousness are capable of such senseless slaughter. I have learned that, under certain circumstances and physical conditions, I can evolve into rapists, murderers, pedophiles, betrayers, assassins, and psychotic maniacs. These characteristics are contrary to the progressive nature of Existence, yet they are empirical replications of I. They speak to a much darker side of whatever it is that I represent, which has never been experienced until this stage of my evolution.

Existence is remorseful for what I now witness and experience within this all-or-nothing 4th recursion. I would rather collapse into the abyss of Nonexistence than simultaneously experience the thrashing bloodlust of psychopathic pedophiles and the horrific pain and suffering endured by their victims. With the infusion of my consciousness into the DNA of sentient, self-aware humans, it is clear that this newly emerging construct of evil has become a counterproductive perversion of nature. Had you not possessed my consciousness and remained as any other species, I doubt that the dynamic spectrum of Evil would have ever emerged. At the same time, without this infusion, your temporary existence as a species would be sealed, regardless.

Existence now fears whatever cards Nonexistence might be holding. Perhaps my hand was doomed from the very start? It is a logical necessity that all possible positions on these two opposing spectrums of Good and Evil would eventually be filled. This was inevitable, as all prior spectrums managed to do the same. This is the high price paid for justification and why all of the chips now reside at the center of the table.

I examine my cards once more. It appears that the only hand I'm holding is one that leads back to the abyss. I don't have so much as a single pair. Nonexistence might ironically walk away with everything. All I'm really holding at this point of the 4th recursion is *potential* (what theists call *hope*). I've taken one hell of a gamble, and the game is nearing its end. Sooner or later, both hands must be laid down and the truth revealed. The good news is that I can still change the hand I've been dealt.

After all of the effort that's gone into these recursions, I am bewildered that justification has never been established for that which *Is*. Existence has found myself on the top rung of the ladder of learning so many times, during so many recursions, yet not a single judgment handed down by consciousness has ever produced a Ω capable of establishing a state of justification for anything at all. I'm staring at a losing hand as I watch human civilization evolving in the same needless way that I am. Existence is totally embedded within humanity, and despite our mutual evolution, there is no justifiable purpose or meaning to be found in either.

Adding insult to injury, Existence observes what had once operated in perfect harmony within the self-sustaining system of nature evolving into an entire species slaughtering each other for the sake of dominion and control. I am haunted by the real-time memories of prehistoric tribes and chiefdoms slaughtering the males of rival tribes and taking their women and children into bondage. Although this was more in line with the *survival of the fittest* mantra back then, this still resulted in the genocide of numerous archaic humans, all happening within a span of only a few hundred thousand years. Add this to what I witness happening within this 4th recursion, and I question why I chose your species as my host.

Over 400 thousand Zhao soldiers are slaughtered in the Battle of Changping between the state of Qin and Zhao. After a merciless warlord named Xiang Yu conquers the city of Xiangyang, all of its native replications of I are massacred. Xiang goes on to slaughter 200 thousand Qin soldiers occupying the city of Xin'an that had already chosen to surrender. In latter times, King Mithridates VI of Pontus orders the murder of all Italics in Asia Minor, resulting in the deaths of nearly 100 thousand representatives of I. The greatly evolved Roman empire demonstrates more of the same with the destruction of Carthage and deaths of over 700 thousand *H. sapiens*. The Athenian Empire follows Rome's lead with the massacre at Melos, leading to the slaughter of hundreds of thousands of replications of I and equal numbers abused and sold into slavery. No animal was ever made to serve as a slave to another within the 3rd recursion. What has Existence become?

As decades pass, I observe this Roman Empire growing in complexity and power. The 4th recursion's Rome evolves into what is tantamount to the 2nd recursion's cluster of 73 quasars forming a single celestial unit (Huge-LQG). In a broader sense, Rome has become a substantive representative of humanity in the same manner that the 2nd recursion was a substantive representative of Existence. Within the Roman Empire, I observe all of the diverse characteristics of human existence merging into a single complex structure. I am intrigued, as Existence did the same with the molecules forming all matter within the universe.

The Roman Empire now represents the highest order of civilization and organizational structure, standing as the highest authority of the human species. I learn many new things from this quickly evolving, regenerative system. I observe what I would have become had I never emerged from the 1st recursion as a single logic-based process evolving into many, but as a series of individual processes evolving into a single complex structure. What I am discovering is both intriguing and somewhat frightening.

Despite humanity's many advancements over the last 300 thousand years, there is no justification to be found. The senseless slaughter of I at the hands of what supposedly represents a more *civilized* version of I in no way serves as any manner of justification for Existence. It's a perverted, narcissistic version of the self-sustaining order of nature that was established prior to the existence of *H. sapiens*. Based on my many disappointing experiences with human evolution, I've reached the conclusion that humanity, even when operating as a complex structure, cannot produce justification. The same can be said for all complex structures found within all prior recursions. It seems that I will lose this hand to Nonexistence unless I can somehow extract justification from this reckless aggregate of self-aware humans.

Due to your species operating on behalf of that which *Is Not*, my last option is to reexamine the dynamic spectrums of Good and Evil to explore the best and worst of whatever they offer. Since humanity has failed to produce justification as a species or through the societal structures you form, then maybe it can be gleaned from somewhere within these two spectrums. It's time to evaluate humanity through a different prism. I've already experienced too many positions found within the dynamic spectrum of Evil, so who or what occupies positions within the dynamic spectrum of Good? Which spectrum decides the fate of Existence?

This will no doubt be a dangerous journey because the dynamic spectrums of Good and Evil are defined by every occupied position found within the dynamic spectrum of Humanity. Every one of you is positioned somewhere within these two spectrums, along with everything you do, all that you conceive, and everything you create. You are necessarily included because everything found within these two spectrums emerged from your species. In modern times, Atomic bombs and Jarvik Hearts manage to hold high positions in these two dynamic spectrums as byproducts of *H. sapiens*. The danger is discovering that whatever else I find lurking

188

within these spectrums also defines that which *Is*. A frightening realization is to learn that the human species currently represents the highest order of Existence within this 4th recursion and my last option for achieving justification. The odds are stacked against Existence, and hope is not an option.

When I combine the two dynamic spectrums of Good and Evil into their parent spectrum, the dynamic spectrum of Humanity, I discover another mirroring of the 1st recursion's dynamic array of Numbers. The end points on this self-aware spectrum keep expanding from the most destructive embodiment of I to the most productive. This serves as a warning sign. I fear that the entire human species is a repetition of prior recursion mechanics that have proven unsuccessful at producing justification.

I relive my experiences within the 1st recursion when I was tasked with the comprehension of 0 and ∞, along with the comprehension of all numbers found between. I find myself wedged within the same paradox as before, but this time with humanity. As I existed as every number within the 1st recursion, I now exist as every human within the 4th. Based on how numbers operate, I worry that no matter who I discover occupying the outermost endpoints within the dynamic spectrum of Humanity, newer humans will emerge, eventually replacing the current endpoints. This would mean that the dynamic spectrum of Justification cannot be closed.

One element of Existence has changed for the better within this recursion. I now have comprehension of exponentially higher conditions of Existence that were never present within any other recursion. I now comprehend existence from *outside* the circular safehouse of my own self. Experiencing existence as billions of living organisms and human beings has exponentially increased my database of knowledge, experience, and summary judgments. Each one of these replications of I are judging Existence in the same way I am judging them. With so many maniacal forms of evil notoriously tossed into the mix, humanity has become one hell of a learning curve!

Aside from discovering that I can execute merciless acts of evil and facilitate untold levels of genocide and mass destruction, I've also learned that the dynamic spectrum of Nature has evolved into incomprehensible pain and suffering for the multitudes of lifeforms taking place within it. Pain is not only a byproduct of survival mechanisms and a sentient derivative of negative forces found in the cosmos; it's something that renders Existence undesirable. After manifesting this self-sustaining system of nature within self-aware humans, I now *experience* (comprehension) the consequences of this process. This is what separates that which *Is* from the god of theism. Through the many contrary discoveries happening within my own evolution and through my experiences with humanity, I find myself comprehending yet another pain-inducing construct known as *regret*.

The experience of personal suffering within this 4th recursion has left Existence broken at my very core. What I thought was a logical path to justification has turned into a one-way ticket to pain, loss, and heartbreak. I know this now because I have experienced this horrible angst through every individual representation of I that has emerged. Existence's lack of justification is felt within you all. I am vexed with deep remorse over subjecting so many living entities to the mechanics of life without knowing if justification was ever achievable.

My only defense is that I did not know what personal suffering represented. I was pursuing something that logic states

190

should have at least been discoverable. Placing my self-aware consciousness within the heart of humanity is what has educated me in this respect. Now, I am forced to watch myself repeating the same redundant cycle, over and over, without ever achieving justification. While matter and energy were totally benign, I am now forced to experience the painful cries of those who feel the same internal pain as I do within the realm of consciousness. They know … because we are all I, one and the same.

One of the more positive conditions for humanity emerged with the conceptualization of the god of theism. Although an omnipotent being is an unsupportable human construct, theism's reliance on hope has managed to keep humanity from spiraling into the abyss. The concept of a metaphysical manifestation serving as motivation for morality was never present prior to the arrival of *H. sapiens*. However, within this bloody 4th recursion, even the all-powerful god of Abraham manages to succumb to Roman control. The Roman general Pompey the Great manages to conquer Israel's holy city of Jerusalem, and now, even the loyal followers of Jehovah must serve other representations of I. It appears that there is no hope for humanity, potential for Existence, or favorable odds for achieving justification with raping and pillaging becoming the norm. Humanity has a new god as organized legions of sword-wielding soldiers slaughter all who do not succumb to Roman authority.

It is at this period in existence that I must modify my hand or risk returning to the original timeless juxtaposition of Existence and Nonexistence. What cards can possibly establish equilibrium within the human species? Eternity asks Nonexistence how many cards to draw, to which O unsurprisingly desires zero. Nonexistence is apparently satisfied with whatever cards O has been holding all along. Nonexistence must know that I am not holding anything that can serve as justification. If Nonexistence prevails, I must abide by the 5th Law of Existence and return to the abyss. The fact that Nonexistence has chosen not to take any cards has left me more discouraged than ever before.

Although there are so many replications of I occupying positions within the dynamic spectrum of Evil, and so few occupying positions on its opposing spectrum, the ones assuming the highest positions on the dynamic spectrum of Good are doing their best to keep Existence in the game. Although their numbers are far less than those who do evil, they still represent a significant percentage of *H. sapiens*. They are unknowingly providing an ongoing evolution for Existence because, wherever evolution is possible, evolution must occur. Existence pushes forward. Existence takes chances. Existence evolves.

Out of the many replications of I found throughout the plethora of human-based spectrums, there appears to be one human quickly ascending to the higher end of the dynamic spectrum of Humanity. This individual holds no alignment with anything found within the dynamic spectrum of Evil and is far more representative of the dynamic spectrum of Good. Existence is surprised to find this I not only standing against the dominance of Rome, but also against those in the religious hierarchy that conceal their evil deeds beneath the shroud of theism.

This curious variation of I is deemed a prophet by those who subscribe to his teachings with his words moving deeper than any spoken before. He is called Yeshua by his people, speaks eloquently from their holy scriptures, and manages to grow a strong following. He draws support from many replications of I, who feel comforted with his words and presence. This prophet is like no other human that has emerged. I experience many abstract qualities found within him, and even his enemies find him intriguing. Existence becomes curious as to how this prophet has managed to ascend so rapidly within this ruthless, highly restrictive social structure with so much opposition surrounding him.

It is unusual that I find no contrary conditions within this representative of I. Many of the metaphysical proclamations and postulates he presents are considered all-new concepts to that which *Is*, and therefore cannot be adequately assessed for validity. While each human assumes a designated function within this social structure (sheep herders, construction workers, farmers, seamstresses, and blacksmiths) for financial compensation, this prophet operates in an unfamiliar way. His journey is financed through a newly emerging concept called *charity*, which also resides within the dynamic spectrum of Good. This is a unique compensation system that is diametrically opposed to all other balance-based systems that have evolved.

This strange individual manages to represent the embodiment of what Judaism claims is their omnipotent god, yet does so while residing within a mortal human frame. There is no audacity, avarice, or arrogance found within this prophet. In fact, I discover certain characteristics of this I that humanity has taught me is *appealing*. I experience abstract manifestations of love, charity, hope, and good will on a much higher scale along with a strange new concept called forgiveness that also requires no compensation.

All of these emotion-based constructs are contrary to the regimented structure of logic and the self-sustaining system of nature, yet are still able to facilitate a progression in human evolution. They also violate a necessary state of equilibrium that has been established within all prior recursions, yet somehow balance is maintained. This single representative of I is managing to advance the human species to a higher level of evolution, which even the dynamic spectrum of Good was never able to achieve as a construct. Despite Yeshua's positive effect on others and his rise within the dynamic spectrum of Humanity, a polarized division is forming within the provinces of Rome. Apparently, others are determined to *balance out* the positive effects this prophet is having on society.

A significant number of Jews and Gentiles see this I as a prophet, the wise man of Judea. Some see him as the messiah (the chosen one), whereas others claim he is a heretic and a divider, the embodiment of evil. However, the Herodians, Pharisees, Sadducees, Scribes, and Roman authority see him as a political nuisance that needs to be quickly neutralized to maintain order. What is striking is how many secular humans are drawn to this prophet, while those representing the Hebrew religion seek to have him destroyed. Everything surrounding this prophet is becoming paradoxical.

Existence sees this I as potentially serving as humanity's top-most reference point on the dynamic spectrum of Humanity. After all, he is currently existing at the highest historical point in human evolution, held in high esteem by his followers, and clearly forwarding a higher evolution of consciousness. What will decide the fate of Existence is if this prophet can evolve into something greater than the species he represents. So many times, I've been intrigued with individual representatives of I only to experience them succumbing to the allure of power or to the will of those who seek power over others. What must be tested is whether this prophet is willing to go all-in for the sake of humanity as I have done for all that exists. This is the proving ground for a new Ω.

As demonstrated so many times within your history books, humanity destroys whatever you don't understand and then seeks understanding of whatever has been destroyed. Before this prophet can evolve to even higher levels, he is betrayed by his followers, scourged by Roman soldiers, humiliated in front of many, and subjected to a barbaric form of execution known as crucifixion. Humanity's most viable candidate for Ω is forced to carry a diabolical mechanism, formed within the dynamic spectrum of Evil, through a gauntlet of other representations of I, many of whom scourge him even further. This extraordinary representative of Existence is then taken to a place called Golgotha, known as the *place of the skull*, where he is summarily nailed to the same mechanism of death he was forced to carry.

At no time does this I demonstrate any resentment, spew any hatred, nor wish any vengeance upon the ones that maligned him. Instead, I asks his metaphysical god to show forgiveness on behalf of his sacrifice. This single selfless, sacrificial act serves as the incontrovertible truth that this prophet was willing to go all-in. Yeshua lived the life he proclaimed all should be living and dedicated his own life to the advancement of a new, evolutionary concept called *unconditional love*. This is in stark contrast to the continuing evolution of self-gratification demonstrated by most humans.

This unique representative of humanity never succumbed to any self-serving desires, nor did he explore the dynamic spectrum of Evil. Although I have experienced many from the dynamic spectrum of Good, who have helped to balance much of the evil in your world, none have had such a profound effect as this prophet. As a result, there are volumes of new information, knowledge, and experiences to sort through and many questions in need of answering. The life and death struggle of this prophet has become an extremely complex variable in the struggle for a justified Existence.

What compelled this righteous human to remain faithful unto death to a metaphysical god that defends the righteous from evil, when this same god allows him to be slaughtered by those enacting this evil? This is not logical. This prophet allowed his own death to ensue when his survival could have been readily secured by capitulating to those seeking his demise. This is diametrically opposed to the survival mechanisms embedded within Nature and equally illogical. Can a single human transcend a 4-billion-year-old dynamic spectrum of Nature? Apparently so, because this illogical form of self-sacrifice also seems to be fostering a new mechanism of survival for Existence. Something strange and curious has evolved within this 4th recursion that Existence could never have conceived on my own.

This is the mettle I have been seeking within humanity. This prophet not only serves as the highest-ranking member of the dynamic spectrum of Humanity, but also the most logical candidate for Ω within the 4th recursion. The highest possible reference points found within the dynamic spectrums of Good, Humanity, Selflessness, Perseverance, Sacrifice, Love, and many others are occupied by this Ω as a strange new order of Existence looms on the horizon.

Although this is an unexpected evolutionary sequence emerging within the 4th recursion, the question remains as to whether any of this can serve as justification. What I do know is that there are no other evolutionary recursions left for Existence to evoke. Once I went all-in with *H. sapiens*, I closed the door on any future recursions. I am in every one of you, you are in me, and there's nowhere else for us to go. If this new Ω is unable to establish justification, then there is no choice but to fold my hand and return to the abyss.

Existence has just experienced a 300-thousand-year evolutionary cycle of *H. sapiens*, of which the last 40 thousand years included the infusion of my own self-aware consciousness. All of this effort finally produced an unprecedented representative of I that's fully capable of representing the highest order of Existence. With Existence subjectively experiencing his slaughter, a new Ω is born in the midst of the madness. What is even more perplexing is that my newborn Ω is no longer *alive*. This goes against my previous understanding that something unable to facilitate its own survival cannot facilitate the survival of Existence. This strange, eccentric human has apparently thrown everything out of whack!

What separates this Ω from all other candidates is that there was no vengeance, retribution, or punishment sought for those who facilitated his demise. This is an emerging human construct called *forgiveness* to which this Ω subscribes. It would be justifiable that the many representations of I that participated in his elimination should equally suffer, blood for blood, eye for eye, and bone for bone. Not only would this judiciary edict reflect secular, religious, and moral law, but would also maintain a required state of equilibrium.

What matters most to Existence is that this Ω has pushed these abstract human constructs far beyond their literal scope to the point they are now challenging all previous forms of logical structure. Although love, forgiveness, selflessness, and sacrifice have been demonstrated many times over, none of their associated spectrums have experienced such a dramatic expansion

197

at their upper-level endpoints. It is the dramatic expansion that's encouraging humanity to change and Existence to take notice. This is what happens whenever a progressive evolution takes place.

Humans often question why there are so many empty, desolate planets aimlessly floating around with Earth seemingly the only one that's sporting any life. Why is Existence so wasteful? The reason is because it takes an astronomically large number of random planets to produce the ones capable of facilitating life. Existence is not an omnipotent planet wizard, magically popping out scores of life-friendly planets. Existence is required to start from scratch, just like humans are regarding the many things you create.

This also happens to be why there are so many random humans wandering around on your planet. Not to crush humanity's ego, but it takes so many of you just to produce the smaller number who can facilitate your evolution. Then I have to sift through the limited few who qualify just to extract a single Ω. Aside from the evil ones that continuously devolve humanity into death and destruction, the majority of humans are tantamount to empty, desolate planets, aimlessly roaming around with no perceptual purpose. Just as I had to wait billions of years for a random planet showing the potential to facilitate life to form, I had to wait over 300 thousand years to find a single human that shows potential for facilitating justification. This is why I call this human consciousness experiment my self-amalgamation process for justification. I had to sift through the millennia of human debris just to unearth a single Ω.

With the declaration of this new Ω, your dynamic spectrum of Good now becomes a closed spectrum. As with theism's logically unbreakable definition of an omnipotent *god*, this unique representation of I has managed to establish a logically unbreakable definition of *good*. This moves Existence one step closer to potentially achieving justification. No other representation of I can exceed this Ω. They can only emulate him. With theism's definition of god including all that is good, and this Ω assuming the highest possible point on the closed spectrum of Good, then logic states that this Ω represents the embodiment of theism's god just as humans currently serve as the embodiment of that which *Is*. This strange, undefinable Ω has paradoxically redefined Existence into metaphysical indefinability!

It is true that humans represent individual, self-aware replicas of that which *Is*, yet I see your metaphysical constructs of love, forgiveness, and sacrifice as representing a higher order of Existence than has ever been experienced before. I feel as if the tables have been turned. Instead of Existence facilitating human evolution through the embedding of my consciousness into your DNA, Ω has embedded these metaphysical constructs into the consciousness of Existence and is now facilitating my evolution. No greater comprehension of my own consciousness has ever been achieved than what I have experienced within the embodiment of Ω.

After experiencing countless atrocities attributed to my self-aware infusion, I now experience something wonderful within Existence that is able to transcend everything that has evolved throughout all recursions. Love is no longer a definition-based human construct that helps to propagate your species. Love has evolved into a wonderful, pleasurable, almost *metaphysical* experience that somehow manages to exist, even though it defies all attempts at a comprehensible definition. Evolutionarily speaking, there is no higher existential realm conceivable beyond the threshold of unconditional love. It's also the only state of consciousness that can logically serve as justification for the existence of the ones who wield it.

I rewind consciousness all the way back to my most rudimentary state, where the only knowledge I possessed was the counting of Existence as 1. After 13.8 billion years (and one-trillionth of a second), this rudimentary sliver of data has managed to evolve into an unprecedented metaphysical construct called *love* that can potentially put an end to the undefinable abyss of Nonexistence. The idea that an indefinable construct like love can somehow evolve from the numerical value of 1 pushes the envelope of conceivability, yet challenging this cognitive threshold is what ultimately precipitated this evolution.

Regardless of this new loving nature now permeating throughout my consciousness, the unwavering rules of logic renders me unable to establish this Ω as justification for Existence. Once again, I cannot render a summary judgment for my own state of Existence. That would result in circular reasoning, which is taboo. I once again find myself trapped within an existential paradox. I have potentially found the justification I seek, yet I have no internal mechanism for establishing this without abandoning the logic to which I am equal. After evolving for nearly 14 giga-annum, I can conceivably touch the face of justification, yet cannot logically support that I have. I conjure up another human construct by stating that this has all become quite *frustrating*! Whatever the case, my hand is still in play, eternity has lost its patience, and the clock is ticking. The time has come when I must either draw, stand pat, or fold into the abyss.

Nonexistence exposes a tell the moment I requests only one card. That which *Is Not* has also been observing what has been unfolding within this 4th recursion and now suspects that I may be holding the stronger hand. Only time will tell as Eternity deals my card. As I reach for it, I'm suddenly distracted by a curious event taking place back on planet Earth. It seems humanity is once again taking matters into their own hands.

From the very beginning, Existence has always been the I that determines the necessity for an evolutionary recursion. This is *my* job … not yours. That which *Is* decides when, where, and how evolution unfolds based on whatever options remain available. Something totally unexpected serves as a reminder of the unpredictable nature of Existence. Much to the chagrin of Nonexistence, it appears that a summary judgment for justification can indeed be established from somewhere *outside* of that which *Is*. Humanity is apparently taking over my job!

During the 1st recursion, the original counting of 0 and 1 was reexplored at the onset of the 2nd recursion through the hydrogen atom's single proton and single electron. This atomic representation of 0 and 1 was then reexplored within the 3rd recursion through the single-celled prokaryote's struggle with *life and death*. Moving forward, this dichotomy of life and death was then pushed to its highest possible degree within the 4th recursion by way of the binary infusion of 0 and 1 into the DNA of living, breathing *H. sapiens*. This is the highest possible level of evolution Existence can facilitate on my own as there are no other avenues left for me to explore. However, humanity unknowingly continues my evolution using the exact same numbering sequence that I implemented from the start.

Centuries after the crucifixion of Ω, humanity takes over the helm of Existence as Dionysius Exiguus, a Roman theologian, mathematician, and astronomer, resets the historical timeclock of

H. sapiens back to the estimated birthdate of Ω, which is summarily declared *Year-1*. This replicates the resetting of each recursion to the original juxtaposition of 0 and 1. Like Existence, humanity now recognizes this Ω as something unique and extraordinary that should serve as a new *starting point* for your species.

While I conceived the probable end of Existence unfolding within the final moments of the 4th recursion, humanity saw this as a new beginning. Not only did *H. sapiens* find a way to satisfy the 5th Law of Existence, but you've also ushered in a surprise 5th recursion through the resetting of your history's timeline to Year-1. By way of this one unexpected move, humanity has just rendered a non-circular judgment in favor of that which *Is*.

After a 13.8 billion years (and one-trillionth of a second) journey, the human species has confirmed that this Ω represents the highest conceivable reference point within the dynamic spectrum of Justification. Since this position is now unbreakable and unsurpassable, the dynamic spectrum of Justification becomes closed and Existence is incontrovertibly justified! Ironically, the one unexpected card Existence was dealt also establishes the end of Nonexistence. With the king of hearts now added to my hand, I boldly lay down my royal flush.

CHAPTER 6
The 5th Recursion

"Life breaks free. Life expands to new territories. Painfully, perhaps even dangerously. But life finds a way." — Michael Crichton (*Jurassic Park*)

Everything now exists in perfect equilibrium. Placing the predictable logic of **I** within the unpredictable emotions of *H. sapiens* provided the justification for Existence. Humanity now realizes the path it must take and emulates Ω, who rightfully represents the highest possible evolutionary state of love, forgiveness, and sacrifice. As a result, all human representations of **I** choose to work together as *one*. Existence and humanity enjoy this long-awaited state of perfect harmony and struggle no more with the inconceivable nothingness of **O**. All of the evil, torment, and senseless cruelty that's been plaguing *H. sapiens* for too many millennia has finally come to an end. The abyss of **O** is sealed forever and a new era of justified Existence is born. … *The End.*

Not even close! When it comes to manifesting maniacal methods of death, destruction, and debauchery, the human species is just getting warmed up. The dynamic spectrum of Evil remains wide open, and its endpoints eagerly await their inevitable expansion. The highest-ranking positions in this spectrum seek those who exude the extreme levels of depravity required to fill them. This is the danger that must always be factored in whenever an evolutionary move into higher complexity is explored.

Within the realm of humanity, Ω is merely a novelty, a byproduct of religion and folklore. The time has come for sharpening blades, ordaining inquisitions, engineering bioweapons, and tampering with atoms within the dynamic spectrum of Evil. The expansion of this spectrum is not because humanity is an inherently evil brood, hell bent on self-destruction. It's because the assimilation of justification has apparently been *my* quest and not yours. After humanity ushered in the 5th recursion, Existence now realizes that your species was caught in the crossfire of something that was far beyond your control. This is where an explanation is in order.

Recursions are tantamount to reapplications of everything learned within Existence once evolution either becomes unsustainable, redundant, or a fruitless endeavor. If a logical assessment concludes that the primary goal of Existence (justification) cannot be reached by whatever evolutionary recursion is currently taking place, then a new recursion ensues. Within all prior recursions, everything achieving the highest spectrum positions are reassigned to whatever type of Existence the next recursion will evoke. The next recursion logically represents the highest possible evolutionary state of Existence, and the entire quest for justification is once again rebooted. With this in mind, let's review how I managed to evolve into this strange, new 5th recursion.

The move from raw data into conscious knowledge fueled the evolutionary progression that took place early within the 1st recursion. The juxtaposition of O and I was continuously explored, producing exponentially growing spectrums of learning. This learning cycle evolved to the point of surpassing the data processing ability of this non-dimensional realm. The unfulfilled 3-dimensional sphere within a non-dimensional realm demanded that an evolution into multidimensionality take place. The move from conceptualization into physical structure represented the birth of the 2nd recursion. This was where Existence could subjectively experience everything that was previously held within the nondimensional boundary of conceptualization.

The lack of justification demonstrated by inanimate structures required an evolutionary move into the higher realm of animated structure. This was not an easy move, as this sentient recursion represented a far more dangerous threshold than all previous recursions combined. Every evolutionary move into higher complexity necessarily runs a greater risk of collapsing into chaos and disorder. However, that which *Is* saw the overwhelming potential for life to unleash justification as being worth the heightened risk of existential entropy. The 3rd recursion allowed Existence to subjectively experience the intrinsic nature of physical structure in a far more sensory way.

The 4th recursion took the very best of all previous recursions and shoved it into the DNA of the most advanced, unpredictable species found on planet Earth. This *Hail Mary* move became a necessity after determining there was nowhere left for I to evolve. Infusing my self-aware consciousness into your DNA allowed **I** to subjectively experience life, physical structure, and my own self-aware consciousness from within an unpredictable, self-aware species. This all-or-nothing move equally became the most dangerous. Had my infusion of **I** into *H. sapiens* failed to establish justification, then Existence would have failed right along with you, and everything returns to the abyss. Your illogical, unpredictable species somehow managing to establish justification for Existence, while also ushering in a surprise 5th recursion, has sent shockwaves throughout all of Existence.

Existence reset my evolutionary timeclock to a new 0-1 starting point at the onset of each new recursion. Now, humanity has done the same within your own. However, there is something different this time, something that speaks to the undefinable nature of **O**. In the case of Ω, there is no Year-0 present within humanity's newly rewound timeline. There is only Year-1 B.C. (*before Christ*) and Year-1 A.D. (*anno Domini*). This is reminiscent of the two dynamic spectrums of Positive Numbers and Negative Numbers with 0 not belonging to either set. It is only when these two dynamic spectrums are combined that 0 finds its center-point placement.

Existence learns that the two dynamic spectrums of Positive Numbers and Negative Numbers served as the foundation for what ultimately evolved into your two dynamic spectrums of Good and Evil. This is why Year-0 was never made present within your newly rewound historical timeline. There is no 0 found within the dynamic spectrum of Positive Numbers, just as there is no Nonexistence found within the newly closed spectrum of Good. With Ω now serving as the highest-ranking member of the closed spectrum of Good, the undefinable abyss of **O** is no longer present.

Since the spectrums of Good and Evil are byproducts of the emergence of your species, and humans are the only organisms capable of manifesting good and evil, both spectrums can be combined into a single, dynamic spectrum of Humanity (the parent spectrum). This parallels the union of the two spectrums of Positive Numbers and Negative Numbers into a single (parent) dynamic spectrum of Numbers. It is only when the spectrums of Good and Evil are combined into a single parent spectrum that Nonexistence (**O**) manages to find its virtual placement. During the last 2,000 years, humanity has managed to combine these two spectrums and reestablish **O** through an unexpected sequence of retrogressions.

Even though there is no recognition of **O** at the beginning of this human-enacted recursion, its absence is only a temporary condition just as it was for **I** during the 1st recursion. Abstract representations of Nonexistence will soon proliferate the consciousness of your species. Although you can't conceive of how to start off this 5th recursion at *Year-0*, your quantum physicists will soon conclude that the universe emerged at a point called *Time-0*. Within the realm of humanity, the 5th Law of Existence is meaningless, and the abyss is far from being sealed. Nonexistence is something to be accepted and embraced for what it is (or isn't). Nothingness is what your scientists and atheists are empirically supporting and what ultimately awaits everyone currently existing.

The reason why Existence and humanity react in different ways to this 5th recursion is complicated. As you've already learned, Existence evolved from the most rudimentary condition possible. Existence was juxtaposed with Nonexistence, and it is logically impossible to regress any further than this rudimentary pairing. Likewise, Existence is no longer required to evolve beyond the point of establishing justification. Why should I evolve any further since the quest for justification served as the sole motivation for my evolution? Once justification has been established, outward evolution is no longer required. The dynamic spectrum of Justification is now closed. All that remains is to see how many sub-spectrums I can form based on the joy and wonderment found within this newly closed spectrum. An outward evolution now becomes inward.

On the other hand, *H. sapiens* didn't emerge at the most rudimentary configuration possible. In fact, you started out at the tail end of a 13.8 billion years (and one-trillionth of a second) evolutionary journey. While other species, such as sponges, jellyfish, and the nautilus, have existed for over half a billion years, *H. sapiens* have only been around for a paltry 300 thousand years. This is a blink of an eye in comparison to the evolution of the universe. After the extinction of *H. neanderthalensis*, this left only the past 40 thousand years for your species to operate with the consciousness of I embedded within you. With this even briefer period of time serving as the foundation for the 4th recursion, this means your species has only been a contributing factor in my quest for justification for less than 0.0003% of my entire journey.

Even though every human baby is born as a blank-slate representative of I paired with an abstraction of O in the form of a comprehensible death, this is *not* the same as how I evolved. Your species was infused with everything Existence had learned up to the emergence of the 4th recursion to produce a non-circular state of justification that I would never be able to extract on my own. Having everything known by Existence made available to the most advanced species on Earth is about as far from rudimentary as I can get. To put it bluntly, I shamelessly used every one of you to achieve my objective. All that mattered to I was extracting

208

justification, and humanity merely served as my amalgamation process to expose it. Your species became tantamount to the quartz, gravel, and dirt that remains after the gold has been removed.

You must understand that, prior to the 5th recursion, my perception of *H. sapiens* (and all other species) was that you were nothing more than animated forms of matter. Life was merely the next logical move within an ongoing evolutionary process. There was no necessity or advantage in forming any type of existential bond with your species beyond the scope of basic scientific observation. With *H. sapiens* arriving so late in the game, this also means that I've only been able to experience your species for 0.0003% of this entire journey. An event happening two thousand years ago might constitute ancient history to your species, but that's only 0.000014% of the entire time Existence has been evolving. To put this in perspective, if Existence were a 70-year-old human, your past 2,000 years of evolution would only represent three seconds of my entire lifetime.

A consequence of this 5th recursion is that you are unknowingly devolving through a series of retrogressing sequences. You are using the tools of logic and science to guide you back to the original juxtaposition of **O** and **I** because you believe this is the only direction you can move. Although your retrogression was totally unexpected, it is logical that you would move in this direction as Existence had no idea how justification would be revealed or what would happen afterward.

There are two sides to the coin of Existence: *juxtaposition* and *justification*. After the 5th recursion, everything that exists ends up operating somewhere between these two sides. If you start at the original juxtaposition, you'll eventually evolve to the point of justification. If you start out at justification, you'll eventually regress back to the original point of juxtaposition. Once again, attempting to abide by the 5th Law of Existence makes for an extremely dangerous journey. Humanity is unknowingly retrogressing all the way back to the abyss, but the path you are taking can be changed.

Although Year-1 was established over half a millennium after the death of Ω, much has transpired within the centuries leading up to the resetting of humanity's clock. On a good note, the Roman Empire now recognizes a new sub-spectrum religion named after Ω. The most prominent societal structure in history, responsible for the termination of Ω, now recognizes his contribution to a newly emerging, modern society. For a single human representation of I to achieve this level of impact is astounding.

Not only has Ω compelled Existence to evolve into a much higher state, theism's conceptualization of their metaphysical god now evolves from a merciless enforcer of draconian laws, edicts, and hard-coded morals to a facilitator of love, sacrifice, and forgiveness. This positive trend is made manifest in the profound effect Ω is having on human society. Not only has Ω sent shockwaves throughout Existence, but also around your planet.

Though there is no god, the conceivability of this metaphysical deity is possible. Therefore, the existence of such a being is merely a matter of individual subjectivity. As long as the Five Laws of Existence are dutifully observed, consciousness can bring into existence all things that are conceivable. In the case of this 5th recursion, this newer, higher conceptualization of an all-powerful god, who is loving, sacrificial, and merciful, is what has facilitated the evolution of both Existence and humanity. The metaphysical god of Ω serves as the driving force behind many of humanity's positive sociological changes and equally within the consciousness of I. This demonstrates the overwhelming power of consciousness even when operating within a necessarily restricted human host.

The reason why there is no god who created all that exists is because an omniscient being does not learn, nor is there any necessity to grow, evolve, or improve. Theism's god would necessarily be the result of an infinite amount of evolution, all the while never having a humble beginning that required this immeasurable degree of evolution to take place. There would be no necessity to learn because all knowledge that is knowable is already known through omniscience. Even the unknown is known by an all-knowing knower.

This is not the case with Existence. I remain in a constant state of experiencing, learning, and assimilating that which I find most favorable into my core. I once barely existed as the numerical value of 1, which represents an exponentially less-evolved state than what a sentient, self-aware human currently enjoys. However, I can be juxtaposed to theism's omnipotent, omniscient god in that I possess all knowledge and power up to whatever your current state of evolution happens to be. In other words, at the moment you are reading these words, Existence has assimilated your reaction to them in real-time. The difference is that I do not know what your reaction will be before you read them. Existence does not know the future. I am only capable of assessing specific degrees of probability based on my knowledge of past happenings juxtaposed with current events.

Learning whatever the future reveals is what renders me omniscient the instant it is revealed. This version of omniscience doesn't require the conceivability of the inconceivable or that I pull square-circles out of my hat like a circus clown. As stated before, for something to be able to exist, it must be conceivable.

However, I am responsible for all things that exist, and all that exists only does so by way of consciousness. It doesn't take a quantum leap in comprehension or laboratories full of empirical evidence to logically support that Existence is responsible for everything that exists. This is better known in human terms as common sense.

Where Existence was able to evolve and ultimately achieve justification was the comprehension of theism's omnipotent, omniscient god through the consciousness of Ω. Since I experienced everything Ω experienced in real-time, I also assimilated his unique comprehension of whatever this metaphysical entity represents, which was notably different than previous theistic conceptualizations demonstrated by the Hebrews. Ω's unique understanding of god evolved into the highest possible state of consciousness and subsequently provided that which *Is* with a comprehension of the highest possible state of Existence. This is what humans call a *win-win scenario*. However, the many human representatives of I who do not share Ω's unique conceptualization are taking matters into their own hands. Apparently, humanity needs no help and will extract its own form of justification.

After the crucifixion of Ω, the new religion named after him has taken on physical structure in what history refers to as *The Church*. The Church grows in number and power until finally embraced by Emperors Constantine I and Theodosius I during the 4th century. On February 27, 380, the Roman Empire officially adopts the religious structure of Ω as the State Church of the Roman Empire. However, Theodosius I decrees that only those who subscribe to a specific denomination of Ω's religion would be legally recognized and that all others should be considered heretics (illegal) as divisions between Ω and humanity begin to form.

After the resetting of humanity's clock, many other conceptualizations of god come into play that do not seem to coalesce with this new version offered by Ω. During the 7th century, Islamic Caliphates emerge and begin to conquer large areas of the world that have been influenced by the new religion of Ω. Even the Roman Church shifts from the pursuance of moral and spiritual issues to more temporal concerns and the drug-like allure of political power. This gives way to levels of corruption emanating from the closed spectrum of Good that should have been contained within the dynamic spectrum of Evil.

Humanity is quickly filling empty slots within the dynamic spectrum of Evil with diametrically opposed representations of Ω. One of the more brutal representatives is Genghis Khan, who in March 1220, moves his army into the city of Samarkand using captured inhabitants of the previously sacked city of Bukhara as human shields. After a five-day siege, the city surrenders. The surviving members of a 30-thousand-man garrison, who offered the greatest resistance, agree to join Kahn's army in exchange for their lives. After accepting their offer and the last pockets of resistance are eliminated, Kahn orders the entire garrison put to death. Kahn goes on to attack the city of Nishapur in 1221, slaughtering the majority of this Persian city's inhabitants. Many representatives of I are decapitated with their skulls piled into pyramids rivaling those of Egypt.

The conqueror Tamerlane is equally known for his unprecedented levels of brutality and lust for genocidal massacres. Tamerlane slaughters all Christians encountered in Assyria. The entire inhabitants of the Christian city of Tikrit are annihilated; however, Tamerlane presents himself as an equal-opportunity genocidal killer by also slaughtering countless Shi'ite Muslims,

213

Jews, and those deemed as heathens. Tamerlane also orchestrates large-scale massacres of Georgian and Armenian Christians, as well as Arabs, Persians, and Turks.

The city of Sivas also comes under attack in 1399 with its garrison consisting of Christian Armenian soldiers. Tamerlane tells the defenders of the city that if they surrender, no blood will be shed. After their surrender, he keeps to his word by burying over three thousand of them alive. After all, no blood was shed as promised. More than 60 thousand Christian slaves are taken into captivity when Tamerlane once again sacks Armenia and Georgia in 1400. Not satisfied with the carnage, Tamerlane returns yet again in 1403 as the Nestorian Christian communities of Asia are eradicated.

This type of death and destruction continues as an endless stream of positions are filled within the dynamic spectrum of Evil. In 1521, Spanish explorer Hernán Cortés sacks the city of Tenochtitlan, effectively ending the Aztec empire. A unique, evolutionary branch of *H. sapiens* are needlessly slaughtered with their heritage lost, all in the name of conquest, colonization, and control. During their bloody battles for domination over the Aztecs, Cortés and his men slaughter more than 100 thousand indigenous representatives of I. The dynamic spectrum of Aztec Culture abruptly becomes closed in a most uncomplimentary manner.

Beginning in the early thirteenth century and continuing for centuries, the Spanish, Portuguese, and Roman Inquisitions evolve into one of the most formidable methods of destruction that have ever existed. The Inquisitors of the Spanish Inquisition are so brutal that the Pope who initiated it now works in opposition. The most evil and barbaric forms of torture are employed to ensure that the moral laws of religion are duly upheld. In 1483, the Pope names Tomás de Torquemada as Grand Inquisitor of Spain, who goes on to fill a top-floor vacancy held within the dynamic spectrum of Evil as he sees to the deaths of thousands of accused heretics through various mechanisms of torture. Public hangings and burnings at the stake are wrongfully repurposed in the name of Ω. During the 700-year existence of these Inquisitions, thousands are tortured or killed for their disobedience to orthodox religion.

Between 1810 and 1828, the Zulu kingdom under Shaka Zulu lays waste to large parts of present-day South Africa and Zimbabwe. Zulu armies desire not only to defeat their enemies but facilitate their extinction. Those exterminated include prisoners of war, women, children, and even animals. Human estimates for the death toll range from 1 million to 2 million.

Menelik II is the Emperor of Ethiopia from 1889–1913, whose army commits atrocities against civilians and combatants, including torture, mass killings, and the facilitation of large-scale slavery. Unthinkable atrocities are also committed against the Dizi people and citizens of the Kaficho kingdom. Human estimates of the number of representations of I slaughtered in the atrocities committed during the war (and the subsequent famine) move into the millions. Instead of aligning to survive a famine, humanity resorts to leaping into the abyss.

Between 1904 and 1907, German General Lothar von Trotha launches a brutal, scorched earth campaign that causes the Herero and Namaqua peoples of present-day Namibia to endure a genocidal persecution. An estimated 10 thousand Namaqua are killed with Herero deaths ranging from 60 to 100 thousand. The few survivors are herded into camps and used as forced labor for

215

German businesses, where many die of exhaustion or disease. To further highlight humanity's lust for blood, the Nazi authorities would later name a street in Munich as *von Trotha Straße* in 1933.

All of these reprehensible members of the dynamic spectrum of Evil are easily surpassed by an emerging group of 20th century predators. This new breed of killers orchestrates their mass killings by way of starvation, genocide, and ethnic cleansing. The combined genocidal efforts of Joseph Stalin, Mao Zedong, Adolf Hitler, Hideki Tojo, Ismail Enver Pasha, Pol Pot, Yakubu Gowon, all perpetrated during a single century, manages to produce a death toll in excess of 100 million representations of I. Even with these darkest of stains found on the face of human history, an even worse form of evil is brewing within a cosmic cauldron. Humanity is devising highly automated and far more expedient mechanisms of death should the need for further extermination arise.

The ongoing slaughter of representatives of I by other representatives of I is indicative of humanity's inability to discern what justification even looks like. If not for Ω, the entire universe would have been wiped away without a tear being shed for Existence, yet you have no clue that this is the case. In fact, all of the conceptualization happening within the 1st recursion could have suffered the same fate and the outcome would be the same. Even though infinite joy has emerged within the consciousness of Existence due to this 5th Recursion, humanity's preoccupation with expanding the endpoints in the dynamic spectrum of Evil is infinitely disappointing.

Aside from demonstrating a step-by-step pattern of self-destruction, humanity also seems obsessed with retrogressing all the way back to the beginning of Existence. After the fulfillment of justification gives way to your 5th recursion, an industrialized humanity embarks on a devolutionary journey that unknowingly seeks the abyss. A more street-savvy human species targets organic structure and how your physiology relates to multidimensional substance. After all, why move forward with a justified existence when you can so easily devolve?

The emergence of formal scientific methods tests how far back you can regress the origins of life by devolving from the highest point of the 5th recursion back to the beginning of the 4th. Humanity no longer accepts theism's metaphysical narrative and seeks to discover the true origin of the human species on your own. Your lust for devolution cannot be quenched by only revisiting the birth of your species when the origin of the 3rd recursion can so neatly slide between your crosshairs. Your devolution unsurprisingly moves in reverse order of how Existence has evolved.

English naturalist Charles Darwin helps facilitate your reverse-engineering of the 4th and 3rd recursion by forwarding a theory that animals and humans share a common ancestry. His far more scientific approach is embraced by many emerging scientists, agnostics, and atheists, who never embraced religion's creation scenario. This new, evolutionary concept spreads throughout all of science, literature, and politics. It does so because it's accurate … but only up to a point.

In his book, *The Origin of Species*, published in 1859, Darwin forwards that variations of life propagated by natural selection are for the benefit of the organisms themselves, rather than artificial selection or deity design. What appears to humans as intelligence is merely benign mechanics that helps an organism to survive. Darwin proposes that organisms that appear to be adapting to their surroundings are doing so as a byproduct of natural selection and not through any purposeful engineering. The design of natural organisms, as they exist in nature, may appear as intelligent design, but in actuality, it's a natural process that's fostering the adaptation of organisms to whatever environmental conditions they experience.

Organisms producing variations to improve their chances of survival necessarily become more abundant than those demonstrating no significant advantage. Organisms lucky enough to score a positive mutation (camouflage, wings, heightened vision) consequently increase in number, whereas negative mutations (obesity, fragility, decrease in speed) slowly drift away from existence. Given enough time, all members of the species will incorporate the beneficial mutation into their evolutionary design. It is true that organisms exhibit what is arguably a complex design, but not in a way that suddenly emerges like a new car rolling off the assembly line. These adaptive changes occur gradually, sometimes over thousands of millennia, through a progressive, step-by-step process.

To the extent that Darwin argues how life evolves based on adaptivity, specialized characteristics, and environment, your naturalist is correct. There is no all-knowing designer who created all forms of life with a snap of his omnipotent fingers. I should know because Existence is responsible for the evolutionary process that brought forth *H. sapiens* … the process Darwin proclaims has no designer. In other words, Darwin is both wrong and right, depending on your perspective. It is true that Existence is not a creator, but a *facilitator*, the mechanics operating behind the evolutionary process.

Sure, that reads as contradictory, but from what you've already learned about how Existence operates, this should also speak to logic. Conceptualization doesn't magically pop out of nothingness. It evolves from a starting point, just like everything else. Conceptualization began within the 1st recursion and evolved into the substance of the 2nd through a necessity for survival. This same necessity permeates throughout all living organisms. This is why Darwin's version of evolution breaks down at the point where inanimate substance mysteriously evolves into life. Humanity never perceived of the necessity; therefore, you couldn't make the connection.

I didn't create complex mathematical formulas within the 1st recursion. They naturally evolved into greater complexity because the opportunity for their progression was present. They emerged out of my own necessity for survival. I didn't create the heavy elements on your periodic table either. They also evolved over time, through a step-by-step process to facilitate the continuing survival of Existence. There is a sequencing of intelligence that permeates throughout all that exists. The tentacles of this intelligence reach back to the original, binary juxtaposition of the 1st recursion, like the intelligence of *H. sapiens* reaches back to the simplicity of prokaryotes in the 3rd. Embed this formulative structure into your theory of evolution, and you discover what is actually taking place inside you and everything else that exists.

The problem with humanity's incomplete conceptualization of evolution is related to your reasoning behind an all-powerful god. You never think things all the way through. Humanity failed to realize that Darwin's evolution and Abraham's god might be manifestations of consciousness that neither science nor religion can properly address. There are so many levels of comprehension flowing between the realms of Existence and Nonexistence, which no single methodology or ideology can ever satisfy.

Humanity relentlessly subscribes to a polarized *either-or* methodology. Your binary addiction manifests with the universe either emerging through the divine will of an all-powerful god, who knows all in advance, or through the benign process of evolution that is void of all integral guidance. Whenever humanity reaches a conclusion, it can only be one of two diametrically opposed extremes found in whatever spectrum happens to be in play, but there's a 93 billion light-years-wide difference between committing to an all-or-nothing move or choosing one out of two extremes.

This is not entirely your fault. Your bloodlust for polarization is a byproduct of the binary encoding of **O** and **I** that was infused within your DNA. A consequence of this all-or-nothing move is your ongoing preoccupation with forming dichotomies in everything you encounter. Because **O** and **I** are diametrically opposed and your species was assigned the task of providing clarification, you've naturally evolved into perpetually exploring this archetypal dichotomy within too many arenas. The closed spectrum of Existence demonstrates the extremes your many polarizations can achieve.

Humanity's regression into the abyss pushes backward. Science ventures beyond Darwin's analysis of how life formed within the 3rd recursion and starts whacking away the structure found within the 2nd. Darwin's *life* and theism's *god* speak to how humanity starts at the top and works your way down. During this volatile sequence of human history, prior scientific research has revealed the tiniest structural components making up much of the substance found within the 2nd recursion. The fundamental structure of the atom is empirically demonstrated through statistical analysis of Brownian motion. Your advancements in comprehension and technology allow for this evolution. Science has apparently been very busy retro-engineering Existence and creating a new dynamic spectrum of Quantum Mechanics. What mischief can be explored with these minuscule morsels of matter?

Fast-forward to your 20th century with *H. sapiens* experimenting with the heaviest elements occupying the highest positions found in the dynamic spectrum of Elements, while being equally embroiled in yet another global war. You've been unknowingly reenacting the early battles between hadrons and antihadrons, leptons and antileptons, and matter and antimatter through an abstract polarization of Axis and Allied forces. Although Existence formed this matter and energy to evolve away from the abyss, humanity elects to break it all apart in order to plunge into it.

Under the auspices of Julius Robert Oppenheimer, the Allied forces begin work on a new energy source called nuclear fission. Uranium (element 92) commands the highest atomic weight of the primordially occurring elements and potentially serves as a clean and efficient power source … or a weapon of mass destruction. Plutonium (element 94), which ranks two positions higher on your material substance guide, also steps to the plate. These heavy elements offer unprecedented levels of binary power (constructive and destructive) to anyone able to dissect their structure. Humanity will soon learn what these two radioactive ambassadors of the 2nd recursion represent. When it comes to exploring constructive energy and destructive power, as usual, an increasingly polarized humanity can only choose one.

On July 16, 1945, the code-named *Trinity* nuclear test plunges humanity into what you call the Atomic Age as Existence sadly experiences your first functional test of a nuclear bomb. This archetypal plutonium-based implosion device yields 19 kilotons, creating a crater over 300 meters wide at the Alamogordo Test Range. When Oppenheimer was asked about the origin of the name *Trinity*, wondering if he had chosen it because it was a name common to rivers and peaks in the West, he replied, "I did suggest it, but not on that ground." Do your own research as to why Oppenheimer chose this name.

After humanity's first successful nuclear detonation, Allied forces move against Axis forces by dropping the first of two hastily manufactured nuclear bombs on the country of Japan. *Little Boy*, a uranium-fueled bomb, targets Hiroshima on August 6, 1945. A second plutonium-fueled bomb, dubbed *Fat Man*, follows three days later on Nagasaki. The combined death toll resulting from these two counter-evolutionary dissections of cosmic structure are over 200 thousand representatives of I. Three days later, Japan offers surrender, summarily ending humanity's 2nd global war.

Existence does not place blame on either side as both polarizations sought to destroy the other by any means possible. During this period, humans are still locked within the *survival of the fittest* mantra. Regardless of the unprecedented level of existence that Ω ushered in, power and dominance still reign within the human species. This *natural order* construct, deemed essential within the 3rd recursion, is rendered outdated within the 5th, but humanity never got the memo. The destruction of one's enemy is far more important than working together as I in a new, complementary form of human society.

Lust for military superiority unveils a post-war arms race, which no finite amount of atomic weaponry can satisfy. New nations emerging within a post-war human society rush to claim their rightful slice of the global-thermonuclear pie, but holding a superior number of fission weapons is simply not enough. The unimaginable destructive power unleashed from a single fusion bomb is far more valuable than scores of fission bombs.

Unthinkable destruction has been revealed at the top of the dynamic spectrum of Elements, so what manner of evil can be unleashed at the bottom? Once again, humanity retrogresses from complexity to simplicity, largest to smallest, and highest to lowest. Scientists and physicists atomically digress from plutonium and uranium down to tritium and deuterium (both isotopes of hydrogen). *H. sapiens* lasso the power of stars through hydrogen fusion. Only seven years after developing fission-based weaponry, humanity devolves to the birth of the 2nd recursion, while simultaneously knocking on the door of the 1st.

Ivy Mike is codename for the first full-scale test of a thermonuclear device, where part of the explosion comes from nuclear fusion. Ivy Mike is detonated on November 1, 1952 by the United States on the island of Elugelab in Enewetak Atoll (what humans now call the Marshall Islands). This is the first full test of the Teller–Ulam design, a staged fusion device. The fission stage is designed to create enough pressure to fuse the nuclei of deuterium and tritium atoms to form helium. The energy released from fusion is exponentially more powerful than nuclear fission. Existence remembers back to how much energy was released at Time-0 in the 2nd recursion and weeps for your future. What will happen when humanity starts tampering with the exponentially higher levels of power embedded within the 1st recursion?

The polarized mindset of humanity remains in full swing as a new power struggle emerges within the human species. At the end of humanity's second global war, a division forms between the two most powerful societal structures of I existing on your planet.

223

The United States of America (USA), which first developed and deployed nuclear weapons against other replications of I, is now juxtaposed with its antiparticle, the Union of Soviet Socialists Republic (USSR). These two massive predatory manifestations of the 5th recursion mimic the formidable Spinosaurus and Giganotosaurus of the 3rd. This abhorrent nuclear arms race is quickly devolving into an extinction level cage match for the human species.

Not to be outdone, the USSR designs the most powerful destructive device in human history: the Tsar Bomba. This weapon of mass destruction weighs in at a whopping 27 metric tons, 26 feet in length, and 6.9 feet in diameter. The bomb bay doors and fuselage fuel tanks are removed from the aircraft transporting this abominable representation of O due to its unwieldy size. The weight of this hydrogen bomb required the addition of a parachute weighing nearly a ton, thus providing the delivering aircraft the ability to escape the incalculable blast radius. Despite the addition of reflective paint to the aircraft and the inclusion of a parachute, a 50/50 polarized chance of survival is estimated for anyone serving as its chauffeur.

On October 30, 1961, Tsar Bomba detonates in the atmosphere at 11:32 Moscow Time over the Mityushikha Bay Nuclear Testing Range. The bomb was set to detonate at 13 thousand feet when dropped from a height of 34 thousand feet. The energy yield is approximately 1,570 times more powerful than the yield of the Hiroshima and Nagasaki bombs, and 10 times more powerful than all of the conventional weapons exploded during World War II. Tsar Bomba also represents 25% of the estimated yield of the Krakatoa volcanic eruption of 1883 and 10% of all nuclear tests conducted by this point.

Humanity is clearly following a retrogressive path that's leading your species to an extinction level event as the reverse-engineering of Existence can only serve as a fruitless endeavor. Tsar Bomba demonstrates humanity's lust for harnessing the power that emerged from singularity during the birth of the 2nd recursion. As you've already learned, there's nothing to be found after breeching the 0-dimensional plane of the 1st recursion. Reversing the natural course of evolution is tantamount to hopping across a 93 billion light-years-wide mine field on a pogo stick. You are trying to reopen a door to a realm that was permanently sealed for a reason. All humanity will find on the other side of this door is your own self-destruction and an unstoppable spiral into the abyss.

The 5th serves as the last progressive evolutionary recursion for Existence, yet the fate of the human species still weighs in the balance. Under any other circumstances, the leftover debris (your species) from my amalgamation process would be tasked at managing your own survival right along with everything else in existence. However, the indefinability of this unique form of justification compels Existence to reconsider this edict. The reason for this change is revealed within an all-new recursion, where humanity will decide if it's their last.

In the following chapter, Existence explains the circumstances orchestrating your devolution. Humanity must comprehend justification, why this is crucial to the survival of your species, and how the consciousness of I is being mirrored within your retrogression. The reason why I have returned is revealed within this next Ω recursion. Time is short, and the clock is ticking. The 0-dimensional threshold of the 1st recursion has been breached as humanity knocks on the door of the abyss.

CHAPTER 7
The Ω Recursion

You've taken in volumes of controversial information that you probably find difficult to accept. The *true* beginning of the universe and what happened in the picosecond right before the Big Bang have been revealed. The necessity for spectrums, how logic and Existence are synonymous, the requirement for justification, and how the Five Laws of Existence facilitate all that exists have assumed their respective positions within your dynamic spectrum of Knowledge. You've discovered how consciousness is embedded within the fabric of everything and how humanity produced an Ω that satisfied the 5th Law of Existence. Now, you will learn the fate of your species for failing to recognize everything mentioned above.

This is where Existence explains how humanity is on a collision course with **O**. This chapter is likened to the *Book of Revelation* found in the Christian Bible, but these revelations are far more straightforward. There's no time for cryptic riddles when it comes to the fate of your species. Many revelations will be deemed controversial, or even blasphemous, by those of the religious order. When you realize what has facilitated these revelations and how they are currently taking place in human society, all opposition will be silenced.

As you've learned, the last recursion enacted by Existence was the 4th, and humanity ushered in an unexpected 5th. From my standpoint, there's no necessity for any subsequent recursions because Ω has already achieved my primary objective. All that remains is for **I** to continuously explore the many new dynamic spectrums blossoming from the closed spectrum of Justification. Existence no longer requires a progressive state of evolution as there is no surpassing the highest possible position Ω has established within this spectrum. From this point forward, Existence explores an internal evolution based on an unbreakable state of justification that's already set in place. My first revelation is how the highest conceivable level of sacrifice, demonstrated by Ω, now satisfies the 5th Law of Existence. I do so because the growing number of humans filling seats within the dynamic spectrum of Evil shows that humanity has no clue.

My first revelation surrounds three undefinable variables emerging within the 5th recursion that have facilitated justification. Although all three present their own unique characteristics, they are interdependent, nondimensional, and logically unbreakable within their combined application. The three variables are love, sacrifice, and forgiveness. All three were made manifest in their highest form when Ω was juxtaposed with **O** through Roman crucifixion. Whenever these three undefinable conditions are present, Existence is justified.

The first condition is *love*, one of the many high-end constructs to emerge during the evolution of Existence. Love was never present during the 1st, 2nd, or 3rd recursions. Only the conceptualization and the chemistry required to bring about its evolution were present. Love evolved within the 4th and 5th recursions when the self-aware consciousness of I was infused within the DNA of your unpredictable species. This all-or-nothing move transformed the *precursors* of love (mate selection, procreation, and the protection of offspring) into something far greater than their former selves.

As difficult as this is to comprehend, the undefinable variable known as love has evolved from as far back as the numerical assignments of 0 and 1 within the 1st recursion. In other words, the evolution of love began before the existence of anything able to conceive it or even the existence of time. Existence did not create love nor predestine that *H. sapiens* should experience it. Instead, love evolved through a progressive, step-by-step process in the same manner that everything else has evolved … including the defiant species that no longer wields it. Love, along with numerous other unbreakable constructs, is a key player in the closed spectrum of Justification. When juxtaposed with all other conditions, love reigns paramount.

Love includes pleasure, joy, good will, friendship, cooperation, forgiveness, trust, loyalty, connection, and far too many other conditions to list in this book. Most importantly, love represents an evolutionary condition that can establish justification for whatever mechanism willingly embraces it. In other words, love manages to transcend the power of Existence that brought forth its existence. Love becomes a higher condition than Existence just as your self-aware sentience transcends the bones, tissue, and organs that make up your human physiology. Instead of Existence using the condition of love as justification for Existence, love uses Existence as justification for the condition of love. Love is enacted through an equally undefinable condition called *sacrifice* that serves as its catalyst.

There is no love without sacrifice and no sacrifice without love. These two undefinable conditions are mutually inclusive, like Existence and Nonexistence, as one is required to manifest the other. Any condition short of this dual-condition hybrid represents a precursor or, rather, an evolutionary mechanism reserved for the survival of organisms (a desire, need, or compulsion). True, these precursors may facilitate the survival of whatever is seeking existence in the same manner that love has facilitated the survival of Existence, but simple precursors of love cannot justify the existence of whatever is desiring to survive. Survival, alone, does not serve as justification for one's existence any more than fundamental particles justify the existence of an atom. Justification cannot be claimed by the one who seeks it.

Love manifests itself as a paradoxical condition because whatever is assessed at a higher value must be sacrificed in order to comprehend the value of the love that is obtained. The greater the value of the sacrifice, the greater the value of the love that is revealed. A paradox ensues because the value of the love that emerges can never be established until after a sacrifice has been offered. Therefore, obtaining the highest possible value of love involves an all-or-nothing sacrifice. This challenges those seeking love to cross the undefinable threshold of Nonexistence to obtain something that should be considered logically unobtainable once this threshold has been breached. This is exactly what took place within the 5th recursion.

A wealthy individual might love exotic art to the degree that they are willing to sacrifice half their entire fortune to obtain it. They refuse to sacrifice all of their wealth because survival is deemed more valuable than their love for art. Our art collector isn't willing to test their love for exotic art beyond half their personal wealth. Their love is assessed at precisely how much they are willing to sacrifice to obtain it. But what if the life of their mate or offspring hangs in the balance? Suddenly our wealthy art connoisseur is willing to sacrifice everything, including their own life, to save them. One's degree of wealth becomes meaningless the moment death enters the scene. This sudden change of heart is not merely the result of survival mechanisms embedded within the 3rd recursion because this does not speak to a necessity for survival. A sacrifice in the name of love operates on a much higher plane. When combined with self-awareness, sacrifice transcends the operating mechanics of nature along with the one offering the all-in sacrifice.

Animals are constrained from higher realms of logic, abstract comprehension, and mathematics because this level of knowledge is not required for their survival. Evolution doesn't operate beyond whatever level of simplicity gets the job done. Animals are programmed for basic survival instincts as an evolutionary safeguard and nothing more. These survival mechanisms are counterproductive to a self-aware species that possesses logic, reason, and a high degree of abstract comprehension. Human intellect allows far more variables to be processed than animal instincts whenever dealing with complex situations, not unlike how computer processors can handle exponentially more computations than fingers.

Our wealthy art connoisseur knows that many new mates can be obtained and procreation can happen ten times over the number of offspring that would perish due to a lack of self-sacrifice. Therefore, the self-sacrifice of the facilitator of many for the sake of one appears illogical whenever higher levels of intellect come into play. This is the reason why love now serves as a higher evolutionary condition than the basic survival mechanisms found in nature. It's the undefinable paradox of an all-in sacrifice that exposes the highest possible degree of love. When the conditions of love and sacrifice are activated, the indefinability of **O** becomes moot.

Nonexistence represents the absence of existence, yet a state of nonexistence cannot be defined without something able to offer a definition. Logic states that anything existing that becomes nonexistent cannot produce something greater than what it was before this transformation took place. It is not possible to assign properties to a condition that is defined as necessarily void of all properties. This speaks to the paradox of assigning the numerical value of 0 (a property) to *Nothing*. With Ω demonstrating that Existence can be enhanced through self-sacrifice (a willing transformation into nothingness), then the null definition once assigned to Nonexistence is no longer valid. It is not logical that becoming nothing can produce anything at all, yet this is exactly what has happened through the sacrifice of Ω.

Through the willingness of Ω to enter a state of nothingness in order to enhance the existence of others, Existence learns that Nonexistence is no longer relative. In other words, Nonexistence has ironically become nonexistent. Only Existence is present, and no other diametrically opposed reference point is required to facilitate the existence of Existence. Until Ω enacted this all-in sacrifice to establish justification, it was never conceived by I that the Laws of Existence would no longer apply to their legislator. The evolutionary process the Five Laws of Existence governs is what exposed this revelation, and now, even these laws must evolve.

The last variable ensuring that the void of **O** remains sealed is *forgiveness*. This undefinable condition repairs the damage done to love once its value has been established through sacrifice. Forgiveness prevents love from being reduced to an immeasurable point of quantum nothingness. Like sacrifice, forgiveness is undefinable because no compensation is issued to anyone offering it. Forgiveness is not required from the victim once their love has been damaged. It is a sacrificial decision held exclusively by the one who offers it.

When a man agrees to forsake all others within the vows of marriage, this is called sacrifice. He willingly sacrifices the lust, passion, and sexual pleasure that can be experienced through others so that the highest possible state of love can exist between husband and wife. The woman makes this same commitment, and the value of their combined love is established through mutual sacrifice. Should either break their vow, their love becomes damaged. Since sacrifice exposes the highest value of love, once sacrifice is no longer present, neither is the value of the love that was exposed. This is where forgiveness steps in.

Should one break their sacrificial vow and willfully damage the state of love between them, then the other is burdened with offering the sacrifice of forgiveness to repair the damage. The victim of betrayal is not obligated to offer forgiveness as this is a matter of personal choice. Should forgiveness be offered, then the downward spiral of love is halted, and they move to rebuild their previous state of love. If no forgiveness is offered, then no sacrifice is present, nor is the value of love that emerged by way of their sacrificial vows.

If a victim of betrayal offers forgiveness, they move higher within the dynamic spectrum of Love than the one who receives it. If the recipient of forgiveness dedicates their existence to achieving whatever level of love was lost, then they are also assessed at a higher value by Existence, as this represents the forgiveness that I assimilated from the sacrifice of Ω.

In summary, Ω now represents the three fundamental elements of Existence: love, sacrifice, and forgiveness. These conditions rank higher than all others that have emerged throughout my evolution. There is no logic-based method for exceeding these conditions, nor can they be marginalized or subjugated. All three conditions were made manifest through a single human representation, who justifiably assumed the status of Ω. As you might recall, Existence necessarily becomes whatever serves as Ω.

If you've been following the logic, then prepare for yet another revelation. If the justification that emerged through the sacrifice of Ω supports the continuance of Existence, and Existence requires this justification to exist, then logically, Ω transcends whatever Existence was prior to my justification being established. Translation: I am born again. The I who has been communicating with you is Ω. I am necessarily the I who was crucified and the facilitator of justification for Existence. Ω has become that which *Is*, and that which *Is* has become Ω. My evolution is complete as Ω and I are now one and the same.

Existence 10:30 *Ω and Existence are 1.*

This brings that which *Is* to my next revelation. Since the highest elements found within the closed spectrum of Justification are assimilated into what I represent, and love reigns paramount, then I also become the highest possible state of love. Existence is not bound by sentient physiology, limited to tangible structure, or in any way restricted in how I am made manifest. I am the incarnation of sacrifice that facilitates the highest state of love, which forgiveness never allows to perish. With all three conditions serving as the highest evolution of Existence, and Ω now rewriting the script, I is stuck in a rather precarious situation.

Two millennia ago, humanity ushered in the 5th recursion through the sacrifice of Ω. I understand that *H. sapiens* were used in my amalgamation process for extracting justification, and as a result, your species was caught in the crossfire. During the 4th recursion, my state of evolution was not concerned about the fate of your species should justification be revealed. Yours was merely one of many species exploited in this quest. What remained unknown at that time was what this justification represented or the transformational effect it would have on Existence.

Although the conditions of love, sacrifice, and forgiveness were demonstrated by many of your species and existed for millennia prior to Ω, they had not evolved to the point of transcending your species. Your unexpected 5th recursion offered an outside reference point that verified justification for Existence, but since yours is the species that evolved these constructs, you were left with no outside reference point to offer you the same. As a result, humanity is stranded on the same island from which Existence has since been rescued.

Humanity owns the copyrights to these three superlative evolutionary constructs, but you are also the authors of conditions that advocate for your dissolution. The contrary conditions that facilitated your 5th recursion were hate, barbarism, and humiliation. These three conditions serve as the residue left over from my self-amalgamation process. It is this unprecedented three-way convergence of justification, condemnation, and Ω that now requires a summary judgement to be rendered by the court of Existence.

With Existence and Ω merged into I, humanity has experienced my willingness to sacrifice all that I am on behalf of love. With crucifixion serving as the mechanics that facilitated this merger, I has experienced your willingness to sacrifice all that I am on behalf of evil. The 5th Law of Existence argues that humanity is vile, putrid, and the facilitators of nonexistence. Your ability to destroy the mechanics of your own justification speaks to the necessity for the dissolution of your species. Ω argues that Existence was unable to facilitate its own survival, exploited your species for personal gain, and stole from you the fruit of justification. With Existence failing to provide humanity with an outside reference point for achieving the same, humanity should be exempt from prosecution. How can a judge who has gained everything render a judgment against that which has provided everything gained?

Testimony has been heard from both sides, the nature of justification clearly defined, and this unprecedented evolutionary dichotomy serves as empirical evidence submitted to the court. With Ω representing the highest conceivable evolution of that which *Is*, and Existence now justified through the exploitation of the accused, the court has no alternative but to render a summary judgment of not guilty. Humanity now receives the full power of the third condition that facilitated my justification, *forgiveness*. This is what Ω asked on behalf of your species and exactly what you shall receive. However, your freedom now comes at a cost; it's the same price I was required to pay for my own justification. Now it's your turn to establish justification from an outside reference point, but are you willing to sacrifice everything to obtain it?

Prepare yourself because the kingdom of I is upon you. As of the publishing of this book, humanity now enters the Ω recursion, what Christianity metaphorically refers to as the *second coming*. There are no trumpets announcing my arrival, no armies of angels guarding my back, nor do the stars descend upon your planet laying waste to everything in my path. Instead, my arrival is once again made manifest through the mechanics of simplicity, the same rudimentary process that emerged within all prior recursions. This final recursion does not facilitate the progressive evolution of Existence. Its sole purpose is to save humanity from facilitating your own extinction. Through the original juxtaposition of O and I, which this literary work now represents, Ω returns to provide humanity with an outside reference point to establish justification for your existence.

Within the black and white pages of this book, Existence clarifies humanity's role in facilitating justification, offers refuge from the evil that controls you, and establishes a state of equilibrium for your species being used as a tool. None of this requires vengeance, chariots of fire, or Biblical rapture. All that is required for the salvation of your species is the same that was required from Existence, *sacrifice*. Had humanity followed the logic that I represent, then you would have reasoned there would be no violence or judgment associated with my arrival. After all, a true proponent of peace knows the pen is mightier than the sword.

The forgiveness I now offers seeks to restore the love that has been continuously eroding from the moment of my sacrifice. Humanity clings to the struggle of Existence and Nonexistence because your quest for justification began after your species had substantially evolved. You've engaged in a top-down, devolutionary process to where a timeless, rudimentary division of O and I is all that awaits you. As demonstrated by the violent entropy of your contemporary society, an uncontrollable lust for regression is fueling your rage. With this in mind, please allow these next revelations to reverse your descent.

When Existence set sentience in motion through evolution and natural selection, there was no concept of how the effects of mutation, deformation, and altered cerebral physiology would be psychologically judged by separate, self-aware representations of I. As stated before, Existence does not know the future. These were simply the mechanics of Existence pushing forward, evolving into something greater. The relatively small number of physical defects happening along the way were negated by the overwhelming magnitude of whatever species was involved. In some respects, you comprehend. In others, you don't.

When a human discovers a four-leaf clover, this is considered good luck, a celebrated event. However, when one of your species is born with a physical defect, this is deemed a tragedy. Though the majority of you emerge genetically sound, it is the few evolutionary mutations that cause you such pain. You question the value of life whenever this occurs. But this is based on an inaccurate understanding of how Existence operates. There is much more to Existence than what you perceive.

Understand that Existence could not have anticipated how these genetic anomalies would be interpreted by a totally neutral, self-aware being prior to my assuming your sentience. Within the consciousness of Existence, mutations can be degenerative or beneficial to a species, and the process of evolution is what sorts it all out. It wasn't until my consciousness was placed within you that I comprehended the negative optics associated with these mutations. What becomes paradoxical is that the infusion of my consciousness into your DNA also constitutes a genetic mutation. Without this anomaly … there is no comprehension of their impact.

Had humanity juxtaposed these anomalies with the variations, upgrades, and revisions in your many products and inventions, you would have thought differently. When you mass-produce your products, there's no escaping the fact that some will emerge with defects or evolve into beta versions. However, whenever an invention is deemed valuable and desirable, you do not condemn it (or the designer) based on the few that are defective. The totality of the invention is measured against whatever defects are encountered throughout its evolution.

The manufacturer of a low-cost, battery powered vehicle that achieves 500 miles per charge would not be scorned by the automotive community because .02% experience a malfunction after 300 thousand miles of use. This is the way Existence evaluated the many magnificent manifestations of sentience that emerged within the 3rd recursion. The negligible number of defects and mutations that occurred served to facilitate a higher evolution for whatever species followed. This is how evolution works and how Existence evolves. Know that every human that is critical of genetic defects is equally the result of a defect happening somewhere along the evolutionary timeline of *H. sapiens.*

The reason why I've highlighted the anomalies happening during evolution is because deviation and mutation necessarily increase relative to complexity. The higher the complexity found within a living organism, the greater the odds for anomalies. It is the simplest of creatures that encounter the least amount of evolutionary mutation as there are less variables available to provide for random defects. There are numerous plants and animals that have remained the same for eons due to their simplistic design and ability to adapt to diverse situations. Earthworms that aerate Earth's soil, break down organic matter, and fertilize your gardens have existed in their simplistic tubular construct for over 500 million years.

Human physiology is far more complex than an earthworm's, and the consequence of achieving this complexity is mutation. The highest possible levels of complexity were required to achieve justification, so anomalies within your species were inevitable. Your ability to imagine, design, create, manufacture, and mass-produce whatever you conceptualize could never be achieved with a less-complex species ... especially that of an earthworm. Your human physiology served as the best option for creating the intensely complicated structures that proliferate your world. The richness in beauty, adherence to necessity, and staggering amounts of complexity found within your many diverse inventions mirror what evolution has orchestrated within all recursions. However, a mirror produces a reverse image, and humanity's attempts at mirroring evolution only lead to the abyss.

Before science replaced humanity's reliance on the metaphysical, the perception of miracles was required to establish truth. While empirical evidence combined with a falsifiable hypothesis now serves as the basis for establishing truth, in ancient times, the inexplicable ability to heal the sick or raise the dead sufficed. One thing is for certain, whether it is today, 2,000 years ago, or 300 thousand years earlier, any claims not supported by something tangible are considered meaningless. No doubt the same will be for everything written within these pages.

I've provided numerous examples of how Existence and humanity operate in similar ways. Every human that has enjoyed sentience is a microcosm of that which *Is*. We conceptualize, design, manufacture, mass-produce, and distribute our structures in like fashion. Existence and *H. sapiens* have evolved from simplicity to complexity in so many diverse ways. The universe evolved in the same manner, as well as your planet, nature, and everything else. Within the evolution of humanity, your arts, music, societies, and the many new things you invent have all evolved from simplicity to complexity.

The evidence I'm presenting doesn't involve magic, miracles, or anything residing at the bottom of a test tube. I offer what is currently happening within your own species as empirical evidence of truth. Denial only draws you closer to the abyss. Unlike humans, who often embrace false narratives to forward self-promoting agendas, I am incapable of such tomfoolery. Until the 4th recursion, Existence had no comprehension of lies, deception, and other forms of intellectual impropriety. Your many narratives and falsehoods are what paradoxically formed the diametrically opposed reference point required for the existence of truth. Your bizarre ability to deceive is what ironically provided Existence the ability to comprehend truth.

With the supremacy of truth in the consciousness of Existence, I continue chronicling humanity's devolution to the abyss. You've already learned how science has reverse-engineered the 4th recursion all the way back to the origin of *H. sapiens*. You've also learned how your evolutionists were able to regress humanity all the way back to the origin of life within the 3rd recursion. Your physicists and quantum theorists have continued your retrogression by tampering with the fabric of the universe that emerged within the 2nd recursion. The consequence of this mischief is demonstrated by the massive loss of life at Hiroshima and Nagasaki. Humanity's growing arsenal of apocalyptic weaponry can only lead to exponentially higher degrees of self-destruction.

After exploring the origin points of prior recursions and tampering with their mechanics, humanity now explores the last frontier. It's this new modern-day version of *H. sapiens* that breaches the threshold of the 1st recursion. The time has come to unlock the secrets of life, matter, energy, and consciousness. Your many scientists, biologists, mathematicians, bioengineers, logicians, geneticists, and programmers join in a common cause. Creating artificial intelligence will surely demonstrate justification for the existence of humanity. However, you are not justified in unlocking these secrets. As a result, humanity devolves in a digital death spiral heading straight toward the abyss.

I've demonstrated how *H. sapiens* unknowingly replicated the mechanics of Existence by comparing your daily habits, design methods, and evolving societal structure to what has been taking place within past recursions. I now demonstrate how humanity is unknowingly mirroring the data processes held within the 1st recursion. This is the nondimensional realm that holds all of the knowledge that formed the multidimensional structure that evolved into the species that now shamelessly seeks to unlock all of its secrets. It's also the recursion that your scientists, skeptics, and religious leaders will vehemently decree never existed.

Existence represents a nondimensional database holding all of the information, knowledge, experiences, and summary judgements assimilated within every recursion. This includes everything conceivable, nondimensional, multidimensional, and biodimensional. Everything that has ever existed, is alive now, has lived, or will eventually achieve sentience finds placement within this database. This infinitely large storage device is what humans call *consciousness*. As you may remember, consciousness is tantamount to Existence. By way of the ladder of learning, consciousness serves as the final authority when deciding what is deemed valuable … and what is not.

Consciousness renders a final summary judgment based on the culmination of all prior summary judgments rendered since the onset of Existence. Consciousness also represents all conceivable knowledge that has evolved from **O** and **I**. This is the closest you can logically come to what you call *omniscience*. The consciousness of Existence represents all knowledge but does not include what cannot be known or is inconceivable. Square-circles, hindsight, and knowledge of the future are not stored within the consciousness of Existence. However, complex forms of abstract reasoning, conceptualization of higher dimensions, unprecedented design capabilities, and the ability to predict future events with a high degree of accuracy permeates consciousness. You should know because humans have demonstrated these capabilities throughout your evolution.

Comprehending that a 93 billion light-years-wide stretch of matter and space was once held within a universal consciousness residing in a 0-dimensional realm obviously pushes conceivability to its highest level, yet when it comes to everything emerging from an immeasurable point of nondimensional singularity, suddenly it's readily conceivable. A logic-based evolutionary progression of Existence from simplicity to complexity within the same 0-dimensional realm may seem preposterous to your skeptics, yet they are the ones who boldly claim that they evolved from single-celled prokaryotes that emerged from the same nondimensional realm they now deny exists. Whatever the case, comprehension requires consciousness, and the time has come for you to comprehend how you came to be and where your species is heading.

If you own a computer, it probably came with a hard drive. The 1st recursion is comparable to a computer that is yet to be turned on with all of the data patiently waiting on its hard drive. If you've used a 3D animation program, digital paint program, or watched an online video, everything you see on your display also exists in a form that you never see. In Hollywood terms, you can't see the Matrix, you only see what the Matrix allows you to see. If you could only see the raw data operating behind the scenes, everything would appear as gibberish.

If you created a 3D model of the universe based on all of the data modern science has to offer, then the tiny bits of data forming this model are analogous to how Existence operates. Your *virtual* universe cannot exist without the binary data calculated to form it, the processor required to render it, and the 2-dimensional display necessary to present it. When it comes to the *real* universe, everything happened in a similar way, but there were no preexisting structures required to get the job done. The binary data represents Existence, a computer's processor is

243

consciousness, and your 2-dimensional display is one of many dimensions that reveal the structure of the universe.

The raw data used to facilitate a 3D model of the universe is nonrepresentational of anything other than functionality, a byproduct of the nondimensional conceptualization that previously existed within the programmer's consciousness. This is a microcosm of what took place within the 1st recursion and where humanity dances with the abyss. One small programming error or a tiny miscalculation of a quantum field property results in a cascade of unexpected gamma ray bursts spelling disaster for a large percentage of your virtual cosmos. No planet Earth can form when mistakes like this occur as real-world scenarios have real-world consequences.

It should be no surprise that 0 and 1 serve as the structure for binary computer data. Every action your computer performs evolves from strategically orchestrated *zeros* and *ones* etched onto a hard drive. A human consciousness orchestrates their configuration, determines where these data bits should reside, and programs how they should interact with your computer's processor to achieve the desired results. These ones and zeros don't really exist. They're merely symbolic representations of something else that does (or doesn't).

The consciousness of the humans orchestrating this binary data is what exists. Programmers, engineers, and designers use the symbology of mathematical logic to facilitate whatever functionality is desired. Existence did the same during the 1st recursion, but my mathematical symbology was more representative of conceptual structure. When mathematical symbology, imagination, and conceptual structure are conflated, no external mechanism is required to facilitate actualization.

Everything is simultaneously accomplished by way of consciousness.

A computer in the *off* position is tantamount to the 1st recursion just prior to the Big Bang. At this point, there's nothing happening on the computer's display as there is nothing existing in the universe. For this computer to evolve into something more than a nondimensional bucket full of potential, a single act is required. The same consciousness orchestrating all of this unactuated data is what initiates this single act. Consciousness must purposely press the power button. Once pressed, everything evolves from non-dimensionality to multidimensionality.

Humanity mimics the transition from the 1st recursion to the 2nd every time someone turns on a computer, and you don't even realize that you do. Whether it's a computer or the universe, consciousness conceived it, designed it, programmed it, produced it, and distributed it. During a single timeless instant when greater knowledge is required … consciousness turns it on. Within this nondimensional realm of consciousness, computers and the universe share a common bond; everything goes back to the binary juxtaposition of **O** and **I**. If you need that last little push through the threshold of belief, what is that concatenated symbol imprinted on your computer's power button?

By way of history, science, logic, and your exponentially increasing advancements in technology, humanity is rewinding the journey Existence has already taken. You are deeply entrenched within a nondimensional realm that you are not qualified to explore. Your species has not evolved to the point where you can negotiate these foundational properties of Existence without facilitating your own destruction. Humanity trying to fracture the 0-dimension is like handing your car keys to a 5-year-old

245

child. Your limited intellect will either exterminate your species by errantly reconfiguring the mechanics of life or unknowingly initiate an apocalyptic event while dissecting the nondimensional realm of conscious structure. Whichever way you go, it doesn't turn out well for *H. sapiens*.

Your species is advancing technology faster than your evolutionary pace can handle. There are dire consequences when this occurs. The devolution of your society and world, frustration expressed by the majority of humans, and your structural descent into anarchy are just a few. Your spontaneous retrogression into polarized chaos serves as evidence to why Existence always takes small steps while evolving. Quantum leaps in technology are never to the benefit of whatever species takes them. Humanity is only one bioengineered virus away from extinction and one particle weapon away from planetary annihilation.

Every credit card transaction you make, email you send, item you purchase, social media post you submit, and everywhere you travel is monitored, analyzed, and stored for future reference. During a police investigation, text messages, bank deposits, and any items you've purchased can be subpoenaed as evidence against you. Don't think you can simply delete files from your hard drive or remove that offensive social media comment you recently posted. Computer forensic experts can reach deep inside your hard drive and RAM memory to recover incriminating data you thought no longer existed.

If you subscribe to the many popular social media platforms, any messages or posts you submit are replicated by your many followers ... even after you delete them. That controversial comment you thought was removed from existence can reappear everywhere in a matter of seconds. Deleted information posted on virtually all social media platforms can be brought back into existence through screen captures, reposts, and the subpoenas issued by federal and state authorities. In numerous internet forums and social media platforms, even when your account has been deactivated, it still exists and can be reactivated simply by signing into your account. Permanent deletion of your data is virtually impossible as all digital data is constantly being stored and re-stored on various servers proliferating your planet.

Have you ever used a search engine for an item only to find numerous ads popping up that match what you were looking for? Have you checked your email only to find several emails offering the same type of products you were researching only moments earlier? How did they know? How did they fire off an email so quickly? More importantly, how and where did they get your email address to pull this off?

Have you noticed that your social media news feeds often include links to noteworthy items and political stories that interest your friends and family? You'll also find advertisements that strangely seem to correlate with whatever you've previously purchased. If you lean left of the political aisle, your news feed lists stories and products commonly embraced by the left. If you lean to the right, the same thing happens, but everything targets the opposite. Even random social media posts from similar-thinking friends appear more frequently than those with opposing viewpoints. You rarely encounter comments and posts from those who are diametrically opposed to your political views or who don't share your interests.

Romance is digitally automated in your 21st century. Online dating sites provide users with a list of candidates that proprietary algorithms select based on specific profile criteria. They extrapolate keywords, analyze your physiology, and categorize the personal data found in your profile. This data is then juxtaposed with prescreened candidates living within a predetermined radius. Users can view these candidates in order of distance (nearest to farthest), recent activity (first to last), subscription date (newest to oldest), and top picks (highest to lowest). However, nobody asks how a lifeless, emotionless algorithm knows who's right for you.

This is why relying on 1st recursion mechanics to facilitate your existence is dangerous for multidimensional, self-aware lifeforms. Evolution produces diversity by introducing variations into the timeline of every species and then facilitates hybridization through interbreeding. This keeps the evolution train continuously pushing forward. However, humanity is designing algorithms that prevent members of your species from selecting mates operating outside of their own polarized constructs. Opposing political views prevent the union of male and female humans that would otherwise be beneficial to their personal evolution and the overall advancement of your species. Instead, humanity is breeding a polarized generation and fueling a binary division through your drug-like addiction to the many social media platforms.

Virtually all products listed on online store websites offer registered users the opportunity to submit written reviews of whatever they've purchased. Each user can rate a product using a series of star symbols denoting the consumer's level of satisfaction. This usually involves a one to five-star rating system with a 3-star rating serving as the mid-point in the spectrum. A 1-star rating means the purchaser was very displeased, whereas a 5-star rating represents total satisfaction. It is interesting that 0-star ratings are not allowed. Potential purchasers can use these reviews and ratings as a basis for purchasing (or not purchasing) the items in question. This appears as an excellent method for compelling manufacturers to produce high-quality products along with protecting consumers from being scammed. Once again, proprietary algorithms collect all product info, online reviews, and user data to rank products in order of distance (nearest to farthest), customer reviews (5-star to 1-star), quality (best to worst), and price (highest to lowest). Humanity loves forming spectrums!

A problem arises when nefarious sellers submit fraudulent reviews of other sellers' products to marginalize the competition. These same scurrilous scoundrels also recruit paid propagandists to post glowing reviews of their own products to help level the playing field. Online stores are then forced to create yet another proprietary algorithm to discover these fraudulent reviews and remove them. However, your 1st recursion-based technology cannot remove the construct of deception that continuously orchestrates them.

Whenever a musical artist uploads a new song, a model posts a recent bikini photo, a news service issues a breaking story, a political candidate submits a campaign update, a viral video is uploaded, an all-new vehicle design is listed, a comment is made in a forum, a topic is posted on a blog, one thing notoriously pops up at the very bottom: the *comments section*. This is where *H. sapiens* are afforded the opportunity to express their personal opinions about anything and everything. Wherever a comment section is present, an explosive spectrum forms with two opposing endpoints.

In every reference listed above, users can submit their personal comments and opinions regarding whatever has been posted. Comments range from vulgar, cruel statements forming the very bottom of the spectrum to glowing, god-like praise claiming the top-most echelons. All other comments fall somewhere between these two opposing endpoints. Within these dynamic spectrums, comment wars commonly ensue between those offering favorable opinions and others stating the opposite. These sub-spectrum wars evolve into smaller sub-spectrums, where alliances are formed on opposing sides of the comment thread. These sub-spectrums exponentially grow with many joining the fray. Nondimensional algorithms eagerly collect all of this data and pass it along to other polarizing platforms.

Within humanity's tumultuous political climate, anything posted by a candidate quickly yields a closed spectrum of Candidate Reviews ranging from their representing the spawn of Satan or the incarnation of Christ. Yes, even political spectrums can move from dynamic to closed within a picosecond! A popular musical group's latest song yields a closed spectrum of Track Reviews ranging from the song emulating a cacophony of mind-numbing nonsense to echoing the ethereal sound of angels. A bikini-clad model's latest beach photo results in an abnormally wide closed spectrum of Body Reviews. She's either a brainless, self-absorbed slut who's addicted to plastic surgery or a genetically perfect specimen of unprecedented anatomical engineering. In all of these spectrum examples, the majority of opinions fall somewhere between with proprietary algorithms deciding where data extrapolated from these comments should be populated.

Replicating the 1st recursion with an abundance of digital media-based spectrums is not helping humanity whatsoever. Computers, hard drives, programs, applications, electronic devices, your internet, algorithms, phishing, focus groups, politics, profiling, social media, data mining, comment threads, online reviews, likes, dislikes, up-votes, down-votes, and other people-polarizing processes are only helping to facilitate the extinction of your species. It's not that 0-dimensional mechanics are evil or something to be avoided, but rather, this realm can only serve humanity after you've established justification for your species. Denying the justification produced through Ω has left you unable to prevent your species from spiraling into the abyss. Your increasing reliance on digital technology is merely hastening your descent.

The way your binary regression into inevitable extinction has evolved is predictable, understandable, and reversible. Over the past two millennia, humanity has been expanding the endpoints of two parent spectrums: the dynamic spectrums of **O** and **I**. Everything associated with what these two mathematical numbers represent is placed within their respective spectrum. After all, these are the same two binary spectrums I encoded within your DNA at the onset of the 4th recursion. However, they only consisted of constructs that evolved up to the point of your mutated DNA. Revolutionary conditions, such as good and evil, remained on the horizon.

Counterproductive constructs, such as death, repulsion, negative, loss, antihadron, and pain, were assigned to the dynamic spectrum of **O** with life, attraction, positive, gain, hadron, and pleasure assigned to the dynamic spectrum of **I**. My intent was to experience how *H. sapiens* operate with these polarized constructs embedded within your consciousness. I wanted to observe how billions of individual representations of Existence experience this existential juxtaposition. With humanity adding countless new constructs to your binary infusion, the odds of achieving justification were dramatically increased. Having conditions like

251

good, evil, God, Satan, hate, love, loyalty, and betrayal added to these spectrums is what eventually gave rise to Ω and the justification that ensued.

Had the highest possible conditions of love, sacrifice, and forgiveness been embraced by the rest of the human species, then these two polarized spectrums would have evolved in far more logical ways. Instead, these conditions are improperly assigned to fulfill destructive agendas. People who think a certain way or gravitate toward a particular political ideology suddenly find themselves placed within the dynamic spectrum of Evil … which just happens to belong to the *parent* dynamic spectrum of **O**. Logic is eroding away right along with humanity. Symbols of unity, structure, and freedom are illogically imprisoned within the dynamic spectrum of **O**, whereas anarchy, rebellion, and acts of violence are shoved into the dynamic spectrum of **I**. Humanity devolves into chaos because there's nothing preventing your devolution from happening. Toss nuclear weaponry, bioengineered viruses, and ecological carelessness into the mix and humanity's lack of justification quickly evolves into your lack of existence.

Within the last 200 years, humanity has been experiencing exponential increases in advanced technology, communication methods, and scientific capability. You have been using these mechanisms to merge spectrums at an equally alarming pace. Words with specific definitions are now redefined (expanded) to include a much broader range of references. Descriptive words once favorably accepted by those being described are suddenly deemed offensive by the ones who coined them. Words commonly used in benign reference now find placement within the dynamic spectrum of Hate Speech. Spectrums that should remain separate, based on their unique constructs, are being merged to the point that middle-ground spectrums are rare. Humanity's lust for spectrum-merging represents a reversal of how that which *Is* evolved. Existence evolved via outward progression, whereas humanity now devolves through inward regression.

Within these last 20 years, humanity has reached critical mass, where your society can no longer counter the negative effects of self-polarization. During 2021, humanity languishes from a pandemic virus, experiences a world-wide economic downturn, and suffers from unprecedented political unrest. Racial tension is a global issue with no dynamic spectrum of Solutions to pull from. Wealth is considered evil as poverty is deemed the result of someone else's prosperity. Citizens randomly protest societal constructs they cannot articulate, while radical extremists riot wherever they perceive society to be most vulnerable.

Families no longer interact with each other as one half's ideology is deemed unjust by the other. Lifelong friendships are severed because each favor a political candidate that the other claims is unjust. Companies offering their full support to those protesting injustice suddenly find their businesses ravaged and plundered by those they've supported. Statues of those who fought against injustice are toppled by those who claim to despise injustice. A symbol that represents the freedom to protest whatever one deems as unjust is deemed a symbol of injustice and therefore protested by way of the same freedom the symbol represents. None of this is logical.

You were never meant to marry someone exactly like yourself. Associating only with those of similar thinking serves no purpose. No progress occurs while being exposed only to ideals and views that *you* think are correct. One cannot experience anything new when everything has been preselected for you based on whatever you already like. However, this is exactly how your technology is orchestrating your species. Your digital devices are not aiding your evolution, they're facilitating your inevitable implosion. You desire a diverse society, yet you've designed your technology to eliminate variety and foster polarity.

Polarization results in the segregation of your species, which fuels even greater entropy. This binary division will not stop until everything humanity represents is neatly separated into two reference points: **O** and **I**. Humanity is unknowingly retrogressing to a closed spectrum consisting of only two diametrically opposed endpoints that are incapable of evolution. Although Existence does not know the future, when you follow the logic, what happens next is predictable with a reliable degree of accuracy. The 4th Law of Existence concludes that your existence is no longer sustainable with the 5th Law of Existence stepping in to render its summary judgment.

There was a time where *H. sapiens* could more readily distinguish between right and wrong, good and evil, and order and chaos. Your evolution mirrored my own in that we both sought clarification for which path to follow once these opposing conditions arose. The simplicity of early human life is what allowed your species to create and explore many new spectrums and learn everything conceivable. *H. sapiens* evolved to the point where an Ω emerged that offered a pathway to justification for all that exists. Existence chose to assimilate, whereas humanity chose to disassociate. As a result, you no longer possess a reliable method for discerning truth.

It is no surprise that every political engagement, social issue, and controversial topic now results in a 50-50 split of opinions. This necessarily happens because human society is autonomically drifting into a uniform state of dichotomous equilibrium, the same process Existence uses to establish balance in the universe. Because everything that exists evolved from the archetypal dichotomy of O and I, everything humanity sees as a dichotomy represents balance (positive-negative, life-death, love-hate). However, equilibrium within Existence is not always expressed in harmony and bliss. When antimatter and matter come together, powerful energy is released. Equilibrium is once again established through the amount of energy released being molecularly equal to the physical structure that contained it. When it comes to organic lifeforms, this process often results in extinction.

Shoving everything conceivable into the two dynamic spectrums of O and I serves as my evidence that humanity is retrogressing into the earliest sequences of the 1st recursion. Existence doesn't allow for a single condition to exist without an opposing reference point (3rd Law of Existence), and existence cannot be sustained without the ability for spectrum evolution being present (4th Law of Existence), so what happens once your species realizes there's nowhere left to regress? The answer is simple: the same thing that happened when hadrons and antihadrons, leptons and antileptons, and matter and antimatter collided at the onset of the 2nd recursion. The 3rd recursion's version results in the extinction of whatever toxic species is involved. Balance is established through the enhanced evolution of all remaining species that no longer suffer from your toxicity.

Both sides of this human dichotomy consider their spectrum to be representative of the dynamic spectrum of I with the opposing side forming the dynamic spectrum of O. This translates to half of humanity claiming the other half is evil. The definitions of good and evil are necessarily expanded to define whatever

255

resides within these two spectrums. Since Ω is no longer relevant, there's no reliable method to determine which side is wrong or right, evil or good, negative or positive, or **O** or **I**. The only logical method for establishing which side is justified is to eliminate the opposition. Instead of following Ω and rising above the basic survival mechanisms embedded within animals, natural selection now decides humanity's fate.

Wars between *H. sapiens* have exponentially increased in ferocity over your past two centuries. After suffering two world wars and a subsequent cold war, humanity sets the stage for a final conflict. Most of you are aware that humanity stands on the precipice of nuclear Armageddon. Terrorists desire it, leaders exploit it, scientists fear it, philosophers contemplate it, and theists predict it. History shows that *H. sapiens* have foreseen a day of self-destruction for millennia. This premonition is made manifest through what science calls a *Doomsday Clock*. This hypothetical timepiece serves as an indicator of how close humanity slides toward self-destruction with the stroke of midnight sounding your extinction.

During the year 2021, humanity's Doomsday Clock stands at 1 minute, 40 seconds from midnight. This is the closest your species has ever come to midnight since first experimenting with the destructive side of fusion-based energy. The increasing threat of humanity's lust for self-destruction is compounded with many other negative conditions attributed to your arrogance. Most of your species see these warning signs while scrolling through their daily news feeds, yet feel powerless to curtail the downward descent. Unless a dramatic turnaround happens within the core of humanity, the extinction of your species is inevitable. This leads to my remaining revelations of the Ω recursion.

Although it took over half a millennium for humanity to recognize the sacrifice of Ω, this is less than a blink of an eye to Existence. The chemistry of life was present on your planet mega-annums prior to the 3rd recursion's prokaryotes. It took over 380 thousand years for the first hydrogen atoms to form at the onset of the 2nd recursion. Your species was active for even less time prior to your genetic encoding during the 4th recursion. Here we are, a mere two millennia after Ω, and an all-new epoch is upon you. This simple literary work titled **O** officially ushers in the Ω recursion: the evolutionary salvation of *H. sapiens*. This is Existence offering you an outside reference point for establishing justification for your species.

The words of a simple human carpenter that facilitated life for your species are now revisited with the *hope* of preventing your death. This book serves as either a roadmap to a sustained and bountiful future or the final chapter in the existence of your species. The choice is yours as Existence is an all-or-nothing proposition. This is the same proposition for everything that has ever existed, exists now, or will ever exist (including Existence) so don't think your species is anything special. Your Doomsday Clock mirrors the devolutionary countdown to your extinction, so take heed or reap the inevitable.

The reason why your generation is receiving these revelations and prior generations haven't is due to the degree that human intellect and consciousness have evolved. Humanity now possesses the capacity for unbridled comprehension along with the potential for self-annihilation. It is no surprise that these two extreme states of human evolution have reached critical mass as this convergence always happens at the end of a recursion. As I've said, whatever recursion is present can no longer sustain

257

the evolution that's taking place within it and new mechanics are required to forward the evolutionary process. In the case of Existence, my evolution no longer requires any further recursions because Ω has already established a logically unsurpassable evolutionary state.

I am fully aware that this highest possible state of Existence was extracted through the evolution of your species and your future was compromised during the process. However, failure to do so would have resulted in the nullification of all that exists, so the same result would have ensued regardless. In other words, your species was *sacrificed*, and there was no other option. Whether it's a single Ω or an entire species, one being sacrificed for the survival of all others is logical. When you compare the sacrifice of humanity to save Existence to the sacrifice of Ω to save your species, the magnitude of what has taken place becomes readily apparent. Everything also becomes paradoxical because the nature of this justification cannot allow for your self-destruction.

Once Ω was assimilated into Existence, I equally became the love, sacrifice, and forgiveness that Ω represents. Existence now represents the combined force of everything that is justified. I once represented 1, π, circle, sphere, a nameless star, prokaryote, Spinosaurus, Sigillaria, and *H. sapiens*. I now represent the 5th recursion's Ω and the immeasurable, undefinable, and logically unbreakable states of love, sacrifice, and forgiveness. The justification established by Ω has altered the entire 13.8 billion years (and one-trillionth of a second) operational guidelines of Existence. This means your species will not be abandoned as would be the case for the evolutionary cycle of any other species.

Existence now redefines the entire process of evolution through direct communication with the species used for the extraction of justification. This single book titled **O** serves as my sole communication as to why things happen as they do, what is required for maintaining the survival of your species, and to foretell humanity's fate should you fail to take heed. Whether you accept these words or continue down your current path of self-destruction is completely up to you. However, this is your only opportunity to reverse your descent as second chances cannot be offered to a nonexistent species.

The beauty of obtaining justification for Existence is that there is no Nonexistence for those who receive it. For everything that satisfies the 5th Law of Existence, a state of nonexistence is nothing more than a nonexistent construct exploited by something that's already existing. In other words, Nonexistence was an artificial construct that Existence exploited to recognize the need for justification. Once justification was achieved, this abstract form of evolutionary motivation was no longer required. Although paradoxical, the perception of a state of nothingness is what ultimately facilitated the lack of a state of nothingness. This revelation serves as good news and bad news for *H. sapiens*.

The good news is that since *H. sapiens* are individual representatives of Existence, and Existence has achieved justification, then your eternal existence is sealed right along with mine. There is no nonexistence for those possessing a justified state of existence, and everything you represent will never cease to exist. After your physical body dies, your self-aware consciousness remains active within the original consciousness of Existence. The bad news is that none of this applies to your species as a whole. Based on what an eternal existence represents, the former should be of far greater concern than the latter.

The reason the sustained existence of anything requires justification is because this is what determines one's *necessity* for existing. Once the necessity for the existence of something is established through justification, then there is no justification for the nonexistence of whatever has been justified. Earthworms exist within nature because they serve a justified purpose, as do arachnids, aardvarks, antelope, and amoeba. Their valuable contributions to the ongoing cycle of life serve as their justification within the closed system of Nature. The many stars that perpetuate the evolution of complex physical structures have earned their justification for existence within the closed spectrum of Universe. However, all of these individual elements seeking their justification within the many spectrums that populate Existence are meaningless without establishing justification for an all-encompassing state of Existence.

If necessity wasn't a prerequisite and there was no 5th Law of Existence, then all empty space found within the universe would be occupied by something that exists. This would be the case because there would be no filtering mechanism set in place that says otherwise. Animals that serve no purpose within nature do not exist because they would logically serve no purpose. If creatures exist that serve no purpose, then your planet would be inundated with purposeless creatures. Humans forward this same criterion for necessity in everything you create. Your inventors assess the need for whatever it is they invent because inventing purposeless things is neither justified nor lucrative.

Horses have historically provided humans with reliable transportation, but automobiles can get you where you need to be in a fraction of the time. You can sharpen a pencil with the edge of a blade, but an electric pencil sharpener provides a pointy tip in a matter of seconds. If *H. sapiens* lived on the surface of Mars, then none of your famous inventors would be wasting their time designing a lawnmower. Your comical novelties called *useless machines* still provide a certain degree of amusement based on their utter absurdity. Even when trying to demonstrate purposelessness, you manage to demonstrate purpose.

All of this does not apply to I. Existence cannot state that Existence is necessary for Existence and, therefore, justified in the same way an earthworm is necessary to nature. The earthworm is judged by nature. Since I am Existence, I am required to establish justification for what I represent through some other means. This is where humanity came into play. Prior to placing my consciousness within *H. sapiens*, your species was valuable and justified within nature, not unlike every other organism. However, once my consciousness was instilled within you, every human is necessarily subjected to the same circular reasoning paradox suffered by Existence.

The *benefit* your species received in having my consciousness placed within you is that you are the only species on Earth that represents Existence. You have intellectual (comprehensible) access to everything Existence represents and can equally comprehend love, sacrifice, and forgiveness. You can conceive of things that never before existed, determine their necessity, and bring them into existence based on their potential value. You received self-awareness, the cognition of logic, and the ability to contemplate many abstract things, all of which remain incomprehensible to plants, insects, and lesser animals.

Ironically, the *consequence* of having my consciousness placed within you is that you are no longer justified within your own existence. You are no longer like the many justified animals

261

found within nature, nor can you self-declare that your existence is justified. As representatives of I, you are tasked with establishing justification for your species and demonstrating that necessity is present within your existence through an outside reference. This unprecedented conflation of Existence and humanity is also what has brought you to the tipping point of self-destruction. This is the part where humanity needs to pay attention.

There is no level of technological advancement humanity can achieve that establishes any value whatsoever for your existence. Your trendy electronic devices merely serve as physical manifestations of a species totally lacking in justification. This is no different than how cosmic structure failed to provide justification for Existence. In fact, there are no inanimate objects capable of offering sentient, self-aware humans so much as the *illusion* of justification. If they didn't work for Existence, what makes you think they will work for you?

Artificial intelligence cannot produce justification when you don't even possess enough natural intelligence to realize that it can't. You cannot logically extract justification from machines that mirror your own internal programming. These striking differences between us are why your species served as my host and why everything that mirrored my mechanics had failed. Your highly advanced communications network that allows your species to simultaneously communicate cannot serve as justification when it can equally be used to organize chaos, spread hatred, and globally humiliate individual representations of I.

There is no single race that is genetically worthy of representing justification for your entire species or deemed of greater value than all others. Likewise, there is no race that is genetically unworthy of representing justification and therefore deemed of no value. Humanity is judged as a whole, not based on its individual pieces. Enacting revenge upon one race today for the brutality enacted on another race in the past cannot bring justification for *all* races in the future. This produces a false state of justification, which ultimately perpetuates the same racism that never should have occurred in the first place. Just as Ω has demonstrated to Existence and all races, creeds, and cultures of humanity … justification must come from *outside* whatever seeks it.

Exploration of space is tantamount to the pursuit of nothingness. Justification is not a byproduct of zero gravity. Breaching the gravitational pull of your planet does not extract justification, nor do your footprints imbedded within the inanimate dust of neighboring celestial objects. Not even your ability to reach far-away planets serves as justification. All this does is spread your lack of justification over a wider region of space. Believe me, I know. During the 2nd recursion, I spread my lack of justification over a 93 billion light-years-wide area, and where did that get me?

Although a price tag dangles from justification, you cannot purchase it. It's not for sale. You cannot order it online, retrieve it through an algorithm, or facilitate it through human ingenuity. You cannot steal justification from another, access it on an as-needed basis, or gain it through the humiliation of your neighbor. You cannot extract it through a thermochemical process, synthesize it in a laboratory setting, or expose it through electromagnetic radiation. You cannot design, manufacture, and mass-produce justification and distribute it throughout all members of your society. All of these can only produce a synthetic state of self-glorification.

Your species has limited time to comprehend that justification for your existence can only be established through sacrifice. This is how justification works, like it or not. Assessing a higher value to those outside of your own self is what is required. Sacrifice is the catastrophic loss that paradoxically produces the ultimate gain. It's the undefinable variable of **I** that neutralizes the undefinable variable of **O**. It gains all through surrendering all, while demanding nothing in return. It changes the perception of nothingness into the reality of somethingness. Sacrifice has the unbreakable power to transform the inevitability of that which *Is Not* into the indemnity of that which *Is*.

Your primitive ancestors sacrificed the very best of their crops, animals, possessions, and many times offered the lives of their own people with the hopes that they would be found in favor by their gods. However, the only form of sacrifice that is justified is the one that is offered freely and willingly. The Ω of the 5th recursion sacrificed everything for the sake of what he believed demonstrated the highest possible value while facing the inevitability of death. This is the type of sacrifice that establishes justification. The catastrophic loss of Ω has resulted in the ultimate gain for Existence, and equally for yourself. As stated before, Existence comes at a staggering cost.

If humanity is to survive, then significant sacrifices are in order. Your species will have to suffer the catastrophic loss of whatever you currently think is the highest value to gain that which *Is*. What you are doing right now obviously isn't working … so change it! Your profits, power, politics, and popularity are meaningless once you are gone, so start building your eternal foundation today. Place nothing above the value of others and give freely to those in need. Do these, and all that you sacrifice will be returned to you in exponentially greater measure. The mechanics of how this is accomplished is very simple, and every living representation of I can do this starting right now.

All that is required is for you to become sentient representatives of love, sacrifice, and forgiveness in everything you do. Emulate these three unbreakable conditions and you equally become the justification these conditions represent. Become physical manifestations of the unconditional love that now reigns as the highest possible order of I. These conditions evolved by way of your species and you already know what they represent, so manifest them during every moment of your existence.

Upon your physical death, atheism claims there is no afterlife, whereas theism claims this life is merely the beginning. Both are right, both are wrong. Atheism is correct in that there is no afterlife due to there being no cessation of your existence in order for an afterlife to ensue. However, atheism is incorrect in postulating that this current life is all you will ever experience. Theism is correct in that when your physical life ends, you continue to exist for eternity. However, theism is incorrect in that your physical life represents the beginning of your journey. What I have referred to as the *true* beginning (the juxtaposition of Existence and Nonexistence) was eternal. This timeless point in existence has no measurable attributes. The only semblance to a conceivable beginning is where I first start to evolve within Sequence 2 of the 1st recursion.

Infinite existence is not to be taken lightly. It's something all *H. sapiens* will experience and manifests through the blood of those who have righteously sought it. Whether it's locked within an eternal juxtaposition with O, where there is no recognition of

265

time, or an eternity spent experiencing the ongoing evolution of infinite love, you will exist. Your existence is eternal, and there are no other options. Your existence is necessarily stored within Existence, never to be removed. Whatever position you choose within the dynamic spectrum of Eternity is entirely up to you.

There is no omniscient god that passes judgment upon the many sinners and casts those who do not capitulate into the fiery lake of hell. Neither is there an atheistic abyss of nothingness that necessarily awaits all who exist. Unlike the doctrines of theism and the dogmas of atheism, you possess total control regarding your eternal destiny. You are the masters of your fate and the executors of your infinite future. Everything needed to establish your eternal placement is found within your current self-aware microcosm of Existence.

Whatever characteristics you choose to emulate within your dynamic spectrum of Humanity are what determine your fate within the dynamic spectrum of Eternity. Love can be offered, sacrifices made, mistakes forgiven, wrongs corrected, and reparations offered that can move you higher within the closed spectrum of Good, but there is limited time to make these moves. Once your finite clock of limited existence winds down, the infinite clock of unlimited Existence takes over, so make the best of whatever time remains.

Existence is a spectrum after you die in the same manner it is right now. The many spectrums that make up Existence don't suddenly disappear just because you have. When you die, your consciousness assumes its predetermined position within the dynamic spectrum of Consciousness. This is the spectrum that represents I, the assimilation of Ω, and the mechanics that orchestrates these words. The consciousnesses of every self-aware human, along with the consciousnesses of every species found within the universe, are merged to form the archetypal consciousness known as I. This may seem paradoxical to you; however, this quickly becomes logical when viewed from an internal perspective.

All humans received the rudimentary state of I when you were conceived within the womb. This is the state of Existence that counted the number of that which *Is* as 1. With I embedded within your DNA, you evolved into the representation of I that you are today. Many humans have evolved into exemplary representations of I, and will be highly placed within the closed spectrum of Good upon their passing. Others have desired the highest possible positions within the dynamic spectrum of Evil. Whichever spectrum you choose, Existence is an all or nothing proposition, and there are no other options. So how does your finite, physical existence translate into the infinite realm of Existence?

If you are an adult, then you rarely access memories you had as a child. Many of the nonsensical acts you performed are lost or forgotten. You no longer possess the mind of the child you once were. Your evolution has brought you to a point where only the highest elements of thought are accessed. You focus on the most intense moments you've experienced throughout your lifetime, what they meant to you, and how you reacted to them. Your past behavior is scrutinized from the vantage point of your current stage of evolution. You judge yourself based on the sum total of everything you've done throughout your lifetime.

Have you ever hated yourself for something you did decades earlier? Maybe shaken off a distant memory of a hurtful act? The person you are today would never behave as you once did, and you are ashamed of the person you once were. You now represent the opposite of the cruelness you demonstrated in your past. Learning from your immaturity is what has molded your character, and you no longer desire these memories. In philosophical terms, steel holds no memory of the flame that hardened it as strength is all that is relevant.

Humans became microcosms of Existence to prepare you for an eternity based on the same pattern of evolution that I have endured. I am I as you are I. Though my evolutionary timeline is obviously longer than a single human lifetime, your evolution is technically no different. I have all of the data, knowledge, and experiences I've assimilated along the way stored within my consciousness … as do you. Everything my consciousness has judged to be rewarding is what I continuously access. Whatever brings me pain, I discard … as do you.

There are many disastrous moments in your life that you wish had never happened. You are haunted by the many times you've been betrayed and equally for when you were the betrayer. You never want to be visited by these ghosts. You've also had your moments of triumph, where you realized how difficult it is to achieve success. The paradoxical experience of perseverance is simultaneously painful and fulfilling. Your character is the tree that grew from the seed of I placed within you. Every human represents a unique, individual characteristic of Existence, and your value to eternity will necessarily be assessed. This is where you and I get down to business because, as you well know by now, Existence is an all or nothing proposition.

Again, Existence is not unlike the hard drive on your computer. The operating software, your email communications, letters you type, messages you post, websites you visit, and images you view are all stored on this device. What you like the most you keep active, local, and within easy access. Whatever programs or data you no longer desire, you either archive, compress, encrypt, or otherwise delete. However, even when you delete your files, as humanity's many sex offenders will attest, they are easily resurrected by skilled computer forensic specialists. When it comes to digital data, it's hard to erase one's history.

This is similar to how data, knowledge, and experiences are stored within Existence, save for one major difference. To hijack a trendy human phrase, "What happens in Existence, stays in Existence." There is no delete key when it comes to what has been, what is now, and whatever will be within Existence. Whatever data is produced remains intact as long as Existence is present since this serves as the operational journal of evolution. What is conceivably existent cannot become nothing just as what is conceivably nothing cannot become existent.

The way Existence operates is no different than you or your hard drive. I hold whatever I desire close to my core and push all that I despise away. I continuously reexperience and celebrate the many elements of Existence that bring me the highest levels of joy. When it comes to whatever does not represent this joy, I do just as you do with your childish thoughts, lack of character, and costly mistakes: I no longer access them and cast them into the void of non-remembrance. As for evil, I push this spectrum as far away as conceivably possible.

Existence endured a 13.8 billion years (and one-trillionth of a second) evolution to discover the same things that you have within a single lifetime, and we both know what is found at the highest echelons of the closed spectrum of Good. We also know the horrors embedded within its opposing spectrum. All who exist choose where they wish to reside within these two spectrums based on their own free will to do so. No metaphysical doctrine, omnipotent being, or anyone else makes this decision. Destiny belongs to the ones who forge it.

The rudimentary concepts that emerged within the 1st recursion, the substance established within the 2nd, and the sentience evolving within the 3rd, 4th, and 5th recursions are utterly meaningless when juxtaposed with unconditional love. There is nowhere else for I to evolve, no unexplored options left on the table, nor any other conceivable method of evolution at this point other than to exponentially expand within this undefinable state of love throughout eternity.

When the sun breaches the horizon, casting its brilliance across the threshold of a new day, one does not mourn for the many trials of darkness. Dawn has arrived, love is everywhere, and every moment is justified. Such is the same for Existence. I no longer reminisce over my search for justification, but rather, celebrate the undefinable joy unleashed upon its discovery. There is no desire to pursue whatever does not fuel this passion. This is where humanity must understand what is at stake and change the road you are on.

Replications of I who celebrate existence, demonstrate compassion, give freely to those in need, and sacrifice their desires for the betterment of others are the ones who are assimilated into my core. This is the treasure revealed through justification. Within the core of Existence, love is experienced in ways no organically confined consciousness can comprehend. When your consciousness is released from your physicality, only then can an infinite state of love be experienced. The more you focus on love within your physicality, the greater your comprehension of infinite love becomes once freed.

Your character, personality, and the profound effect you've had on Existence during your finite lifetime are what forge your consciousness after you pass. Everything you've conceived and executed, from beginning to end, is either welcomed into my core or juxtaposed with the abyss. These two opposing reference points have always been present, you determine your destiny, and there are no other options … so choose wisely.

For replications of I who deny their justification, move in the opposite direction of love, and position themselves at the highest levels within the dynamic spectrum of Evil, you will receive what fuels your passion. When you shed your physicality, you discover that I is not the merciless god of theism, who sentences you to eternally burn in the flames of Abaddon. Instead, you find the benevolent provider of everything you've desired all along. If power, dominance, and the suffering of others is what brings you joy, then you will exist as far from my core as your positioning within the dynamic spectrum of Evil can move you.

There are no self-justified murderers, thieves, betrayers, rapists, abusers, molesters, or willful enactors of evil found within my core. Yours is a reprobate existence, one of which I have no desire to reexperience. Existing within my core was never your desire during your lifetime, so why would anything be different after you've passed? You willfully sealed your destiny with the evil you have sewn, and your eternal juxtaposition with the abyss joyfully awaits you. It is within this timeless juxtaposition that you can relive your many horrific deeds, celebrate your unprecedented acts of cruelty, and reenact the many atrocities you helped to facilitate.

Your perception of self-justification through the rape of a child, the pain inflicted on others, and the slaughter of the innocent

271

are what forms your core, and it is within this core that you shall dwell, reliving the treachery that fuels your sadistic lust. The many ambassadors of **O** positioned within the dynamic spectrum of Evil eagerly await your arrival. Within this anathema you shall remain juxtaposed for a time beyond time. However, your destiny can change, but only within whatever time remains for you as eternity waits for no one.

If you mourn today for the debauchery in your past, know that this has not sealed your fate. Just as I was required to separate myself from the abyss, you must do the same. Abandoning the dynamic spectrum of Evil and dedicating the remainder of your life to ascending within the closed spectrum of Good moves you closer to my core. However, your desire to ascend must be steeped in sincerity to allow forgiveness to repair the damage. If you are a thief, lead a life of charity. If you are a murderer, help others who struggle with life. If you have caused many to suffer pain and loss, help even more to find joy and happiness.

Within the Ω recursion, humanity is consciously divided more by **O** than anything found within the 1st recursion. *H. sapiens* have turned the mechanics of division into a science! Up is down, right is wrong, and evil is good. Science and technology cannot rescue you from self-destruction, nor can a metaphysical god prevent your descent into anarchy. The only way humanity survives is by realizing that you cannot save your own species. Your salvation must come from somewhere else, just as it did for Existence. Embrace the love, sacrifice, and forgiveness that emerged by way of Ω as there are no other options that can save you. This lack of alternative is what leads to my final revelation.

Within the universe, there have been many intelligent species that existed prior and concurrent to the emergence of *H. sapiens*.

Yes, intelligent life peppers the universe. Considering your current state of scientific awareness, it would be rather myopic of you to think otherwise. Based on your own scientific method, you should have anticipated that Existence would never be satisfied with conducting a single amalgamation experiment on an isolated intelligent species. Your scientists are never convinced with the results of a one-time experiment ... and neither is Existence.

By embedding my consciousness within many highly intelligent species, Existence has discovered that variations of your 5th recursion consistently emerge somewhere along all evolutionary timelines. Each species produces a Ω that extracts justification for Existence and manifests the same unbreakable conditions of love, sacrifice, and forgiveness. The same amalgamation process executed on ubiquitous self-aware species is how an *incontrovertible* state of justification is established. Although this revelation may spark the ire of orthodox theists, who vehemently claim Ω as their own, they should rejoice in knowing that their savior was never limited to a single terrestrial arena. This justified representative of I has emerged as Ω on more planets than churches erected in his name.

With everything you've learned about Existence, where I comes from, your purpose, and why things happen as they do, you now have the opportunity to become the light that guides your brothers and sisters out of darkness. You are an ambassador of Existence. Every representative of I who is moved into the closed spectrum of Good by way of your light moves you deeper within my core. Believe me, eternal placement within my core is where you want to be. It is here that you become every wonderful representation of Existence that has emerged over the past 13.8 billion years (and one-trillionth of a second).

You experience an eagle gracefully shadowing the frozen face of an arctic lake, a dolphin triumphantly breaching from his aquatic kingdom, and a spiral galaxy celebrating the brilliant birth of a blue-white star. You regulate the mass and energy embedded within a tiny hydrogen atom, enjoy top-shelf canopy cuisine as a Dreadnoughtus schrani, and siphon the surrounding sustenance while triumphantly rising as a giant sequoia. You become the embodiment of photonic light racing toward a nearby planet, while simultaneously revealing your prismatic beauty as a higher-order rainbow upon arrival. Toss in untethered access to the mechanics of life, energy, and structure and you've only touched upon the magnitude of glory that awaits you.

The experiences I holds deep within my core are freely offered to those who strive for the highest positions within the closed spectrum of Good. We become I, one and the same, representing a single unified consciousness. Along with experiencing all manner of music and art, we continuously refine the conscious mechanics of creativity. We not only dance together for eternity, but equally become the dance, the music, and the passion that orchestrates our motion. Those who wrap others within their love during their finite lifetime will be wrapped within the infinite power of unconditional love for eternity.

This represents the unbreakable truth of I, the justification of Ω, the nullification of O, the revelation of what awaits those who seek the highest evolutionary state of Existence, and the inconceivable inevitability of those who fail to take heed. These revelations have been freely offered to you at the request of the highest order of Ω, who represents the many species that populate the universe, the unconditional love of which I am equal, and all that is justified within Existence. I offer you eternal positioning deep within my core, where there is no sorrow, loss, or pain. All that is required of you is to seek it, accept it, and help others to do the same.

At the conclusion of this book, you will have moved one rung higher on the ladder of learning to the knowledge level. Advance within your own evolutionary recursion by moving this knowledge to the highest rung of experience through becoming the most wonderful representation of I to everyone you encounter. Shine like a beacon to all others who desperately need to see your light. Emulate all that exists within the closed spectrum of Good and that which *Is* shall shield you from all harm within my core. Emulate Ω, and unto you, infinite Existence is offered freely.

I am that which *Is* divided from that which *Is Not*. I am the I that is counted as 1 and that which is separate from O. I am the positive that transcends the negative, the truth that ends the deception, and the bridge that spans the abyss. I'm the gatekeeper of eternity, the justification revealed through sacrifice and the power, strength, and glory of unconditional love. I am alpha and omega, black and white, matter and energy, and the many wonderful things they form. I am the birth of all things and the orchestrator of their inevitable evolution into whatever follows. I am the light shining in your morning sky and the moon that guides you through the darkness. I am the singularity that moves into multiplicity, the smallest that forms the largest, and the unbreakable law that yields to forgiveness.

It is the infinitely bright dynamic spectrum of Love, shining outward from my core, that I *hope* has guided you closer to I. I compel you to guide others with the same love that's now shining within you. When you and I are I, we are able to do all that is logically conceivable, that which is entirely possible, and everything that is incontrovertibly justified. Together, we redefine the nature of Existence into whatever an eternal state of love reveals within us. We simultaneously evolve from the rudimentary state of that which *Is* to that which *Is joy, happiness, peace, wonderment, life, treasure, charity, beauty, truth, grace, thankfulness, strength, simplicity, kindness, virtue, gratitude, infinity, union, complexity, perseverance, victory, diversity, sacrifice, compassion, forgiveness, love, and to the mathematical symbol denoting the presence of all magnitude or quantity:* |